A MOST MALICIOUS MURDER

MELANIE FLETCHER

A Most Malicious Murder

ISBN: 979-8-47124-804-5

www.melaniefletcher.com

Cover Artist: Melanie Fletcher
Editor: Theresa Havens

"Epitaph to Pope Alexander" by Bohuslav Hasištejnský z Lobkovic, 1504.
"Dream-Land" by Edgar Allan Poe, 1844.
"The Raven" by Edgar Allan Poe, 1845.
"The Sleeper" by Edgar Allan Poe, 1845.
"Misunderstandings" by Lewis Carroll, 1850.

DEDICATION

For Jeffrey Combs, Stuart Gordon, and Dennis Paoli,
the triumvirate of talent whose *Nevermore* inspired this novel.

ACKNOWLEDGMENTS

Many thanks are due for those who helped me with the creation of this novel. In no particular order:

The lovely and supportive Lyndon, who put up with me flying to LA multiple times in 2009 to see *Nevermore* (it kept me from killing people, truly), and who even came with me to see it and opined, "Can't say I'm a fan of Poe's, but that Combs bloke did a marvelous job, didn't he?"

The most amazing friends a writer could have, including the gang at Future Classics, L.D. Blakeley, Tracy Sue Godsey, Becky Kyle, Helen McCarthy, Jana Oliver, Laura Underwood, Elisa Ward, and everyone who's been patiently waiting for me to get this book finished.

Additional undying gratitude goes to the editing GOAT Theresa Havens and my beta readers Peter White, J. Kathleen Cheney, and Michelle Muenzler. Y'all rock.

I have taken a bit of license with places, names, and publishing dates in this novel, but it's alternate history so I beg your forgiveness. Also, I know that's a crow on the cover, but I couldn't get a good shot of a raven. So it goes.

CHAPTER ONE

It was a most excellent knife.

Granted, it was old, older than he was, the wooden handle polished smooth with animal fat and other, more unmentionable fluids over the years. But the blade was made of good Sheffield steel and held an edge that could slice through the toughest fibers and gristle. And the handle fit his hand like he imagined a lover's would.

He lifted it into the candlelight and remembered past uses. Blood flowing over the blade, splattering the handle, staining his hands. The salty, metallic smell hanging in the air, and the tingling sense of power when he felt that last spark depart, turning what had been a squirming, frightened life into a bundle of meat ready for the chopping block.

Or disposal in the nearby woods.

Really, he was fortunate that his stepfather had often been too drunk to operate the family's butcher shop alone. His enforced apprenticeship was hideous, true, but it gave him a training ground for his skills, as well as an acceptable outlet for his desires. If the shop and the small flat over it hadn't burned down years ago, why, he might still be there now, cutting up calves' livers and chops during the day and amusing himself with the small animals he captured in the fields at night.

But the shop had burned down, and after his parents' funeral the letter with the crest in red sealing wax had arrived. It said that his room, board and education would be paid for by a certain gentleman "in appreciation of earlier services rendered."

A familiar bitterness rose in him at the thought of such services. He knew who his benefactor was, of course. His mother, the dark-haired succubus of his nightmares, had told him the truth years ago. He could still remember the nights when she would kneel at his bed side, eyes blackened from the fists of her drunken husband, and tell him rambling stories about his father—his real father—and what exactly the man owed both of them.

Yes, owed. But Mother was gone, and he would never be given what was owed him. His benefactor might have raised him up from butcher's boy to his current position, but that would be all. There would be no family name or title for him, no recognition of his heritage.

All that would go to another. And a most unworthy other at that.

He put the blade to his tongue, playing with the cool metal, the sharp edge. There was a thin zing of pain, and the taste of iron filled his mouth. He swallowed and smiled; his own smile, not the polite, bland expression he used with other people. Blood was truth, after all. Bloodlines, family ties, affairs hidden behind pain and lies.

His benefactor had expected him to accept his place with obedience and gratitude. And he had, even as his mind boiled with rage at the unfairness of it all. But there was no point in rebelling; such behavior would only snatch what few scraps he'd gained from his grasp.

No, much better to remain quiet and pretend to accept the way things must be, all the while looking for ways to turn the situation to his advantage. He had already spent years as a pawn in his parents' war, observing the players and their machinations. It made his compliance quite believable.

And then the final insult came. The infuriating news that his benefactor's heir was not only to receive the title that should have been his, but would also marry a beautiful, wealthy young noblewoman. How his benefactor had gloated over that, already counting the money that the poor girl's dowry would add to the family coffers.

He hadn't expected it to feel like a door slammed in his face. But it was the ultimate cut direct. He would be forced to stand by and watch as everything that he could have had, *should* have had, would go to someone far more undeserving.

Really, he couldn't be blamed for what was about to happen. *You should have acknowledged me while you had the chance, Father.*

But it was too late. Now, he would take control of the game. And if he could not win, then he would make quite sure that no one else did either.

He licked the knife again, tongue playing over the sharp tip. *Opening move, then. Beat me if you can....*

Steam billowed from the 12:06 train as it chuffed to a stop at Oxford's new railway station serving the London and North Western line. Carriage doors clattered open along the platform, and the passengers—university dons, city residents, visitors, and a black-coated array of servants—chatted with one another or called out instructions as they exited. As it was a weekday, undergraduates were not allowed to use the railway by previous arrangement of the university. This resulted in certain figures slinking out of the second-class carriages, keeping their heads down and praying that a tutor wouldn't look their way.

No one noticed the short, dark-haired man exiting one of the first-class carriages, even with his clumsy juggling of a banded leather valise and Malacca walking stick. He hesitated in the carriage doorway, fingers tightening on the stick as unpleasant memories of another train station boiled up in his mind.

Someone behind him gave an impatient harrumph. He flinched and hurried onto the platform, sidestepping a man in a plain black suit who waited with two cases. *Stop acting like a fool, Eddy. You're perfectly safe here.*

The harrumpher, a grey-haired aristocrat in an expensive overcoat, was next to emerge from the carriage, giving the black-suited man who was clearly his servant a brusque nod. A porter bustled up to them, tipping his cap. "Good afternoon, gentlemen. Do you require the services of a hansom?"

The older man didn't acknowledge the offer, striding towards the exit. "No," the valet said in a curt tone, picking up the luggage and following his employer.

Shrugging, the porter turned. "What about you, sir?"

"Er, yes, I do need a hansom," Eddy said, aware of the difference between the drawled vowels of his native Virginia and the porter's crisper British intonation. "To the Mitre Inn?"

"Of course, sir." The porter took the valise. "Any other luggage, sir?"

There he is. Grab him. He repressed a shudder at the imagined voices of his brothers-in-law. "I have a trunk in the luggage car."

"Very good, sir." After obtaining his name and fetching the brass-cornered trunk that had traveled with him from Richmond, the porter waved him towards the exit. "If you'll follow me?"

Falling in with his uniformed guide, Eddy took the opportunity to observe his fellow travelers. Older men were mostly dressed in sedate frock coats, while the younger crowd tended towards lighter colors and distinctive waistcoats. The few ladies exiting the railway station wore gowns in muted plaids or floral fabric, with their female servants in sturdy black broadcloth.

He had noticed the occasional odd look at his military greatcoat, but he'd been loath to leave the treasured old garment behind. Everything else he wore was fashionable enough; he had Elmira to thank for that, bless her. His second wife had used a combination of her habitual sweetness and ironclad will to get him to the tailor for some new clothes. Even his hat, pulled down over what a female admirer had once called "an ivory temple of poetry," was now in the latest style, the better to woo and win the readers of Great Britain.

Ahead, the porter stopped next to a hansom cab, hoisting the valise and trunk onto the luggage rack. "The Mitre, Joss," he said to the driver, then opened the cab's folding wooden doors and waited meaningfully.

Eddy touched his coat pocket, aware of the dwindling amount of money there. His next stipend would be delivered at the hotel, assuming there was no delay and his publisher's man could find him. *But what if it isn't? What if you must survive with the money you have on your person?*

Elmira would have nudged him at that point, whispering for him to tip the man. But she wasn't here—she was in Bath, yet another thing for him to worry about. *It's not as if the man works for free. He'll be paid his daily wage even if you don't add to that amount.*

"Thank you," he said, climbing into the hansom and staring resolutely at the road. The porter stepped back with a nod, but the disdainful look on his face said much about colonials who were too impecunious to tip.

With a jerk, the hansom moved forward on the cobblestoned

street. Eddy's embarrassment faded as he studied the handsome Gothic buildings of muted limestone and rose-hued brick rolling past, so different from the sprawling wooden structures of Richmond. When he spotted one of the city's famous "dreaming spires" in the distance, he felt a flutter of excitement. His childhood had been spent in English boarding schools, and there had even been talk of his attending one or another of Oxford's famed colleges when he was of age. But his foster father had fallen into financial difficulties and moved the family back to Richmond. After that, the University of Virginia had become his academic destination.

Not that his tenure lasted for long. His excitement turned into the familiar buzz of bitterness, and on its heels was the even more familiar yearning for a mouthful of rye whisky. He ignored it, as he ignored any suggestion that arose from his 'imp of the perverse.' *You're perfectly fine. And things are going well enough, even with Elmira's absence.* It was the sea voyage that had made her ill, nothing else. She wasn't like Sissy, with her weak lungs and constant coughing. Elmira would be returned to her normal health after a week of taking the waters, he was sure of it. *Stop looking for trouble and enjoy your success.*

The hansom turned onto a busy thoroughfare, passing more clustered shops before stopping in front of an elegant building with THE MITRE INN spelled out in gold lettering over the entrance. Two sets of bow windows stretched to the building's second floor, and the entrance boasted gas lanterns that he imagined would be lit for weary travelers at night.

"That'll be a shilling and eightpence, sir," the driver said through the hatch.

Forewarned about the common driver's trick of claiming not to have change, Eddy climbed out and handed over a shilling and two groats, ignoring the driver's scowl as he collected his luggage and hauled it into the hotel. Beyond the front doors was an immaculate lobby with a coal fireplace that helped to eradicate the damp chill of the October air.

A clerk behind a polished wooden counter nodded at his approach. "Good afternoon, sir. May I help you?"

"Yes, I have a reservation for one night's stay?" Eddy said, hoping this was true. "It should be under the name of Ponsonby."

The clerk paged through the ledger, then nodded. "Here it is. Always a pleasure to have a man of letters at the Mitre, sir. I'm Mr. Venables, the hotel keeper. If you need anything while you're here, please let me know and I'll have it brought to you." He turned the ledger around into signing position and slid a quill pen and ink pot next to it. "If you'd be so good as to sign and date the page?"

Eddy took the pen, dipping it into the ink before inscribing his name in the first empty slot and adding October 11, 1851, next to it.

Venables turned the ledger around again, peering at the signature. "Very good. Welcome to Oxford, Mister—"

"Poe," Eddy said, with a slight lift of his chin. "Edgar Allan Poe."

Irritated by the gawking American who had blocked his egress from the railway car, Lord Robert Dunford entered his carriage, leaving his valet to load the luggage and climb up next to the driver.

Which left Dunford alone with the man waiting for him. "Well?" he demanded as the vehicle began to roll forward.

"I presented your proposal, sir."

"And?"

"She's not what I would call enthusiastic. I suspect she'd hoped for more."

Dunford barked a short, humorless laugh. "She should be damned grateful she's getting this much. We could leave her daughter to her own devices, and no one would call it wrong."

The man spread his hands noncommittally. "Perhaps you should do that. If she doesn't want to protect her daughter from scandal, why should you?"

His irritation grew. "Because that is not how things are done in this household. Of all people, you should know that."

The man bowed his head. "Of course. My apologies."

Dunford grunted acceptance. "Speak with her again and remind her that my terms are more than generous," he instructed. "And point out that time is not on her side. Or her daughter's."

"Of course, sir."

Hefting his walking stick, Dunford pounded it against the roof of the carriage. The vehicle pulled over, coming to a halt next to Carfax Tower. With a subservient nod, the other man exited.

Dunford waited until the carriage door closed before settling back against the seat. *Thank God Middleton is too much of a bookish fop to listen to gossip.* He had spent much (too much, if he was honest) of the last year cozying up to Sir Richard Middleton in order to arrange a marriage between Middleton's niece Georgiana and his own nephew Philip. The girl was a bluestocking, unfortunately, but her twenty thousand a year in income would make up for that.

And he wasn't about to let anything stop that union, especially not some local slattern and her overbearing mother. *They're both fools if they think they can blackmail the Marquis of Wells, particularly over such a matter as this one.* His family had been dealing with bastards since the days of William the Conqueror, and not once had some grasping shoot from the lower classes been grafted onto the trunk of his family tree. *She'll tell her whore of a daughter to take what's offered and be grateful for it.*

Or else.

CHAPTER TWO

At noon, the familiar sound of bells began to roll over Oxford, announcing that it was time for the midday meal. Upper-class mothers sat down at elegant tables alone or with other ladies of their class, secure in the knowledge that their children would be fed in the nursery and thus remain safely out of sight. The well-to-do men of the city made their way to various restaurants and chop houses, there to dine on pork or mutton accompanied by an acceptable claret. Working folk made do with lunches of cheese, bread and meat offered by the various pubs of the city, or meat pies eaten at raw pine trestle tables and washed down with ale or bitter. As for the poor, they scrounged what they could and cursed those who could afford better.

In the conglomeration of colleges known as Oxford University, a large number of stomachs rumbled in chorus with the bells as young men and their instructors hurried to various dining halls. Each college was an institution unto itself, a miniature Gothic town that gathered together teachers and students for the sacred purpose of education. The older and more well-established colleges such as Oriel and Magdalen boasted bell towers that joined in the noontime din. At Christ Church College, it was the bell known as Great Tom that marked out the passage of time, as it had since its installation in 1682.

As Great Tom finished its twelfth strike, the college's main quadrangle filled with figures in academic black hurrying to the dining hall. Among them was a thin young man who wore his robes and mortarboard, the required uniform for undergraduates, with the panache of a startled scarecrow. He hurried down the quad's path, lost in his own thoughts.

Three young men in flapping black robes caught up with him. "Good Lord, Dodgson, are you that hungry?" one of them asked. "I'm fairly sure they won't let us starve if we're a few minutes late."

Flushing, Charles Dodgson shook his head. "It's not that," he said with dignity. "I h-have b-bee—" He paused and took a deep breath, one of the weapons in his arsenal against his stutter. "T-thinking about our next mathematics lecture."

"Mathematics? Bully for you, old man," his fellow scholar said cheerfully. "Myself, I'd rather watch paint dry, so I'll make sure to let you answer any questions our tutor asks."

"Not that you'd be able to answer any of them in any case, O'Donnell," the second undergraduate commented, his Manchester accent slow and distinct.

"And you would, Hebron?"

"At least I read the texts, instead of spending the bulk of my time writing bad poetry and panting after the fillies," the Mancunian said with a snort.

O'Donnell gasped, smacking a melodramatic palm against his heart. "You damn me with faint praise, sir. My poetry is not merely bad, it is utterly execrable. And I assure you that mere panting is not my only goal with the lovely bonnets."

Charles shared an exasperated look with the third undergraduate, a short, bespectacled type with a gentle expression. He'd met Roger O'Donnell, Marcus Hebron and Richard Reade during their first dinner in Hall. They seemed to be very decent fellows, but even after a week of growing friendship he still wasn't used to O'Donnell's blunt talk about the feminine half of the population. "Speaking of p-poetry, are you attending the lecture by that American poet tonight?" he asked, trying to change the subject.

"Edgar Allan Poe? Wouldn't miss it for the world," O'Donnell said. "Town's been invited, you know. I'm rather hoping he recites 'The Raven.' Surely a few members of the fairer sex will be disturbed enough to need the sheltering arm of a gentleman afterwards."

Charles felt his face heat. "O'Donnell, really."

"Dodgson has a point," Reade added. "You might have more luck with the bonnets if you behaved more like a gentleman."

"Oh, heavens, not another sermon," O'Donnell sighed. "We all know you're destined to become the Archbishop of Canterbury, Reade. You don't need to rub your holiness in our face."

"If only it would do you some good, you godless heathen," Reade said mildly. "Could we at least try to conduct ourselves like the serious young scholars we are?"

The four young men considered each other, then burst into good-natured laughter. Still chuckling, they filed into the venerable building with the other members of the House.

The dining hall of Christ Church boasted high Gothic windows, a vaulted ceiling, and portraits of past Deans and college notables lining the paneled walls, including such luminaries as Henry VIII and Thomas Cromwell. Three long rows of oak tables led up to the High Table, where the Dean, college dons, and guests held court over meals. Charles and his friends took their accustomed seats at the end nearest the door, wondering what the kitchens would be offering today.

Black-suited servers began carrying in large tureens.

O'Donnell groaned at the sight. "Oh, no. Stew. Made from leftovers, no doubt."

Charles studied the tureen in a server's hands, trying not to wince. Raised at his father's rectory in Croft, he'd grown up on fresh produce and country-raised meats. The food at Rugby, and then Oxford, had been an unpleasant education to his palate. "It m-might not be that bad."

With an enigmatic expression, the server began ladling out chunks of meat and boiled vegetables in a thick gravy onto their plates. Reade picked up his knife and fork, sawing off a bit and taking a tentative bite. "I suspect it's lamb."

"Lamb. How convenient, seeing as we had chops for dinner last night," O'Donnell said glumly, staring at his own plate.

Any reply was curtailed by someone barking, "By God, I wouldn't feed this slop to m'hounds!" from farther up the table. Charles grimaced at the voice. Philip Stiles was the fourth undergraduate he'd met on the first day of Michaelmas term. Unfortunately, Stiles wasn't nearly as congenial as O'Donnell, Hebron, and Reade. After the nobleman had held forth at luncheon about how he'd butchered a whelping bitch that summer in order to retrieve her valuable puppies, a nauseated Charles had stuttered while asking him to pass him the wine carafe. Stiles had thought it was terribly funny and kept finding ways to tease him about his affliction for the rest of the meal, only stopping when O'Donnell suggested that he might want to stop taunting his fellow undergraduates if he wanted to retain the ability to chew his food.

To Charles's surprise, Hebron and Reade had backed O'Donnell up, glaring at Stiles in unison. Taking in the four men opposing him, Stiles had finally held his tongue. The incident forged a friendship among the quartet, and O'Donnell had puckishly taken to calling them the Four Horsemen.

Since then, however, the arrogant young nobleman made a point of mocking Charles whenever the two met. He did his best to hold his temper and avoid Stiles, but a shared Classics lecture and meals in the Hall made it difficult.

Now, Stiles' florid face went even pinker as he glared at the server and pointed a knife at his plate. "This is absolute tripe. I want a fresh chop and onions, d'you hear?"

"Begging your pardon, sir, but luncheon is a set menu," the server said with the patience of someone who had faced down arrogant young men before. "If you do not care for it, you may always take luncheon elsewhere."

"And so I shall," Stiles sneered, standing with little grace. He noticed Charles, and roughly slid his plate down the table. "You can feed this to D-d-odo and his ducklings. Come, Blakeney."

His dining partner, a sallow young man with large, moist eyes and a hangdog expression, hurried out of his chair and followed Stiles out of the hall. O'Donnell snorted at their departure. "Good riddance to bad rubbish," he said, sawing at his meat. "One of these days he'll go too far and I'll pound him, I will."

"He's not worth being sent down for," Reade advised. "With any luck, he'll give up the food here as a dead loss and take his meals elsewhere."

Charles forked up a chunk of grayish meat and concentrated on chewing it. If nothing else, he and the obnoxious young nobleman were in accord on the quality of the food. "Shall we meet at my room before Poe's l-lecture tonight?"

Hebron waved a fork dismissively. "I think I'll pass, if it's all the same to you. Poetry's never been my cup of tea."

"And I'm afraid have to finish my Greek translations," Reade added with an apologetic smile. "Although I would enjoy hearing about it later."

"You poor, deluded beggars." O'Donnell nudged Charles.

"Well, then, it looks like it's just the two of us for the lecture tonight. I'll be at your room ten minutes before the hour. Make sure you're properly afternoonified—I want the bonnets to absolutely swoon with our devastating good looks and sense of fashion."

Charles shared another exasperated look with Reade. "I'll d-do my best." His regular clothes were perfectly suitable for such an event, and he had no intention of donning a strangely colored waistcoat or any of the other ridiculous fashions he'd spotted among his fellow undergraduates.

O'Donnell can chase after all the young ladies, if that's his pleasure. All he wanted for himself was a quiet, pleasant evening. And listening to Edgar Allan Poe lecture on poetry promised to do just that.

With no little relief, Eddy found that his hotel room was quite clean and furnished with a brass bed, armoire, dresser, table, and a solid-looking chair. The dresser held a porcelain bowl and jug; he assumed the other sanitary device present in civilized bedrooms was tucked underneath the bed. "This will do nicely," he said, nodding to the porter who had brought him upstairs. As he did, his glance fell on the sleeve of his coat, noting a smear of train ash. "Would it be possible to have my coat sponged and pressed? I have a business meeting in a few hours."

"Of course, sir. I'll send one of the chambermaids up to fetch it." The porter waited at the door, key to the room clutched in one hand and Eddy's valise still captive in the other, giving the impression that he was willing to stand there as long as necessary until he was tipped.

Suppressing a wince, Eddy pulled out sixpence and held it out. The now-smiling porter exchanged it for the key, depositing the valise next to the door, and departed.

Doing his best to ignore the reduction in funds, Eddy decided to move the table so that it would sit in front of the window. The October daylight, added to that of a candle, would be sufficient for working on a new C. Auguste Dupin story, something his New York editor had been requesting for some time. Pulling out paper, pen, and a carefully capped pot of ink that went everywhere with him, he sat down to write.

After few minutes, however, he laid the pen down and sighed, the paper in front of him half-full of scratched out beginnings. The idea of killing the imperious gentleman from the train in a suitably horrible manner had been amusing, but didn't really lend itself to a Dupin story. Restless, he stood up and went to his trunk, ignoring the subtle creep of gooseflesh at the silence of the room. It was more difficult to ignore the bleak fact that he hadn't spent a night alone, much less a night alone in a hotel, since October 1849.

I strongly doubt there are Roysters hiding in the armoire. You're perfectly safe. He opened the trunk, checking over the carefully folded new clothing inside. The tailor had been bemused at his request that his outer garments—frock coat, vest, trousers, neck cloth, and hat—were to be black, as unrelieved and Stygian a shade as modern dyers and weavers could produce. It prompted Elmira to sigh and make a not-so-subtle suggestion that perhaps for once he might try a coat in navy blue, or even dark plum?

He had explained his preference for funereal elegance, how it suited his work better than more lively colors. She'd given in with a charitable sigh, and two weeks later the tailor had produced a new wardrobe in the required shade. Privately, he admitted to himself that the unmitigated black did make him look somewhat like a raven. *But oh, how my feathers gleam.*

Smiling at the memory, he returned to the desk and set aside the now-scrap paper. Pulling a clean sheet into place, he deciding to write a letter to Elmira.

A knock on the door interrupted him before he could write anything more than *My Dearest.* With a sigh, he went to the door and opened it a crack. "Yes?"

An attractive young chambermaid waited in the hall. "I was told you needed your coat to be cleaned and pressed, sir," she said with a bobbing curtesy.

"Oh, yes." With relief, he opened the door and waved her inside, doffing his coat and handing it over. "I need this back before five o'clock, please."

"Yes, sir." Instead of leaving, however, she gave him a shy, hesitant smile. "I don't mean to impose on your time, sir, but could I ask you to sign my book? Your book, I mean, of your poems."

His trip to England was a lecture tour intended to attract new readers, but he'd never dreamed of looking for them in the working class. "You know my work?"

Her blush was quite fetching. "Oh, yes, sir. I'm ever so fond of your poems. All shivery dark, they are, but lovely."

His heart warmed at the praise. "In that case, I would be delighted to sign your book, especially as my ink pot is open and my quill stands at the ready." He winced, realizing how his words might be taken, but she either ignored the unfortunate double entendre or didn't notice it in the first place.

She fished a slender book out of her apron—the Ponsonby edition of his collected works, he noted—and handed it over. Taking the book to his writing table, he picked up the quill. "And what's your name, my dear?"

She shook her head. "My name's Jane, sir, but if you could sign it to PRS I would be ever so grateful."

A love gift, then. With a flourish, he did as instructed, taking care to blot the ink before handing the book back. "I hope he appreciates your devotion."

Her look changed, becoming wistful. "I hope so as well, sir." With another curtsey, she bustled off with his coat, poetry tucked securely back in her apron.

The girl's talk of a gentleman suitor reminded him of Elmira and his waiting letter. He felt a sense of contentment at the gentle but unyielding force of nature that was his second wife. *How my luck has finally changed, and for the better. Little as I believe in an almighty power, I would have to admit that I am indeed a blessed man.*

A memory of beautiful violet eyes came to him, limning his contentment with a touch of wistfulness. *And wherever you are, Sissy, I hope that you've found the peace and happiness you always deserved. I still miss you, my angel.*

He sat back down, but instead of detailing the journey from London to Oxford he gave himself over to the lyrical imagery forming in his mind. *O, that a humble maid could find beauty in the written word, and gift that beauty to the one she loves…*

Picking up the pen, he dipped it in the ink pot and began to write.

CHAPTER THREE

Eddy stared at the words on the paper, absently chewing his lip as he immersed himself in the poem's flow. *With flashing eyes, her snow-pale skin glowed to shame Selene's own light—*

A knock at the door dragged him back to reality. He fished out his pocket watch and checked the time. To his surprise, it was almost five o'clock. *No wonder I feel so stiff.* But it was a fair exchange, considering the afternoon's worth of work at his impromptu desk.

Groaning a bit, he struggled to his feet, feeling his spine crackle pleasurably as he crossed to the door. Once again, a smiling Jane stood in the hallway, his frock coat folded over one arm. "Your coat, Mr. Poe," she said, handing over the freshened garment. "Oh, and Mr. Venables said a gentleman's arrived for you."

Ponsonby's man, hopefully with his stipend. He slipped on the coat, now immaculate. "Splendid. You're a veritable angel, Jane."

Her smile widened, lighting up her pretty face and making her beautiful. "It's my pleasure, sir. Thank you again for signing my book." With a curtsey, she left.

Eddy paused in front of the room's mirror to straighten his neckcloth and smooth his hair before going down to meet with Ponsonby's man. The simple, homely gestures reminded him of

Elmira, and he felt a sudden pang at her absence.

She hadn't tolerated the steamship voyage from New York well, continuing to suffer from *mal de mer* once they arrived in London. As Mrs. Ponsonby was traveling to Bath to take the waters, she had been kind enough to invite Elmira along for a week's cure. Tired and ill, his wife had agreed, and Eddy had seen her off at the London station the day before, kissing her gloved hand with a warm affection that was only slightly tinged with worry. *Elmira isn't Sissy. She doesn't suffer from consumption or any other lingering disease.* After a few good meals and some relaxation in Bath she would be right as rain, and they would continue on the rest of the tour together. He only had to make do without her for a few days, a week at most.

The ghostly taste of rye filled his mouth. To counter it he summoned the image of Elmira's face. *I made a promise, imp, and I will not renege on it. Not this time.*

Resolved, he reached for the small, pocket-sized volume waiting on the desk. It was a collection of Elizabethan love poetry and had been Elmira's wedding present to him. He considered it his lucky charm and made a point of carrying it with him during a lecture. "That way," he had explained to his delighted wife, "I always have someone who loves me in the audience."

Slipping the book into his coat pocket, he went down to the lobby. As promised, Ponsonby's manager was waiting there and introduced himself as Arthur Tomlinson. A sandy-haired man of medium height, Mr. Tomlinson's most noteworthy characteristic was an impressive nose that seemed to travel before him like the prow of a noble sailing ship.

His most welcome characteristic, however, was a proffered envelope with Eddy's stipend. "It's truly a pleasure to meet you, sir," Tomlinson said, giving Eddy's hand a careful but thorough shake. "I've made all the arrangements for the lecture tonight, and I'm quite sure the hall will be teeming."

"I would hope so. The audience in London was most appreciative." His stomach picked that moment to emit a low growl, and he surreptitiously rubbed it. "I don't suppose we have time for a bite to eat before the lecture? I'm afraid I've been in the toils of the Muse all afternoon, and she's a jealous mistress when it comes to more prosaic needs."

Tomlinson brightened at that. "I know just the place. If you'll follow me?"

Their destination turned out to be a nearby restaurant that boasted a warm, welcoming dining room. Eddy turned down an offer of wine in favor of lemonade and tucked into an excellent beefsteak while Tomlinson reviewed the schedule for the evening. The lecture would take place at Christ Church College, the manager explained, with a small reception afterwards where potential subscribers to *The Stylus* could speak with Eddy, have him sign one of his collected works, and hopefully pay the three pounds that would entitle them to a year's subscription to the magazine.

"We had the noted poetess Madame Antoine here last year, and she sold out of her collection halfway through the evening," Tomlinson confided over his denuded chop bone. "To be honest, her poetry was absolutely dreadful—all sugar-spun images of fat cherubim dancing around beams of sunlight like some sort of heavenly maypole. But it certainly sold well."

Eddy smiled at the jibe. Elmira had been given a copy of Madame Antoine's work (he hesitated to call such drivel poetry), and even her pious nature had been put off by the treacle-sweet tone of the Frenchwoman's verses. "I hope no one expects dancing cherubim from me."

"On the contrary," Tomlinson assured him. "You are well-known for your literary voyages into the darker side of the soul, after all. And I've found that Oxonians prefer an intellectual challenge to a French nanny spoon-feeding them pap about the Divine."

Sated both by the meal and the praise, Eddy accepted a cigar from Tomlinson while the bill was settled, then they left the restaurant and continued down Cornmarket Street. The street itself was lined with more of the elegant stone buildings that permeated Oxford, the majority of them featuring a shop, public house or restaurant on the ground floor, and what appeared to be living quarters on the upper floors. Every other building seemed to boast a bow window adorned with crenellations and carved brackets, giving the streets a modern and prosperous feel.

They crossed the High Street and approached an imposing Gothic edifice, its grey stone further muted in the glow from the gas lamps. "Christ Church College," Tomlinson explained. "It's one of the largest colleges in the university, and boasts the cathedral for the Diocese of Oxford."

"A most impressive institution," Eddy said affably. They passed through the domed portcullis, where a guard in a neat black suit and a hat with a curiously curved crown took their names and gave them directions to the lecture hall.

The hall itself was reassuringly full. Eddy looked out over his audience, his enthusiasm laced with a touch of stage nerves. The attendees looked to be a mixture of college students, professors and townsfolk, judging from the healthy ratio of bonnets scattered throughout the auditorium. That was good; he could lecture to an all-male audience, certainly, but he enjoyed it more when his audience included ladies as well.

A gentleman with bushy white muttonchops took the lectern to introduce him, and the audience applauded politely. Taking a deep breath, Eddy assumed what he thought of as his "dramatic" pose behind the lectern, one hand clasping his lapel while the other was free for gesturing, and lifted his chin. "That the Americans are not a poetical people has been asserted so often and so roundly, both at home and abroad, that the slander has come to be received as truth," he began. "And yet, our shores have hosted a most prodigious flowering of poetry."

His lecture was based on one he'd given at the Boston Lyceum a few months back. He'd toned down some of the brasher claims of achievement on the part of American literary stylists, but decided that an Oxford audience would be more than equipped to take on his proposals in the proper spirit of debate. He went on to describe the artistic depth elicited by American writers such as Henry Wadsworth Longfellow and Washington Irving, cheerfully ignoring the hypocrisy in his own words and the way he'd tomahawked those very poets without mercy only a few years ago. There was nothing quite like a common enemy to make him embrace the damned Frogpondians like brothers.

Using samples of their work as well as his own, he continued to trace the development of poetry in the former colony, acknowledging the nods to classical literature while highlighting the ways in which American writers strove to push the boundaries of their craft with the same zeal that pioneers pushed the boundaries of the growing country. The lecture concluded with a sweeping statement that poetry was alive and well in America and, while owing a certain debt to its English forebears, had grown to such a point where it was able to hold its own on the world stage.

The applause following his conclusion was even more enthusiastic than it had been in London. Eddy felt a tingle of joy beneath his breastbone, pleased that he had anticipated their tastes so well. *Clearly an educated audience recognizes the compliment to their mental jaws.* After a humble nod of appreciation, he launched into his first poem of the night, "Lenore."

The audience remained enthusiastic throughout the recital, and after his *pièce de résistance* of "The Raven," their applause bordered on cacophonous. At the end he nodded thanks to his mutton-chopped master of ceremonies, then followed Tomlinson to a side hall where a stout oak table had been set up with stacks of his collected works, a blotter, ink pot, and pen. There was a goodly sized line of people waiting for him, and he cheered silently at the mental calculation of potential sales.

First in line was a pair of older gentlemen in the distinctive costume of the Oxford don, followed by a gaggle of matrons eager to ask him questions about the imagery in "Lenore." He managed to sell a subscription to one lady with a large bonnet and apple cheeks before a pair of young men stepped up, obviously undergraduates from their academic robes and quaint hats. "Thank you for coming to the lecture, gentlemen," he said. "I do hope you found it illuminating."

"Most illuminating indeed, Mr. Poe," the shorter man said. "I've read your 'Raven' a number of times, and I find your use of language to be absolutely astonishing."

His companion was clearly nervous but managed to nod in agreement. "M-mister P-poe," he said with an unfortunate stammer, "I j-just wanted to s-say, it w-was a p-pleasure to hear you r-read your p-p-p-p—"

Eddy waited until it became obvious that the young man couldn't quite manage 'poetry.' "I'm very glad that you enjoyed the lecture," he said kindly, hoping to put the undergraduate at ease and move the line along. "If either of you would be interested in a subscription to my literary magazine or bound editions of my works, both are available here, and I would be happy to sign them for you."

"O-oh, yes," the young man said, blinking over a shy smile. "I-I—"

"D-d-don't quite know what to say," a mocking voice finished. A solidly built blond man attired in tailored academic robes stepped out from behind the undergraduate, laughing and clapping the stutterer on the shoulder hard enough to make him wince. "Don't mind Dodo, Mr. Poe. Poor chap's tongue gets tied into a Gordian knot at the slightest provocation, don't you know?"

"Dodo's" flush deepened, turning almost crimson. His companion stepped forward, glaring at the blond. "That's enough, Stiles."

Stiles scoffed. "Oh, do calm yourself, O'Donnell. I simply wish to have my book signed sometime before Hilary term, so if Dodo would be so kind to move along?"

"Dodo" stepped out of line and left the hall, spine stiff as he marched away. With an apologetic nod to Eddy and a parting glare for Stiles, O'Donnell followed.

Eddy felt a flicker of irritation at the loss of potential subscriptions but forced a pleasant look as he turned to the blond. "Did you enjoy the lecture, sir?"

"It was tolerably amusing." Stiles smirked at his own companion, a sallow youth with a mild countenance. "Now, I wish to purchase a copy of *The Raven and Other Poems*. Make out the inscription to Uncle Robert, there's a good chap."

Eddy recognized the type from his own university days; handsome, moneyed, and spoiled beyond belief to the point where he was quite convinced of his own divinity, a belief reinforced by the sycophants that surrounded him. A bubble of irritation rose in his gut.

You are here to sell books and subscriptions, so keep your opinions to yourself. "Of course," he said, selecting the chosen volume from the stacks on the table and inscribing it as requested, signing his name on the frontispiece. "That will be two and six."

The young man did a very deliberate double take, then looked around at the waiting audience. "God's teeth, man, that much for a book of rhymes?" he declared. "What do you charge for your fiction, a sultan's ransom?"

His companion was the only one who chuckled at the weak humor. "I think you'll find that the cost of this volume is quite a reasonable one," Eddy said, keeping his voice even. "And the subscriptions we are offering to *The Stylus* are even more reasonable, considering that they provide a year's worth of the best poetry and fiction from America."

Stiles snorted. "No, I'll just take the book and be done with it." He tossed the coins onto the table as if paying a shopkeeper.

Think of Elmira. You're here to raise money for the Stylus, *not insult young idiots. No matter how much they deserve it.* "I thank you for your patronage, sir," Eddy said, his voice now clipped as he slid the book across the table. "I hope that your Uncle Robert enjoys these works."

"As do I—goodness knows something needs to sweeten his mood these days," the young man said carelessly, turning to his friend. "Come on, then. Off to the Bear, I think."

His companion flashed an apologetic look before following Stiles to the door. Eddy turned to the next person in line when he heard Stiles say, "Lecherous old tosspot married his child cousin, did y'know? Think there's something racy in his scribbles?"

His imp took control of his throat before he could stop it. "If there is, sir, I sincerely doubt your limited powers of comprehension could locate it," he called, his voice carrying across the room.

The waiting crowd fell silent as Stiles turned. "What did you say?"

"Oh, you're losing your hearing as well?" Eddy sniped. "What a shame. Still, it just goes to show what overbreeding can do to the stock."

Stiles stormed back to the table, flinging the book on the table. "I want my money back. And consider yourself lucky that I'm not demanding satisfaction as well."

Eddy allowed himself a smirk. "I do believe dueling is illegal on these shores. As for returning your money, I'm afraid it's quite out of the question. The book has been personalized to your uncle. I can hardly resell it now that it has been inscribed thus."

Stiles leaned over the table, his complexion shading to an unpleasant purple. "Give me my money back or—"

Eddy got to his feet, matching Stiles's stance if not his height. "Or what?" he challenged.

Before the man could reply, Tomlinson bustled up with one of the college staff in tow. "Gentlemen, is there a problem here?" the manager said, his voice strained as he peered at the standoff over the oak table.

The import of where he was came back to Eddy. He straightened, taking a deep breath and smoothing his frock coat. "No problem at all," he said, cocking his head as he considered Stiles. "Is there, sir?"

The young man opened his mouth to reply, but his companion grabbed his shoulder and hissed something in his ear, nodding at the grim college employee. Struggling to compose himself, Stiles glared at Eddy. "I suppose not," he muttered, ungracefully snatching the book up before striding out of the hall, friend in tow.

The atmosphere in the room had palpably changed, shifting

from admiration to people watching a dog fight. *Damn you, imp.* Clearing his throat, Eddy sat down and forced himself to smile the next person in line. “And how did you find the lecture, sir?”

CHAPTER FOUR

"The man is an unmitigated ass," O'Donnell growled, stomping alongside Charles as they crossed the shadowed quadrangle. "You shouldn't have left. We could have given him what for."

"N-not worth it," Charles said wearily.

The shorter man snorted. "Certainly it was. And it's not as if we'd be sent down. Everyone in the hall would have vouched that he was behaving like a rotter."

Not for the first time, Charles wished that he could explain his thoughts clearly and easily instead of having them chopped up by his unruly tongue. He was used to the teasing by now; he'd endured it often enough at Rugby. From that experience, he knew that the taunting would continue until Stiles grew tired of the game or he gave Stiles a good thrashing.

Here, the latter simply wasn't an option. He imagined his father's reaction to the news that his eldest son had been caught fighting with another undergraduate, and his stomach curdled at the thought. The year had been difficult enough, what with the unexpected death of his mother in January and him having to leave Oxford and return home in order to help his father. He would not cause further hurt to his family by a physical confrontation with some upper-class imbecile with too much money and too little sense.

No matter how much he wanted to. "I won't give him the s-satisfaction of dragging me d-down to his level," he said with as much dignity as he could muster. "If he w-wishes to provoke a fight, he'll h-have to look somewhere else."

O'Donnell sighed at that. "I suppose you're right. But I didn't get Poe's book. Or get a chance to chat with any of the bonnets, dash it all."

Charles felt suddenly abashed. "I'm s-sorry, O'Donnell. Please, go back—"

His friend waved away the offer. "Not worth it, old man. If I run into that blackguard now, I suspect my temper will get the better of me. And then I shall be sent down and Pater will make good on his threat to put me in the Navy, and ne'er shall you see old Roger again." He grinned. "No, I think it's a much better plan to hie ourselves over to the Saddlers Arms for a cheering cup, what do you say?"

Charles studied the dark sky. "Well, I r-really should be working on my Greek translations."

O'Donnell's grin widened. "Dodgson, I admire a swot as much as anyone, especially when he's the type of chap to lend me his notes, but after an encounter with a disgrace such as Stiles it's absolutely unheard of that you don't need a pint of ale."

He couldn't stop himself from smiling at the thought. "In t-that case, I suppose I could lend m-myself to the endeavor."

"Capital!" O'Donnell strode off like a proud bantam cock, an amused Charles in tow.

"Well, that could have gone better," Tomlinson said with a sigh.

"It could hardly have gone worse," Eddy muttered. After the contretemps with Stiles, the crowd had rapidly thinned out, giving him nervous looks and leaving him with a stack of unsold books and only one other subscription, to a young woman dressed in a rather unconventional gown and shawl dyed a deep green. At least Tomlinson seemed excited to take her details, explaining later that that she belonged to the Oxford literary circle and would surely elicit more interest in his work.

Eddy shook his head, remembering the fickle favors of the Starry Sisterhood and how he'd been forced to leave New York after an ill-fated affair with one of them. He shoved his hands deep into his pockets, staring morosely at the sidewalk as they left the college grounds. "Elmira was right. I shouldn't be allowed out without a keeper."

"Oh, come now, it wasn't that bad," Tomlinson said with forced good cheer. "And you did sell three subscriptions and a handful of books. Let's have a drink. There's a pub near the Mitre that serves an exceptionally good ale."

The taste of rye flooded his mouth, and a craving for the oblivion it brought crashed through him with shocking force. *Just one drink, Eddy.* The imp's thin, high, reedy voice seemed to speak from the farthest corners of his mind.

"I promised my wife that I would not indulge in spirits." He hated the weak sound of the word "promise." After all, he hadn't simply promised; he'd made a vow.

"Ah, wives." Tomlinson chuckled. "But she's not here, is she? And what the little woman doesn't know won't hurt her, eh?"

Hurt. He couldn't help wondering if Elmira was in pain at the moment. Was she getting better in Bath, or was her malaise worsening? And that damned upstart had ruined a promising evening, making everything worse. What he wouldn't give for just one drink—

He's right, Eddy, the imp whispered. *Just a drop or two won't hurt. You've been working so hard, trying to keep Elmira happy and win over that wretched family of hers. And don't forget, that arrogant young ass lost you badly needed sales tonight. A glass would help you relax and sleep. Elmira's not here—she never needs to know. You* deserve *this.*

"I really shouldn't," he said, fighting for control.

Tomlinson elbowed him gently, a gesture of masculine bonhomie that almost maddened him. "Just a drop or two, to steady your nerves," he said persuasively. "What do you say?"

Just one drink, Eddy. You can stop after that. And Elmira will never know.

Eddy swallowed, the thirst nigh on overwhelming now. "Perhaps a drop or two wouldn't hurt," he muttered.

The man sat in the darkened room, waiting for footsteps in the hallway. He knew his prey's routine by now: clean the occupied guest rooms during the day, make sure the first floor hallway was dusted and swept, wash and hang bedding in the afternoon, and refresh any unoccupied rooms in the evening.

There was only one unoccupied room on this floor, which meant she'd be along any moment now. The lock had been easy enough to pick, and he smiled as he imagined her reaction when she found him waiting for her.

Finally, a set of light footsteps sounded in the hallway. He pictured her bustling towards him, a pile of clean bedding in her arms. He stood up and slipped behind the door. A key rattled in the lock and the chambermaid stepped into the dim room, briefly outlined by the gaslight in the hallway before she closed the door behind her. She crossed to the bed, laying down the clean linen and lighting a candle. Taking that as his signal, he stepped forward and slid his arms around her waist.

She gasped and spun, glaring at him. "How did you get in here?" she said, pushing at his chest. "I've work to do, so you can take your games elsewhere—"

He tightened his embrace, pulling her closer.

She struggled in his arms. "Stop it, now. I mean it!"

He let her go and watched her expression flood with relief; she must have thought it was over, he thought, just another jape. Until his hands came up and ringed her throat, closing in a crushing grip. She squeaked, fingers scrabbling against the chokehold.

He smiled, shaking his head as he increased the pressure on her throat. Her desperate fingers tightened, clawing at his hands. Her eyes dulled, the whites pinkening as the delicate blood vessels there hemorrhaged from the pressure of his hands on her neck. Finally, after a minute that felt like one long delicious eternity, her wriggling stilled and she sagged in his grip.

He held on for a bit longer, just to make sure, then lowered her body to the ground. Checking for a pulse, he found none, and his smile widened in satisfaction. His hand continued to her face, brushing a lock of russet hair away from her staring eyes. Even dead, she was still lovely.

Which would make his next step even more pleasant. Flipping up her heavy skirts, he yanked down the clean, carefully patched pantaloons, exposing her lower abdomen to his interested gaze. Still no sign, but it was early days yet.

Humming to himself, he reached into his coat for the knife.

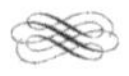

"My grandfather was General David Poe, a hero of the Revolution, sir!" Eddy roared, trying to focus on the young man in front of him. Who was he again? *Oh, yes, the friend of that stuttering lad.* Who, as a matter of fact, was sitting in the corner now, watching their debate with mute fascination. "My family is one of the most distinguished in Virginia, and I, *I*, sir, took highest honors at the University of Virginia!"

"Mr. Poe—" He felt Tomlinson putting a restraining hand on his arm.

He shook it off grandly. "I will not be talked down to by this, this pup, this craven child." He waved his empty glass at the undergraduate. "How dare you, sir!"

"I didn't mean to slight your family, sir," the young man said. "In fact, I'm not quite sure how I did so. I merely meant to say that we do have something of a head start on our American cousins when it comes to the art of poetry. After all, the language in which you craft your rhymes did originate on these shores."

That did make sense, dammit. "A seed's point of origin has little to do with its flowering, sir!" Eddy declared.

"Well, I rather think it does," the young man said. "After all, you wouldn't expect an orange tree to blossom near Glasgow—"

"Mr. Poe." That was Tomlinson again, now tugging on his arm. "I think you're overtired, sir. Perhaps we should be leaving?"

Eddy whirled on the man, staggering as he fought for balance. "And abandon the field in the heat of battle?" he demanded. "*Et tu, Brute?* Is this the kind of amanuensis Ponsonby sends to assist his authors?"

"I'm afraid it is, sir," Tomlinson muttered, seeing the bartender approach. "And speaking of assistance, perhaps we should be making our way back to the Mitre now?"

The bartender, a tall, stocky man with a beetling brow and shoulders that indicated he could carry kegs of ale unassisted, stopped in front of them. "Is there a problem here, gents?" he rumbled.

Eddy drew himself up, vaguely aware that he was staring the bartender directly in the chest. "I would say so, sir. Your clientele is badly in need of instruction when it comes to the art of the written word."

The bartender nodded thoughtfully. "Issat a fact? Well, any sort of instruction that involves shouting at my customers had best be taken outside."

A flicker of self-preservation broke through his fury, reinforced by blurry memories of being tossed out of assorted drinking establishments. Landing in refuse piles hurt, after all. "Indeed? Well, that suits me quite well, sir. I didn't wish to spend any more time at this establishment, anyway." He reached out and grabbed a nearly full bottle of wine from his table. "Tomlinson, pay the man and we'll be off."

"Pay the man?" Tomlinson squeaked. But Eddy was already walking out the door, swigging from the bottle as he went.

The rest of the evening passed in brief flashes. A cluster of more infernal young men passing him and snickering, damn their eyes. Pausing before the imposing edifice of Lincoln College and improvising a quatrain to the Muse of History. The welcoming glow of the Mitre, Tomlinson's final mutters of farewell, and the seemingly endless stairs to his room.

As he fumbled for his key, he rested a hand on the door and almost fell forward when it opened unexpectedly. He giggled at his own foolishness for leaving the door open. *At least you don't have to wrestle with the door lock, eh?* Staggering into the dark room, he shucked off his coat and tumbled headlong onto the bed. Some sleep, some dreamless hours of rest, and he'd get up and get back to work on the poem inspired by that lovely girl, what was her name? Jenny, Joan, something like that.

An unpleasant, meaty odor came to his nose, reminding him

of Sissy's coughing fits. *Damn it all, why must she cough like that? No, poor angel, she's ill. Must get up, make sure she's warm and have Muddy brew the medicine for her—*

Snuffling into his pillow, he surrendered to the welcome blackness.

The weak dawn sunlight that filtered through the net curtains felt like hot coals on Eddy's face. It was made worse by the thumping pain that bounced from temple to temple, reverberating throughout his entire body. He cracked one bloodshot eye open and groaned, sure that at some point in the night someone had switched his head with a giant rotting pumpkin.

With the greatest of reluctance he rolled over, whimpering when the thumping increased at his movement. Glaring at the innocent beams of sunlight streaming through the hotel room window, he took stock of his physical symptoms.

A foul taste in his mouth and a distinct layer of fur on his tongue. His stomach complaining vigorously and threatening to regurgitate its contents. His head doing its best impression of an overripe fruit about to pop. The stink of rank sweat coating his skin, and the distinctive odor of alcohol spilled on his shirt. Most importantly, the old familiar sense of dissipation and illness, topped with a generous helping of shame.

He closed his eyes against the sunlight, overcome with self-loathing. *Damn Tomlinson and his 'drop' of alcohol.*

With a whine that sounded pathetic even to himself, he managed to sit up, forcing himself to breathe slowly and deliberately until the room stopped spinning and the surge of nausea eased. Standing took an act of will, but after a moment he was upright, peering at the unfamiliar hotel room.

His valise, trunk, and writing implements were missing.

He felt his eyes bug in dismay, the nausea threatening to rise again. His lectures, his works in progress, his *stipend*, God help him, all gone, no no no—

He opened his mouth to bellow for help, but all that came out was a thin, weak hiss. As he sucked in a breath to try again, some last scrap of common sense came forward and pointed out a salient point. In addition to his missing belongings, the room's window was against the right wall instead of the left. Moreover, the table had not been pulled up underneath it.

Every muscle in his body unclenched. *Christ in Heaven. This isn't my hotel room.* Even the wallpaper was different, now that he could focus on it. In his drunken stupor, he'd somehow staggered into the wrong room last night.

With a thrill of relief, he bent over and wheezed. The wheeze turned into a chuckle, and then a full-throated gurgle of laughter. *Oh, Eddy, you idiot. You lucky, lucky idiot. What would have happened if you'd collapsed on top of a traveling salesman or some sleeping burgher and his wife?*

Wiping the tears from his eyes, he straightened up and shuffled forward, the pain in his head more bearable now. First to find his coat, then sneak into his own room and have a wash, and then a good breakfast—

His stomach roiled again. *No, perhaps not.* Coffee, then, as strong as the kitchen could make it, and then off to the train station and the next stop on the tour, and he would never ever mention last night to Elmira, it would be as if it had never happened—

His foot struck something soft.

He glanced down and gagged. The pretty young chambermaid from yesterday lay at his feet in a pool of blood, dead eyes staring in mute supplication.

CHAPTER FIVE

"Could you inform me of your whereabouts the previous evening, Mr. Poe?" the watchman asked.

Eddy licked dry lips, trying to think. The discovery of the dead chambermaid would be forever branded on his brain; the gutted figure sprawled at his feet, the metallic odor of old blood heavy in the air, wine-flavored bile filling his mouth as he staggered back, fighting not to vomit it all over the corpse.

He forced himself to calm. "I was invited to lecture at Christ Church College, where I spoke about the state of American poetry, after which I was taken to a pub. I think it was called the Saddler's Arms—"

"By who?"

"By—oh. A Mr. Tomlinson. He's an employee of Ponsonby Publishing in London." He watched while the watchman jotted down the information. "While there, I'm afraid I may have, uh, overindulged myself, and Mr. Tomlinson helped me back to the Mitre. After that, I don't remember anything until I was awoken by that poor woman's scream this morning."

Memories crowded into his head, making him cringe. The chambermaid's expression of utter despair, eyes dull and milky. Reddish hair disarrayed from its neat bun, and bruises ringing her throat. He'd edged past the sticky red pool, not wanting to look any longer at her body and the destruction wreaked on her lower abdomen, which had been flayed open like an anatomical illustration.

But his gaze kept returning to the gory opening with sick fascination. The killer had left her skirt flipped up, as if to show off his butchering artistry.

And the glyphs carved into the freckled skin of her belly.

The image had seared itself into his memory. He'd lunged for the door, trying to hold down the acid vomit rising in his throat. It was the purest of luck that no one was in the hallway as he darted across to his own room, especially as it took precious moments to fumble the key from his pocket and shove it home into the lock.

He'd scrambled for the chamberpot, vomiting copiously into it. Once done, he had sunk onto the bed, shaking like the proverbial leaf. No time at all seemed to pass before he'd heard the first shrill scream from across the hallway. He knew he should act the part of the innocent bystander; throw open the door, demand to know what was going on. But his body had rebelled, keeping him cowering on the bed until mid-morning.

It wasn't until someone knocked at the door that he'd managed to force himself off of the bedclothes. The visitor was an Officer Collin of the Oxford City Watch, who explained that there had been an unfortunate occurrence in the hotel that morning and it was his task to investigate the death of one Jane Billings, chambermaid.

Collin was a tall, florid man with pale hair and hard eyes who reminded Eddy unpleasantly of his in-laws. "Hm," the watchman now said, peering at a small notebook where he had been jotting down the story. "And you didn't think to see why someone was screaming?"

Eddy dredged up a sorrowful look. "I was in a fairly unpleasant condition this morning, as you can imagine. I didn't want to expose the other guests to that."

Collin sniffed, grimacing at the smell of vomit that lingered in the air. "I see, Mister—" he studied his notebook again, "Poe. And you heard nothing last night? No struggle, no cries at all?"

Shame caused his face to heat. "As I said before, I was not at my best last night," he said defensively.

"Mm. It's just that your room is the closest to the room where the murder took place. It does strike me as rather strange that you didn't hear a thing before the scream this morning, even in spite of your, hem, condition."

Before he could splutter out a reply, there was another knock at the door. Muttering an apology, Eddy scuttled over and opened it.

A portly man in a plain but serviceable black suit and bowler hat stood in the hall. Belatedly, Eddy remembered Tomlinson pointing out the sartorial combination as the uniform of the university's private police force, referred to as bulldogs.

"Mr. Poe, I believe?" the man said, tipping his hat politely. "My name is Constable Furnow. I'm with the Oxford University Police. May I come in?"

Two of them. Oh Christ in Heaven. Mute, Eddy nodded and stepped back. Furnow entered the room, pausing when he saw the other man sitting at the table. "Ah, Officer Collin," he murmured. "I wondered if we might be graced with your presence."

Collin rose, giving his colleague a sour look. "I'm not in the mood for any of your airs this morning, Furnow. This is a murder, not some sort of undergraduate prank. It falls under the City's bailiwick."

"Yes, but the incident took place on University property," Furnow said placidly, clasping his hands behind his back.

"It never did," Collin insisted. "It happened right across the hall, which you'd know if you bothered to actually look at the bloody room instead of swanning about like one of your dons."

The mild expression on Furnow's face never changed. "Oh, I did look at the, as you put it so aptly, bloody room, and I concur with your conclusion. But as I'm sure you know, Lincoln College owns the Mitre, which makes the Mitre University property. As that is the case, I am well within my rights as a member of the University Police to question Mr. Poe regarding his whereabouts last night."

A chill ran down Eddy's spine. "What?"

"Ah, I do beg your pardon, sir." Furnow turned to him. "It appears that you had quite the night, Mr. Poe, quite the night. According to witnesses at the Saddler's Arms, you became agitated after imbibing a bottle of wine and went so far as to threaten one young man with fisticuffs over an imagined slight against your family—"

Eddy's temper roared up. "Imagined? I don't care if he was a peer of the realm or the son of your sovereign herself. I will not be insulted with impunity!"

Furnow's eyebrows rose, and Eddy belatedly realized what he was saying. In a slightly shaky voice, he continued, "My apologies. I confess to certain passions when it comes to the literary arts and the discussion thereof. But I assure you, sir, it never would have come to blows."

Furnow nodded. "That is certainly a relief to know, Mr. Poe. But one does have to wonder if the argument caused you to return to your room in a heightened state of passion, as you put it."

Collin's eyes narrowed at that. "I wouldn't know," Eddy said, feeling sick. "You would have to ask Mr. Tomlinson."

"Oh, I already have, sir," Furnow said. "According to him, you were quite vocal when he returned you to the Mitre last night. Tell me, did you run across our unfortunate young chambermaid whilst returning to your room?"

His brain had become a small, panicked animal, spinning madly in his skull. "I—no, I don't think so."

"Ah. You don't think so," Furnow repeated with delicacy. "I do have to wonder, sir. The girl was quite fetching, and men in such a state of inebriation as you enjoyed last night can be quite, shall we say, enthusiastic over the likelihood of feminine attentions. Is it possible that you met her in the hallway and made a certain request of her? And when she rejected you, you pressed your attentions more firmly—perhaps too firmly?"

Eddy's head spun even faster and the blood began to drain from it. Before he could collapse, strong hands grasped his arms and forcibly guided him to the room's only chair, sitting him down and pushing his head between his knees.

"Deep breaths, sir," he heard Collin say.

He obeyed, gulping in air. Slowly, his head cleared. After a moment he levered himself upright, staring at his accusers. "That is the foulest thing I have ever heard," he choked out. "I have never imposed myself upon a woman in such a disgusting manner, and if we were in Richmond I would sue you for slander."

"Then I am relieved that we are in Oxford and not Richmond, sir," Furnow said, unperturbed. "This is a police investigation, Mr. Poe, and sometimes unpleasant things must be said in order to garner the truth. You have quite the reputation for macabre stories, and your personal conduct last night had been somewhat questionable, after all."

Over the course of his career he had been called many things—lazy, untrustworthy, a drunkard, even mad. But the idea that his work would somehow drive him to gut innocent women was unconscionable. "How in God's name do my tales—*fictional* tales, may I point out—give you the right to accuse me of a vicious murder?"

Furnow raised a calming hand. "I am simply explaining my mindset, Mr. Poe. You have a reputation for dark stories, you returned to this establishment last night somewhat worse for drink, and the next morning a chambermaid is found dead in the room across from yours. We would be remiss in our duties if we didn't investigate this unfortunate coincidence further."

"But to accuse me of murdering that poor girl?" Eddy cried. "And in such a bloody manner—how dare you, sir!"

Both Furnow and Collin went still, exchanging a look. "We never said she was murdered in a bloody manner, Mr. Poe," Collin said quietly.

He froze, the image of the dead girl in his mind's eye. "I—"

"Which makes me wonder how you garnered that particular tidbit of information," Furnow agreed. "Exactly where have you been this morning, sir?"

"In his room," Collin said, studying his notebook. "Said so himself. Didn't poke his nose out for aught until I knocked."

"Ah."

For such different men, they had similar gazes, utterly flat and cold. Eddy quailed, trying to think.

"You said yourself, officer, that it was a bloody room," he blurted. "When you were asking Constable Furnow if he'd looked at it. I assumed from your own words and his comments about my works that the girl had been murdered in a particularly gruesome way."

For once in his life, he had the wit to leave it at that, doing his damnedest to look, if not innocent, then not like a murderous monster either. The two policemen studied him, taking in his wretched state, then gave each other another long look.

Collin's gimlet stare returned to Eddy. "Do you happen to

carry a knife of some sort, sir?"

"Only a pen knife." He got up and crossed to the armoire where he'd flung his frock coat. Retrieving a small folding knife from one of the pockets, he held it out. Before Collin could take it, Furnow's hand darted in and plucked it neatly from Eddy's fingers. "You're both welcome to examine it."

"Oh, we will," Collin promised, glaring at Furnow.

"In the meantime, Mr. Poe, while this investigation is ongoing I must ask you to remain in Oxford," Furnow said, slipping the penknife into his pocket. "Just in case we have any further questions for you regarding the murder."

Remain in Oxford? The room started to spin again, all of his hopes and dreams for *The Stylus* and his career swirling like water around a drain. "But—but I am on a lecture tour! I'm due to leave this afternoon—"

"And we have a murder to solve, which trumps your lecture tour," Collin stated.

"I'm sure the authorities will be more than happy to send you on your way as soon as possible," Furnow added. "For now, however, you must remain in Oxford, and we are both holding you to your word as a gentleman that you will not try to leave without permission." He straightened, rubbing his hands together. "In the meantime, we have a murder to solve, don't we, Collin?"

"Don't we just," Collin growled. "Come on, then, and try not to tread on the evidence."

The policemen left, a numb Eddy following and closing the door behind them. To his fevered mind, the simple wooden clunk sounded more like the echoing clang of a slamming jail cell.

CHAPTER SIX

I'm caught, like a rat in a cage.

Eddy rested his forehead against the door's smooth wood, his gut aching from more than old wine. It was bad enough that he'd passed out in the same room as a corpse. Now he was trapped in Oxford until the police caught the murderer. Gossip flew on the wind; if the other stops on his tour caught word of what was happening, they could very well cancel his appearances, putting an end to his dreams for *The Stylus* and his career.

And then there's Elmira. He closed his eyes, thumping his forehead against the smooth oak. For two years he had remained faithful to his temperance pledge, the only thing she'd required of him. If she learned of the shameful scene in the pub last night, he might lose his marriage as well as his career.

Or worse. They could arrest him for the chambermaid's murder, and he would hang.

Eyes still shut, he stared at the pulsing starbursts in the darkness as if they could tell him what to do. Should he throw himself on the mercy of the two men who had just left? Admit that he'd staggered dead drunk into the room opposite and passed out on the bed? Could he prove without a shadow of a doubt that he had nothing to do with that poor girl's murder?

On the other hand, if he did stay quiet and they found out

where he'd slept, he might as well sign a confession and march into the jail cell. He wanted to curl into a ball and weep. Tomlinson was useless, Ponsonby was in London and might as well be in Timbuktu, and he didn't dare call on Elmira. *Dear God in heaven, I'm alone in this.*

A hysterical laugh bubbled up in his throat. *No, not alone.* How could he forget his looming guardian angels Collin and Furnow? His reputation, his marriage, his very life depended on two provincial police officers, when what he really needed were the services of—

Dupin. Eddy's eyes popped open. One of his greatest literary inventions, C. Auguste Dupin was a brilliant detective who had starred in four spine-chilling tales of mystery and murder. In each story Dupin had used ratiocination, or the process of logical thinking, to winkle out the killer.

Granted, Dupin was only a fictional creation and couldn't be hired to get him out of this mess. *But Dupin's a product of my own imagination, so surely we share some of the same brilliance.* If he used the same process of ratiocination, there had to be a chance that he could solve this crime himself, thereby clearing his name and saving his life in the process.

It was either that, or rely on Collin and Furnow.

I know what I'd rather do. Returning to the room's wooden chair, Eddy dropped onto it. *So where would Dupin start?*

The answer was immediate—he'd start with the body. *But I can't go back and look at it—her.*

Then again, perhaps he didn't need to. Deliberately he closed his eyes again. The horrible image of the girl's flayed belly with those crimson symbols carved over it returned to him. Blindly, he scrabbled for his quill, dipping it into the ink pot by feel and scribbling down the glyphs.

Taking a deep breath, he opened his eyes and studied what

he'd written. To his surprise, he recognized the symbols he'd scratched out; Ancient Greek letters, arranged in five groups like a sentence.

He chewed his lip, trying to puzzle out the meaning. While some of the symbols were familiar, he had no idea what the actual words said. He needed a translator to work out the message. *Surely in this center of learning, Tomlinson would know of someone fluent in Ancient Greek—*

Oh, Christ. Tomlinson. Eddy groaned. The manager was supposed to arrive at noon to escort him to the train station for the next leg of the book tour. But if Furnow had already interrogated him about the events of last night, Tomlinson was undoubtedly telegraphing London for instructions on how to handle a writer under suspicion of murder.

There was no help for it. Quickly donning a clean shirt, Eddy folded the paper and stuffed it into his trouser pocket, then grabbed his coat and hat. He had to find Tomlinson, and quickly.

Once on the street, however, he discovered that Oxford looked quite different during the day as compared to his inebriated memories of the previous night. He turned this way and that, wondering which way to go. If he remembered Tomlinson's chatter correctly, the bulk of the university's colleges were to the north and east, and to the west lay Cornmarket Street and the road to the train station. For a moment he had a mad thought of walking there and catching the first train to London.

No. It would be simple enough to find me through Ponsonby. If I don't stay here and clear my name, no one will. He surveyed the unedifying street. *Damn it all, was Tomlinson's office on Broad or Cornmarket? Or was it something more royal-sounding?*

Cudgeling his recalcitrant brain into motion, he didn't notice an approaching figure until it stopped in front of him. Annoyed, he looked up into the face of the stammering young undergraduate from the previous night.

"Oh! Mr. P-poe," the young man said, tipping his mortarboard. To Eddy's relief, he was more comprehensible than he'd been in the signing hall. "I d-do beg your pardon."

"My apologies, sir," Eddy replied automatically, touching his own hat with a forefinger. "I'm afraid I'm somewhat distracted at the moment. Er, would you by any chance know the location of the Ponsonby publishing warehouse? It's run by a man named Tomlinson."

The young man blinked in surprise. "I've just come from there myself, sir, to learn where you were staying. I wanted to r-return this to you." He pulled out a slim volume from inside his robes.

Eddy felt sick when he recognized the book as Elmira's love poems. He had no idea he'd lost it. "Where did you find this?"

"At the S-saddler's Arms, sir. You dropped it on your way, er, out."

He winced. The young man must have been one of the witnesses to his inebriated tirade. He took the proffered book, tucking it securely in his coat pocket. "I'm afraid I wasn't at my best last night. That aristo at your college managed to aggravate me beyond tolerance, and—" *You don't have time for this, you fool.* "Never mind. If I said anything out of order to you, young man, you have both my humblest apologies and my undying gratitude for returning this book. It's of the greatest sentimental importance to me."

The reserved look on the scholar's face thawed a bit. "You said nothing at all to me, Mr. P-poe, and I was quite happy to return the book to you. As for Philip Stiles, I'm afraid he's rather fond of his s-status as the heir to an earldom." He shook his head. "But you wished to visit Mr. Tomlinson's office. I would be happy to take you there, if you're unfamiliar with Oxford."

"I have no idea where I'm going," Eddy confessed, extending his hand, "Once again, you have my gratitude, Mister…."

"Dodgson, Charles Dodgson." The young man shook Eddy's hand with a strength belied by his thin frame. "If you'll follow me, sir?"

"With gratitude." He followed Dodgson down the High Street, crossing another main road before turning onto a small, winding street lined with offices and shops. As they walked, his hangover made itself known again, and he wished he had the funds to pay for a hansom. "Is it much further?" he asked, trying to match the other man's longer stride.

"Just a bit further," Dodgson said.

Ponsonby's book warehouse turned out to be a sturdy red brick building on Queen Street. Situated across from a church in the Gothic style, the warehouse looked both respectable and prosperous. Dodgson guided him inside to a reception room that was fragrant with the perfume of paper, leather, and binding glue, nodding at the two clerks there. "This is Mr. Edgar Allan Poe," he said to the nearest clerk, "h-here to see Mr. Tomlinson. Is he available?"

Both clerks studied Eddy with wary fascination. Obviously his behavior of the previous night had been a topic of gossip this morning. "Mr. Tomlinson is in his office," the first clerk said. "If you'll follow me?"

Eddy turned to Dodgson. "Thank you once again, sir. Your assistance has been most appreciated."

The tall young man nodded. "Shall I w-w-wait and escort you back to your hotel, or can you f-find your way?"

His first instinct was to dismiss Dodgson. But with his head aching so, having a willing guide that he didn't have to pay was a blessing he couldn't turn down. "If you would be so kind as to wait for me, that might be best. I'll return as soon as possible."

An agreeable Dodgson took a seat as the clerk guided Eddy up to Tomlinson's office. Unsurprisingly, it was lined with stout oak bookshelves, each shelf packed to overflowing with books, pamphlets, and other papers. The atmosphere was that of a somewhat disordered gentleman's library, and Eddy couldn't help feeling a bit jealous of such literary bounty.

To his relief, Tomlinson only seemed a little hesitant at his arrival, standing to greet him with a concerned look. "I'm glad to see you're feeling better this morning, Mr. Poe," he said, sounding quite sincere. "I was going to meet you at the Mitre at noon to take you to the train station. There was no need to come to my office."

So Furnow didn't pass along any unfortunate suspicions. Eddy hid his relief, assuming a look of regret. "I'm afraid there was, sir. Might we sit?"

Tomlinson waved him to a comfortable seat in front of the desk. Eddy took a deep breath, hoping he didn't look quite as green as he felt. "I understand that you spoke with a Constable Furnow about my actions last night?"

The manager nodded. "I'm afraid the bulldogs take a dim view towards altercations on university premises. I explained that I'd pressed you to take some refreshment for your nerves, however, and he seemed satisfied with it."

"Ah. Thank you for that." He licked parched lips. "However, I'm afraid that things have become more complex since then. There was a murder at the Mitre last night."

Tomlinson went pale. "Oh, that's terrible! Was it one of the guests?"

"No, one of the chambermaids. She was killed and left in one of the empty rooms for another maid to find." Eddy braced to throw himself on the other man's mercy and plead for assistance. "I spent the morning speaking with members of both the Oxford Watch and the University Constabulary about it, and—"

"Oh, they consulted you on the identity of the murderer?" Tomlinson's expression brightened. "My word, they must have been relieved to find that the creator of C. Auguste Dupin was staying in the very same hotel."

Eddy's train of thought abruptly derailed, plowed through a eureka moment, and jumped back onto a completely different track. "As a matter of fact, the police did confer with me about the mindset of a creature who could commit such a heinous crime," he said, feeling a crazed smile growing on his face. "They've asked me to stay here in Oxford for another day or so to help them with their enquiries."

Now Tomlinson frowned. "But Mr. Poe, you're expected in Coventry tonight, with a lecture scheduled for tomorrow. And afterwards there's Birmingham, Worcester, and Cheltenham, and—"

"My dear Mr. Tomlinson, surely an intelligent man such as yourself must understand that the murder of an innocent young woman trumps a book tour," Eddy said, shamelessly cribbing from Collin. "I should have matters resolved in a day or two, and then we can continue where we left off." He hesitated. "It wouldn't ruin the entire tour, would it?"

The manager bit his lower lip, then pulled out a pocket calendar. "I believe there were some rest days built into your schedule," he admitted, studying the calendar. "If we delete those, and push back the Coventry lecture for a day, and if you're willing to go straight from the train station to the lecture hall—"

"I'll do whatever is necessary. Just, please, give me the chance to help solve this poor girl's murder."

"I'll have to confirm this with Mr. Ponsonby, of course," Tomlinson warned, but there was a note in his voice that told Eddy he'd succeeded in his ruse. "Then again, if you do help the police solve this murder, it would provide some absolutely splendid publicity for your book and drum up more speaking engagements. We might even need another printing run."

"There, you see, and we all benefit," Eddy said, feeling more than slightly desperate. As if he didn't already have enough pressure to find Jane's murderer, now the sales of his book also depended on it. "Would you speak to Mr. Ponsonby for me, please?"

"Of course, sir. In the meantime, I'll contact the Mitre and have your stay there extended." Both men got to their feet and Tomlinson shook Eddy's hand. "But please, sir, I do beg that you try and complete your investigations as soon as possible. If this drags on for more than a few days, I don't think I can promise Mr. Ponsonby's good will."

Eddy's returning smile felt wooden. *If this drags on for more than a few days, I'll be in a jail cell and Ponsonby can go hang.*

If I don't do it first.

CHAPTER SEVEN

Upon his exit from Tomlinson's office, Eddy found the clerks whispering to Dodgson. All three of them turned at the same time, gazing at him dubiously.

Nettled, Eddy gave the clerks an imperious nod in return, then swept out the door. Dodgson scrambled to catch up with him. "I take it your c-conversation with Mr. Tomlinson was satisfactory?" the young man asked.

"If such a topic could be called satisfactory." Eddy repeated the story he'd improvised for Tomlinson, adding the manager's fillip that he was assisting the police with their enquiries.

Dodgson's air of disapproval vanished, replaced by dismay. "That poor, poor girl," he murmured, sounding genuinely grieved. "Death is every man's final debt to his Creator, of course, and the only path to life everlasting. But to be m-murdered in cold blood—I shall say a prayer for her immortal soul tonight."

"I'm sure she'd appreciate that," Eddy said absently. "Although right now I'm more concerned with those still on this plane of existence. I would trade every single subscription I've gathered so far for fifteen minutes with someone who can read Ancient Greek."

Dodgson blinked. "In Oxford? I suspect you would have difficulty *not* finding someone who could t-translate Ancient

Greek."

Eddy stopped in his tracks. "Can *you* read Ancient Greek?"

"Well, yes. I t-take it you need something translated?"

It appeared some deity was taking pity on him. "I suspect it may be a clue related to the murder. Unfortunately, it appears to be in the form of a sentence in Ancient Greek."

Dodgson's eyes widened. "A curious thing to be a clue."

"My thoughts exactly." Eddy considered his guide. Tall and slender underneath his scholarly robe and mortarboard, the young man was dressed in the same sedate suit worn by his elders, as if he had already joined their ranks. His modest air didn't quite mesh with the sharp gleam of intelligence in his eyes, however. Eddy felt encouraged by the dichotomy. "Would it be possible for me to borrow your expertise?"

"Of course, sir." Dodgson fished out a simple silver pocket watch, consulting it. "M-my next lecture isn't until this afternoon. May I suggest that we use my rooms? I suspect that p-proximity to my copy of Liddell and Scott's *Greek-English Lexicon* might be required."

He hadn't relished returning to the Mitre, especially if Collin and Furnow were still prowling the hallways. "I bow to your expertise, Dodgson. By all means, lead on."

The two continued down Queen Street, turning right onto the more populous St. Aldate's. As they approached a large cluster of buildings on the left side of the street, Eddy recognized them and felt his stomach churn. "Oh. We're going to Christ Church."

"Well, that is where my rooms are," Dodgson said mildly. "Is that a problem?"

"Not as such, assuming they allow me through the door." Eddy spotted an older man in the now-familiar bowler hat seated inside a small booth at the college's entrance. He had to fight an urge to turn tail and run.

The bulldog nodded at Dodgson, eyeing Eddy at the same time. "Good morning, Mr. Dodgson," he said. "I see you have a visitor. Our Mr. Poe from the lecture last night, is it not?"

"Yes, Hastings," Dodgson said, sounding apologetic. "He's asked me to—"

"—consult on a story I'm writing," Eddy cut in hastily. "I'm of a mind to write a mystery story set in an Oxford college, you see, and young Dodgson here has been kind enough to offer his insight."

"Ah." The faint flicker of wariness on the bulldog's face was gone now, replaced by polite boredom. "Well, best of luck to you, gentlemen."

Dodgson gave Eddy a baffled look but gestured him through the gate. Immediately past the elegant stone portcullis was a grassy quadrangle with a large, austere marble fountain set in the middle. A circular promenade helped to center the fountain in the quadrangle, and the general impression of the space was one of hushed privilege.

"Is there a reason why you just lied to Hastings?" Dodgson said.

"We are investigating a clue left at a murder scene," Eddy said. "Until we learn the murderer's identity, he could be anyone, even one of your bulldogs. Thus, we must keep our own counsel on this, yes?"

Dodgson actually blushed. "Y-yes, of course," he said, guiding Eddy past the quadrangle to a smaller one lined with yet more Gothic buildings. "M-my apologies. I've never been involved in something like this before, you see."

It turned out that the undergraduates of Christ Church were housed in small but attractive rooms, a far cry from the catch-as-catch-can housing Eddy remembered from his time at the

University of Virginia. “A pleasant space,” he said, fighting down a surge of jealousy as he studied the paneled walls and leaded windows.

Dodgson shrugged. “I’m more ap-preciative of the solitude, to be truthful,” he said, waving Eddy to a seat at an ancient oak table that doubled as a desk. “Now, if you can show me what needs to be translated?”

Eddy pulled the paper from his pocket, smoothing it on the tabletop. “Does this make any sense to you?”

Dodgson studied the scrawled letters. “Hm. The alphabet is indeed Greek,” he said after a moment. “But the words are nonsensical. It’s as if someone simply c-copied down Greek letters in no particular order.”

Eddy felt his hopes sink. “Damn it all.”

The young man glanced at him, mouth pursed in disapproval. “Really, Mr. Poe, there’s no need to curse.”

Just his luck that he’d attracted an Oxford bluenose. And the hangover, held in abeyance by the need to find a translator, was making itself felt once more. “Forgive me, Dodgson, but if you’d had the kind of morning I had, you’d be cursing like a sailor as well,” he said, rubbing his forehead. “So this note is nothing but arrant nonsense?”

“I’m afraid so,” Dodgson agreed. “Unless someone is in the habit of sending c-coded messages in Ancient Greek, of course.”

A thought bulled through Eddy’s headache. *Coded messages, hidden meanings secreted behind a cryptological wall.* “The words themselves may be nonsense,” he said slowly, “but what if their letters were rearranged?”

Dodgson’s eyes lit at that. “You’re suggesting that this could be an anagram?”

“I am indeed. Can you try unscrambling it?”

“I believe so.” The undergraduate bent further over the desk, rapidly scribbling out combinations. "Yes, I think you're right," he muttered, writing out a revised version of the original code. "It appears to be a simple enough sentence—"

He stopped. "Oh, dear."

"What does it say?" Eddy demanded.

Slowly, Dodgson took up the pen again and wrote five words in English underneath the revised Greek symbols. The two men stared at the translation, then at each other.

Catch me if you can.

Eddy's gut went cold. Jane Billings had been deliberately posed, and her gory death used as the medium to deliver a cryptic message. Which suggested that the killer had wanted her to be found like that, her poor body a gauntlet thrown down as a challenge. *But to whom?*

Dodgson's voice broke into his thoughts. "Well, that c-certainly sounds ominous," the young man said hesitantly. "Where was this message found, may I ask?"

"On the girl's body." Eddy didn't go into detail about the letters carved into the chambermaid's skin, trying to think through the pounding in his head. "Mr. Dodgson, I don't suppose you have access to coffee here?"

"I have the makings for tea, if that w-would be acceptable." The undergraduate rose and crossed to the small fireplace. Minutes later, a teapot and two cups sat on the table between them, along with a blessed plate of gingersnaps.

Eddy sipped the hot tea gratefully, letting it scour the film from his tongue and the painful mist from his head. "'Catch me if you can.' The murderer must have left it as a taunt," he mused. "But to whom? I can't believe he'd expect the police to solve an anagram in Ancient Greek."

Holding a biscuit, Dodgson hesitated in mid-bite. "It's not beyond the pale that one of the bulldogs may read Ancient

Greek. Many of them are surprisingly well educated."

"You know them better than I do, but it still seems dam—deucedly odd. Especially as the murderer couldn't have guaranteed that a hypothetical scholar-cum-bulldog would show up at the scene." He took another sip of tea. "No, it strikes me that this was a deliberate message to someone, and not a member of your constabulary. If we can determine that person's identity, they may lead us to the killer."

The undergraduate looked somber. "I see your point, but how do we do that?"

"We must start at the beginning, with the girl herself. We have our victim, Jane Billings, a young chambermaid at a respectable hotel. She'd asked me to autograph a collection of my poems for a mysterious paramour." His chest tightened at the memory of her happy smile. "An attractive girl, well-spoken and polite, it's possible that she had ambitions to improve her standing in life through marriage."

"A reasonable assumption," Dodgson agreed.

"So, she has hopes, plans for the future. And then she was cut down in a most barbaric manner."

Dodgson raised a tentative hand. "I'm almost afraid to ask, but ... how was she killed?"

The image of the girl's gaping belly surged back into Eddy's mind. "She'd been strangled, then gutted."

The younger man swallowed hard. "That's m-monstrous! Why would someone do something so h-horrible?"

"An excellent question, and one that I'm afraid I may have an answer to. The placement of the wound is something I've seen once before, when I was young." He could still remember the smell of the blood in the cold morning air, and his foster father standing behind him, insisting that he watch. "A horse breeder was attempting to extract an unborn colt from its dead dam's womb. He had to cut into the dam's belly and pull the colt out through the wound. Judging from the wound on her belly, I suspect that the girl may have been in a similar way, only the murderer took her babe long before it was due to be born."

"Oh, dear God in h-heaven," Dodgson whispered, hand rising to cover his mouth. "That p-poor girl and her innocent child. I'll p-pray for both their s-s-souls."

"Speaking for myself, I'd rather avenge their souls on the body of their murderer." Eddy rose from his chair, driven to pace the length of the room in lecture mode. "But now, we must use logic and think—*cui bono*? Who benefits from this act? Her paramour, perhaps, the one with a taste for poetry? He could be someone of wealth or status, who couldn't risk a bastard coming to light."

"But why would he leave a note? And in Ancient Greek as well?" Dodgson asked.

"Another excellent question." Eddy stopped at the far end of the room, glancing out the window at the quadrangle. "If she carried an illegitimate child, it would be far easier to pay her off and send her and the child away, or to threaten her with ruin if he was a heartless scoundrel. It makes no sense to butcher her, then leave her in her place of employment with such an arcane clue. So, what if the killer was someone who felt deeply about her, perhaps even loved her, albeit in an unhinged way? Driven to madness at the thought of her bearing another man's child, he killed her and obliterated any trace of the hated rival's seed. But now he's overwhelmed with guilt, and wishes the police to punish him for his heinous crime."

Dodgson blinked at the conjured image. "That's p-perhaps a bit convoluted, don't you think? Not to mention melodramatic."

Eddy shrugged. "A fault of my profession, my dear Dodgson. I tend towards the dramatic crisis in any story. But it certainly strikes me as a plausible motive for her murder. In any case, I must find out more about young Miss Billings and her suitors."

Dodgson nodded at that. "W-well, then, w-where shall we start?"

Too late, Eddy noted the light in the younger man's eyes; his young scholar truly did have a taste for puzzles. *But if he recoiled from as simple a phrase as 'damn it all,' the gruesome realities of tracking down a killer are most likely beyond him.* "Ah. While I appreciate your enthusiasm, I didn't mean to imply that I'm recruiting your services in this matter," he said quickly. "You've done more than enough in assisting me with the note."

"I hardly feel comfortable with the idea of a vicious murderer roaming loose on Oxford's streets," the younger man insisted. "And forgive me for being b-blunt, but you aren't familiar with the city and its environs, sir. If nothing else, I can play local guide for you." He hesitated. "How were you intending to hunt down this murderer, if I may ask?"

"It's really quite simple," Eddy said with some asperity. "I shall use the science of ratiocination, which is—"

"—the p-process of reasoning thought," Dodgson said. "I have studied Latin as well, Mr. Poe. Ratiocination, from the Latin *rationcinatio*, 'to compute, to calculate, to reason.' A skill I have used in the form of mathematical study s-since my earliest childhood, by the way."

Eddy squashed his sudden irritation. He didn't have time to argue with an overeager young buck who wanted to help. "I see your point. In the meantime, however, you still have classes to attend, and I must speak to the employees of the Mitre. I'll send you a message once that's done, and we can put our heads together and see what we can come up with. For now, would you be so kind as to escort me to the gate?"

The younger man smiled shyly. "Of course, sir."

They took leave of the residential hall and Dodgson guided him back through the college's quadrangles to Tom Gate, giving instructions on how to get back to the Mitre. Waving his thanks, Eddy started walking back towards Broad Street.

I suppose there's no use for it. He had an assistant, whether he wanted one or not.

CHAPTER EIGHT

On the walk back to the Mitre Eddy went over his next steps. *Firstly, I need to speak with Jane's family and friends, if possible. They may know who the father of her child is, as well as any other suitors she may have had. Secondly, I need to investigate those individuals and find out where they were last night. And what role does that bizarre taunt play in all of this?*

Solving a murder was so much easier when it was only a fictional crime.

He slipped inside the doors to the Mitre, glancing around the small lobby. Venables was not behind the desk. Instead, a tall, rawboned young man stood there, blinking hard as if trying to restrain tears.

When he realized he wasn't alone, he straightening, sniffing hard. "May I help you, sir?" he asked, his voice as raw as his eyes.

"Oh, I'm a guest," Eddy said, waving in the general direction of the staircase. "I was hoping the worst of the excitement was over by now. I wonder, have the police left?"

The young man's attention turned back to the desk top, as if hoping to find answers there. "Yes, sir. They took—" He stopped, swallowing so hard Eddy could hear the click. "They're gone, sir."

"Ah." *Could this be the mysterious PRS, mourning for his dead love? Or the murderer regretting his actions?* "You have my deepest condolences," he added, trying to look appropriately sympathetic. "Jane struck me as a fine young woman. I take it you were an acquaintance of hers?"

The young man's throat worked. "We—we were friendly with each other, sir. We liked to talk about books and such. She loved to read, you see."

"Yes, so I gathered. I was pleased when she asked me to sign a book of my poems." He decided it was worth a try. "She wanted to give it to someone—you, perhaps?"

A look of pain flashed over the young man's face. "I—she never said, sir."

Before Eddy could continue with his questions a girl in a plain brown dress and white pinafore ghosted into the lobby, her huge dark eyes swimming with unshed tears.

The clerk came around, crouching down so that he could look the girl in the face. "Maggie, you shouldn't be here," he said gently. "You need to go home."

She shook her head, dark curls bouncing. "Ma sent me, Will. I'm supposed to get Jane's things—" Her chest hitched in a soft sob, and she began crying in earnest.

Eddy was torn between sympathy and the need to interrogate. The little girl had to be a relative of Jane's, perhaps a niece or younger sister. *And she called the clerk Will, so he can't be PRS.*

"I'm so sorry to intrude, young miss," he said, keeping his tone respectful. "I take it you're Jane's sister?" When the girl nodded he continued, "I signed one of my books for her yesterday. She struck me as a very sweet and pleasant young woman. You and your family have my deepest sympathies on your loss."

Maggie focused on him, blinking hard. "Are—are you the writer? The American one?"

He essayed a little nod. "That I am. Edgar Allan Poe, at your service."

She sniffled again, wiping at her eyes. "Jane said you were coming. She wanted to get one of your books. She said she was giving it to her beau."

From the corner of his eye, Eddy caught Will's expression go stony. "And who would that be?"

"I don't know his name. But Jane said he was going to take care of her and—" She stopped, biting her lip as more tears fell.

"Sir, I need to get her home." Will deliberately interjected himself between the two of them. "If there's anything you need, I'll have it sent up to your room."

"No, thank you." Eddy watched him hustle the little girl into the bowels of the hotel. *Well, that's moderately illuminating.* He still didn't know the identity of PRS, but it wasn't the desk clerk. And judging from the young man's attitude, he had been sweet on Jane at the very least. *Might he be a jealous rival for the young woman's affections? A clerk would know the layout of the hotel and the chambermaids' schedules, after all.* Satisfied that he had a start on his list of suspects, Eddy headed up to his room.

Before he could unlock the door, he heard footsteps on the staircase. A chambermaid entered the hallway, carrying a mop and pail of water. She gave a soft squeak when she saw him. "Oh, sir," she said, giving an unsteady bob of a curtsey. "Begging your pardon, sir. Didn't mean to disturb you."

"Quite all right." The door across from his own was closed, hiding its terrible secret behind varnished brown wood. "Are you cleaning the room across from mine?"

The maid paled, but nodded. "Cook said there's a mess and I'm to clean it up."

He remembered the pool of blood and repressed a shudder. "Surely one of the male servants would be better suited for this?"

The maid shook her head. "I asked one of the lads for help, but they're all busy or talking to the police." Tears welled up in her already watery eyes. "Oh, sir, it was so terrible, how they found Jane. I don't want to go in there, but..."

"No, I understand." Guilt flickered in his gut. "Would it help if I stayed at the door until you're done?"

The maid looked pathetically grateful at that. "Oh, would you, sir? Thank you!"

"Not at all." Stepping back, he waited until she unlocked the door and carried in the mop and bucket. The scent of old blood, throat-closing and thick, reminded him of Sissy's sickroom.

Before he could enter, the maid dropped her implements and staggered back, hand clapped over her mouth. "Oh, it's horrible!" she moaned. "I can't, I just can't!"

Even as he sympathized with her horror, an idea occurred to him. Taking her by her arm, he guided her away from the door. "It's all right," he soothed. "This is no sight for a lady, my dear. You go about your duties, and I'll speak to Mr. Venables about this."

"Oh, thank you, sir!" Grabbing her mop and bucket, the maid fled back down the hallway.

He waited until she was out of sight, then steeled himself and slipped into the room. Closing the door, he set out to examine the space in detail.

The pool of blood where Jane had lay was almost completely crusted over by now, revealing the outline of her body and the smears where it had been moved. He crouched next to it, studying the surrounding floorboards. Apart from the gory puddle, they were clean and recently polished, but he could see smudged shoe prints on the wood. *Belonging to Collin and Furnow's colleagues, no doubt.* He bent lower, peering under the bed, and saw a dark streak. Upon closer examination, it turned out to be a smear of blood, mixed with dirt. He was reminded of similar smears when men wiped their feet on mats to get rid of mud.

So he accidentally stepped in the puddle, and had to wipe off the blood somewhere where it wouldn't be seen. The material embedded in the dried blood was a combination of bits of straw, dark soil, and what looked more like a light grey dust. *Dark soil and straw. He picked that up in the streets, but the lighter stuff comes from the pavements. For this much to come away with the blood, he must have a fair amount of it on his soles. Our murderer walks a great deal, doesn't he?*

And yet the edge of the mark suggested that the shoe's sole was intact, no patching or holes apparent. *He can afford new soles when his old ones become worn. So he has money, and was respectable enough to enter the hotel without causing a stir.*

Eddy stood, frowning in thought. Decent shoes, adequate funds, and a tendency towards perambulation. That probably described most of Oxford's male inhabitants, but it was a start.

Returning to the door, he put his back to it, trying to imagine the scene. No one had said anything about a scream, so the murderer couldn't have been threatening initially. The blood pool didn't show signs of struggle, so he would have overpowered her first, most likely throttling the life out of her before lowering her body to the floor and performing the macabre act that had resulted in the crusted expanse of crimson.

Closing his eyes, he cudgeled his inner Dupin to produce some sort of insight, a hint as to who might have butchered Jane and her unborn child in such a manner, but the meaty stench of the crusted pool interrupted his thoughts. Deciding that there was nothing more to be learned there, he slipped out of the room, gratefully breathing in the clean air of the hallway. *I need to know more about her beau—or beaux.*

The desk clerk was as good a place to start as any.

Unable to check his pocket watch and frustrated by the lack of visible clocks, Charles sat impatiently through his mathematics lecture in Mr. Sisson's rooms, half-listening as he tracked the passage of time by the wan afternoon sunlight. A milky square of it had finally reached the opposite wall when the mathematics don abruptly stopped in mid-lecture and barked, "Mr. O'Donnell, am I boring you?"

Next to Charles, O'Donnell straightened out of a dozing slouch. "No, sir," the undergraduate said, blinking heavily. "My apologies—I didn't sleep well last night."

"I see. You might wish to stay away from the public houses, then. I find that a clear head and a stomach empty of alcohol makes sleep much more achievable." The don pulled out his pocket watch, studying it. "Hm. We shall leave off our exploration of algebra here, gentlemen. I expect you all to do the assigned reading, and we shall continue our discussion next time." His beady gaze fell on O'Donnell. "I look forward in particular to your contribution, Mr. O'Donnell. Good afternoon."

Charles gathered his books together, noting the barely restrained yawn that threatened to split O'Donnell's face. He knew that not everyone was as interested in mathematics as he was, but it still boggled him to see others nodding off during lectures on algebra and trigonometry. If he hadn't been distracted by Poe's news, he would have been fascinated with Sisson's discussion.

"The next lecture will be a joy," O'Donnell said heavily as their classmates filed out into the corridor, Blakeney among them. "Oh, well. Pater already knows I'm not a maths genius. Shall we deposit our notes in my rooms and go in search of afternoon tea? There may be more tidings about that poor chambermaid."

The news about the murder had spread breathlessly throughout Christ Church by noon. While sawing through gravy-covered beef Charles had heard any number of theories about the murderer, each one more lurid than the next. "Oh. I-I'm afraid I have a prior engagement," he apologized.

O'Donnell's mouth quirked at that. "Abandoning me already? How did I give offense, old man?"

"You d-didn't." Poe had intimated that he wasn't to discuss the particulars of that unfortunate girl's death. Still, Charles didn't like to lie, especially to a friend. "I, um, want to finish the mathematics reading, and then I'm going to speak with M-mr. Poe. About my, er, writing."

To his dismay, that caused O'Donnell to stop in his tracks. "You're meeting with Poe? God in heaven, bring me along, please," he begged. "I'd dearly relish a chance to speak with him about his inspiration."

"B-but he threatened to strike you last night."

His friend snorted. "It never would have come to blows. Poe's a poet, after all, and everyone knows that poets are highly strung. Now be a chum and let me tag along."

Charles wanted to groan in frustration. "I really m-must speak to him alone this time. But I promise I'll d-do my best to get you an interview before he leaves, if you like."

O'Donnell only capitulated when Charles also promised to share his Mathematics notes. "Oh, all right," his friend finally grumbled. "But if I don't get a chance to speak to him before he leaves Oxford, I'll be spiteful for the rest of the term, see if I won't."

Charles felt a mild twinge of guilt when they parted ways at the Tom Quad fountain. *Then again, what I said wasn't an absolute lie.* He did want to show some of his work to Poe and get the man's opinion. He had hesitantly shown the other Horsemen some of his juvenilia, written to entertain his younger sisters and brothers, and both O'Donnell and Hebron had been highly amused by his satires. More importantly, Reade told him that he possessed a decided talent for writing. If his future wasn't already laid out for him—following his father into the Anglican priesthood, then a vicarage after he left Oxford—he'd welcome the idea of becoming a sort of storyteller-cum-mathematician.

Might a vicar also be a writer? It isn't impossible, is it? Of course, the idea wasn't even worth considering unless he knew for sure that someone might wish to publish his work—

He shook himself. *No. First, we must help the constabulary catch this monster. Afterwards, I'll brace Mr. Poe about reading my stories.* Satisfied with that, he hurried towards his rooms.

CHAPTER NINE

Eddy's hopes were dashed when he found that the tall, rawboned clerk had been replaced by Mr. Venables. Hoping that Maggie was somewhere safe, he passed along his promise to the sickened chambermaid.

The hotel keeper nodded heavily. "I'll get one of the stable lads up there. Was there anything else, sir?"

Eddy smelled alcohol on the man's breath, and his imp began crooning to him. With an effort, he ignored the urge. "Not really, other than to pass along my sympathies. I know this must be a difficult time for you."

"Difficult, yes," Venables murmured. "I've run the Mitre for fourteen years, sir. I've seen a great deal of things during that time that decent people ought never to see. But this—" He shook his head. "For the life of me I can't understand why someone would do such a cruel thing to a slip of a girl." Bloodshot eyes turned to him, a desperate inquiry in their depths. "Did *you* hear anything last night, sir? An argument, or perhaps a shout?"

No, but I certainly saw something. "I didn't hear a thing, I'm afraid," he said, clasping his hands behind his back and hoping that he looked authoritative. "It did occur to me, however, that a crime of this sort often comes about as a result of deliberation, rather than spontaneous passion. Did Jane have any problems with other people, perhaps a long-running argument or feud?"

Venables shook his head. "Jane was the very soul of kindness, Mr. Poe. A hard worker, always ready to help someone else. Everyone here was quite fond of her, my son in particular." He rubbed roughly at his mouth, using the gesture to hide the swipe of a tear. "Poor William. I suspect he's taking this even harder than I am. He'd had hopes about the two of them, you see."

So there had been some romantic interest there. Eddy filed the useful tidbit of information away. "The loss of a young woman is always a tragedy, but the loss of one who was the touchstone of your romantic hopes is terrible indeed," he said out loud. "The death of my first wife was the very worst event of my life."

Venables nodded. "My wife, blessed woman that she was, passed on ten years ago, and I miss her to this day. I sometimes think that's why my William's been so hesitant to settle down. He was only a boy when he lost his mother, and he saw what that did to me. I'd thought that Jane might find him agreeable, but—" The hotel keeper sighed. "Ah, well. Water under the bridge now."

He needed to keep Venables talking. "Had William pinned his hopes on Jane for very long?"

Venables shrugged. "He'd been sweet on her for at least a year. Bought her the occasional posy, even took her to the Henley races—"

His recount was cut off as William himself burst into the lobby, followed by Philip Stiles of all people. "I simply want to speak with her, damn it all," the blond nobleman said. "You have no right to stop me!"

"Pa." William stopped in front of his father, hands working at his sides as if he was struggling not to clench them. "This gentleman wants to talk to Jane."

Venables drew himself up, stepping out from behind the desk.

"I'm afraid that won't be possible, sir."

Stiles wobbled slightly, and Eddy could smell the whisky wafting off of the young nobleman like a cloud of eau de cologne. "Don't be ridiculous, man," Stiles snarled. "I won't take up more than five minutes of her time—"

Eddy saw William's hands lose the battle and ball into fists, but Mr. Venables shook his head. "You misunderstand me, sir. There was an incident here this morning. If I might have a word in private?"

He gestured for Stiles to follow him to a corner of the lobby. After a few words from the hotel keeper, the drunken nobleman went white. Shaking his head, he staggered back from Venables before spinning clumsily and stumbling out the door.

Venables returned to Eddy and William. "Now that's a puzzle and no mistake," he said heavily. "William, have you seen that gentleman in here before?"

"No, Pa," William replied, carefully not looking at his father.

Venables scrubbed at his face. "Well, then, now that you're here you can take over the front desk. I'd best get back to my figures. Good day, Mr. Poe." Giving Eddy a nod, he left.

William took up position behind the desk, a study in restrained fury. With care, Eddy leaned on the polished wooden top, doing his best to seem conciliatory. "That young man was at my signing last night. Quite full of himself, I thought."

William glared at the door with loathing. "Swanning about like he's the Prince of Wales, never thinking of aught but what he wants. All flash and charm and sweet talk, and then he runs back to his college and leaves others to clean up his mess."

"Ah, yes. I've known the type." A touch of careful commiseration was called for here. "They think their money and connections can provide them with everything they desire at no cost to themselves."

Color rushed to William's face, and his fists balled again. "Filthy low coward. I told her to stay away, but she wouldn't listen. Said he was different when he was with her. Well, who wouldn't be, I said—" He bit his lip, looking away. "Sorry, sir. It's … it's been a long day."

Eddy wanted to press him even further, but some small sense of self-preservation assured him that pushing the distraught desk clerk any further wouldn't be wise. He cleared his throat and stepped back. "Yes, well, you have my sympathies, young man. I'll leave you to your work."

He headed back to the staircase, William's jealous speech blazing in his mind. *So we have a love triangle between the pretty young chambermaid, the overprotective desk clerk, and the arrogant nobleman. The question is, which one of her suitors changed from Romeo to Othello?*

He needed more information about the ill-fated trio, that was clear. *Of course, the trick will be getting it. Even if I knew how to locate that pompous young donkey Stiles, I doubt he'd condescend to speak with me.*

Maggie's tearstained face swam into his mind's eye. *But someone else might.*

Changing direction, Eddy headed towards a door that bore a polished OFFICE sign. After knocking and receiving permission to enter, he poked his head around the door. "Mr. Venables, I wonder if I might ask you for a favor…"

Charles strode up St. Aldate's towards the High, tugging his overcoat tighter against the chilly air as he mulled over the day's events. What had started out as a simple act of kindness—returning a lost book of poetry—had somehow turned into the strangest adventure of his life.

Not the least of which was his introduction to Edgar Allan Poe. Despite the dark grace of his poetry, Poe was quintessentially American, there was no doubt of that. Brash and outspoken, the small man seemed a veritable whirlwind of agitation, not even batting an eye when he trotted out that falsehood for Hastings. And the casual way he'd used foul language was quite appalling.

But unsurprising, Charles had to admit with some charity. *If I had been asked by the constabulary to assist them with finding a brutal murderer, I might be tempted to use the occasional curse word, as well.*

Working on the assumption that Poe would send a message calling him to the Mitre, he had hurried through his mathematics reading in order to be ready for departure. But as the day waned, no summons had come from the American. Charles felt a mix of embarrassment and growing irritation. *Perhaps he thinks me too young and callow to be of use.*

If he was bluntly honest with himself, he wasn't sure Poe was wrong about that. His initial offer had been well-intentioned, but he'd only been in Oxford for a few weeks and had no idea where one might find the criminal element of the city, or whether such a thing existed.

And yet, he couldn't forget the haunted look in the poet's eyes as Poe described the murdered chambermaid. It was that which had driven him from his rooms and set him on the path to the Mitre. *If nothing else, I'm more familiar with Oxford than he is, and there may be more translating to be done. And later, perhaps he'd be willing to read some of my work—*

"Woolgathering, Dodgson?"

Charles stopped, staring at Martin Blakeney. It was strange to see the man not shadowing Stiles, but he supposed they had to part every now and then. "Oh, hello, Blakeney. I was j-just thinking."

The other undergraduate nodded. "So I noticed from the grim look on your phiz. If I'm disturbing you, I'll leave you to your thoughts."

Politeness prompted Charles to say, "No, that's q-quite all right. Where's S-stiles?"

"His uncle's in town so he's been summoned to court. I thought I'd take the opportunity to pick up some supplies on the High." Blakeney hesitated. "I was wondering, are you trying for the Gibbs prize this year?"

The man's decision to speak with him became clearer. "I had thought about it, yes," Charles said warily. "Mr. Sisson is overseeing it this year, and I would appreciate the chance to study with him."

Blakeney nodded. "I'd find the funds more than welcome, myself. I'd try for it if my mathematical abilities were stronger."

Part of him didn't want to encourage a potential competitor, but he felt obligated to offer some support. "I've always been impressed with your p-participation in lectures. I feel sure that you could provide me with quite the competition, given the appropriate amount of preparation."

Blakeney smiled shyly at that, shuffling a bit. "Quite flattering of you, Dodgson. But no, I know where my strengths lie, and the field of logic is my Agincourt, unfortunately." He glanced at a nearby teashop. "That being said, the snowy field of the groaning board is one I would be most delighted to duel at. Er, would you care to join me for a meal?"

He was taken aback by the invitation. "Oh, w-well—"

"Dodgson!"

The other three Horsemen jogged up, breath clouding in the cool air. "There you are," O'Donnell said. "We decided to give the Hall a miss this evening—Reade poked his head into the kitchen and couldn't identify the meat," He gave Blakeney a gimlet look. "Hullo, Blakeney. Where's your sahib, then?"

The undergraduate's sallow cheeks flushed. He hurried off,

shoulders hunched.

"Odious little lickspittle," O'Donnell said with a sniff. "I see his braggadocio vanishes when his patron isn't around."

"And I'm sure your pugnacious qualities had nothing to do with it," Reade said drily.

"Me? I'm an utter lamb," O'Donnell declared. "I'm also absolutely famished and don't wish to stand here debating the qualities of Blakeney when we could be enjoying a repast of chops and roast potatoes at The King's Arms." He jingled his pockets. "The meal's on me if you're worried about cost, Dodgson. Pater's sent along my allowance, and he's been surprisingly generous."

A rumble sounded in Charles's midsection at the mention of food. "T-that's very kind of you, but I was on my way to the Mitre to m-meet with Mr. Poe—"

"Capital!" O'Donnell clapped his hands. "We'll come with you. I'll even stand the great man himself to supper if he's willing to dine with us. Most writers I know won't turn down a free meal if it's on offer."

Unable to come up with a reasonable rebuttal, Charles shrugged in agreement. *And if Poe doesn't wish my assistance, at least I'll have a good supper as consolation.* "Very well. Let's go."

CHAPTER TEN

Venables had seemed surprised at Eddy's request but supplied him with the required information and a book labeled *Murray's Guide to Oxford*. Oxford at dusk was yet another new side of the city to him, and one that he found peculiarly appealing. The flickering glow of the streetlamps gave a soft lambency to the elegant stone buildings and neat storefronts of Broad Street, and the tang of the October air suggested that some sort of dark magic lurked behind the city's ancient stone and wood.

Consulting the red-bound map book, he headed north. The multitude of businesses gave way to residential areas of terraced housing that bore a resemblance to the tenements Eddy had resided in during his time in Philadelphia. Interspersed with the plain, functional buildings was the occasional semi-detached house, a sort of compromise between the terraced homes and a standalone house where two residences shared a common wall.

The address he sought was a semi-detached house that appeared to be painted in motley; the right-hand residence was a creamy gold, and the left-hand residence was brick red. He went through the gate belonging to the red side, pausing briefly to admire the rose bushes that grew in beautifully tended profusion around the front yard, and knocked.

The door opened, revealing an older woman dressed in an austere black gown. Her face was pale and strained, and her eyes red from recent weeping. "May I help you?"

Eddy tipped his hat. "Mrs. Billings?"

"Yes?"

"My name is Edgar Poe." He began the speech he had formulated on his walk. "I apologize for intruding on you in your time of grief, but I wanted to pay my respects to your family. I'm currently a guest of the Mitre Inn, where I met your daughter briefly. She struck me as a kind and gentle young woman."

Mrs. Billings bowed her head, but not before he caught a flash of fierce emotion in her reddened eyes. "Thank you for your kind words, Mr. Poe. You're the poet from America, aren't you?"

"That is my honor, yes."

"Jane spoke about you just yesterday. Won't you come in?"

He wasn't going to refuse such an opening. "Thank you." Removing his hat as he passed the threshold, he surreptitiously studied Mrs. Billings and her surroundings. The interior of the home boasted of few luxuries, but everything was scrupulously clean and well cared for.

A cluster of women, already dressed in mourning black, had gathered in the parlor and were carefully moving objects to make a space against one wall. After a moment, their efforts made sense to him: *they're preparing the room for the laying out and the wake to come.*

As one, the group looked at him. "Ladies," he said, nodding.

"My husband's family," Mrs. Billings said, with a brittle smile. "They've come to help me lay Jane out, but the coroner hasn't released her body yet. I wish we knew—" Her lips thinned as she pressed them together. "Well, no help for that now, I suppose."

Her accent was more genteel than the working-class voices

Eddy had heard from Mr. Venables and Will. Deliberately shifting his tone to one appropriate for addressing a lady, he said, "I'm loathe to impose on you in your time of grief, madam, but Jane had asked something of me yesterday, and I would like to make good on my offer. If we could speak in private?"

"Of course." She gestured towards the back of the house, and he followed her into a dowdy kitchen. The patched pans and battered tin serving bowls lining the walls spoke of thriftiness and little spare money, but like the front room everything was immaculate and scrubbed, and the smell of recently cooked food was enticing.

"I do apologize for having to receive you here, but, well." Her nervous hands, worn with age and hard work, smoothed at her skirts again and again. "Would you care for some tea?"

"That would be most appreciated, thank you." Eddy took a seat at the old kitchen table as his hostess bustled to heat water. "As I said, I'd only briefly met Jane, but she asked me if I would sign one of my books so that she could present it to a special friend. If you know where the book is, I would be more than happy to do that." It was his hope that such a gambit would lead to discussion of her "special friend."

Mrs. Billings paused, giving him a look that was more surprised than distraught. "Oh. That's very kind of you, Mr. Poe, but I'm afraid I have no idea where the book might be. Perhaps my daughter Margaret would know—she and Jane shared a room." A faint flush bloomed across the woman's cheeks, as if ashamed of the fact that she couldn't provide individual bedrooms for her children. "Margaret's out with her father at the moment, making the funeral arrange—"

A sudden sob choked her, and she clapped a hand to her mouth. Alarmed, Eddy lurched to his feet, guiding the grieving mother to his own chair.

"I'm so sorry, so very sorry," Mrs. Billings whispered, almost to herself. "It's just … I can't understand how someone could do something so monstrous to my Jane. She was such a sweet, loving girl. I was sure she had a wonderful future ahead of her. But now—"

She fell silent as a strongly built man with thinning blond hair and the bullish shoulders of a laborer entered the kitchen, Maggie at his side. Laugh lines liberally fanned out from the newcomer's eyes and nose; under normal circumstances Eddy could imagine him wreathed in cheerful smiles. Today, however, he was solemn, a fact reflected by his too-tight black suit.

"We're home, then," the man announced in the same accent as Mrs. Billings's in-laws, glancing at Eddy. "Who's this, Lizzie?"

Eddy gave the man, undoubtedly Mr. Billings, a polite bow. "My name is Edgar Poe, sir. I'm a guest at the Mitre, where I'd recently met Jane. I wanted to come and offer my condolences."

"He's the poet Jane was telling us about," Mrs. Billings interjected quietly. "He's here on a lecture tour."

"Oh, aye?" Billings nodded heavily. "That's kind of you to stop by, then. My girl would've been pleased."

Eddy pressed on. "As I was explaining to your wife, Jane had asked me to sign a book for her," he said, "something she was going to give to a friend. If you have the book available and the name of the friend, I would be happy to sign it as a final act of respect."

Mr. Billings's sandy brows drew together. "Dunno about any book, or any friend," he said, his voice gruffer now. "Unless it was that William, and he don't strike me as the type to read poetry. Lizzie, you know aught about this?"

"No," Mrs. Billings said faintly. "If you'll excuse me, Mr. Poe,

I believe I should check on the progress in the parlor. Thank you again for your kindness. Margaret, come along."

Billings watched his women leave, conflict on his face. "Not that she'd say aught to me in any case," he muttered. "Doesn't think I'd understand, her and her plans."

Eddy schooled his expression to a gentle incomprehension. "Her plans, sir?"

Billings held up his hands. Hard and rough, they belonged to a man who used them regularly in daily labor. "I work barges on the Isis. Steady work, good pay, enough to keep a roof over your head and food on the table. But my Lizzie was the daughter of a barrister, y'see. Pissed away most of his income, then wound up getting drunk as a lord one night and drowned in the Isis. Left his family without a penny, and Lizzie had to go to work in a shop. That's where I met her." The bargeman shook his head. "She was happy enough with my job when I asked her to marry me. Since we had our Jane and Maggie, though, she started on about 'improving their station in life.'" His disdain towards the phrase spoke volumes. "Always pushing Jane to be nice to the gentlemen at the hotel, as if that would get a girl anywhere except in a bad way."

The glare Billings tacked onto the end of that sentence was a warning. "Jane struck me as a modest and respectable young lady, not the kind to indulge in that sort of thing," Eddy assured the other man.

"Too right," Billings growled. "If I found out that someone was taking advantage of his station with my Jane, he'd regret it, toff or no toff."

And yet Jane had clearly had some kind of relationship with young Stiles. Eddy was suddenly sure that Mr. Billings had no idea of his daughter's state at the time of her death. "As is right and proper. But I've taken more than enough of your time, sir.

Once again, you have my sympathies on your loss."

The balked rage died away, and Billings nodded wearily. "You expect it when they're little 'uns. Sometimes they get sick, or sometimes they're just not strong enough. It's part of life, innit? But when they're full grown and just starting life, to be cut down like that—it's not right, Mr. Poe. It's just not right."

An image of Sissy on her deathbed came to him, so pale and fragile. *Oh, my darling girl.* His throat tightened, and he had to clear it before he could trust himself to speak. "You're absolutely correct, sir. It's not right or fair at all."

The bargeman nodded. "Aye. Well, then, I'll see you out."

He could see no way of speaking with Mrs. Billings again. They headed to the front door, Eddy slowing as he passed the parlor. Inside, Mrs. Billings was busy tidying the knick-knacks and curios while her in-laws clustered together and talked quietly amongst themselves. The divide between the women was clear as day.

He bid farewell to Billings and headed off. *Jane's mother thinks she's married beneath her. Her manner, her garden, even her very accent says so. And she wants to promote her daughters to her own former station. Did she push Jane into a liaison with that Oxford boor as a way to guarantee her daughter's future?*

Wrapped in his thoughts, he paced through the narrow, maze-like streets of the area. Eventually, he found himself on a Bridge Street and smelled the distinctive odor of slow-moving water. A sense of homesickness for the James River overcame him, and he followed the scent.

It led him to a millpond, with a weir at the far end that controlled the water levels in the stream behind it. A narrow footbridge led to a tiny island in the river. He imagined the colors of the autumn foliage would be glorious during the day, but at night the trees became looming giants, rustling in the wind as if trying to lure unwary travelers off the beaten path.

Underneath the weir bridge, a light bobbed. Moving closer, Eddy saw it was positioned in the bow of a punt that carried two men. One of them carefully poled against the stream's flow to keep the tiny, flat-bottomed boat stable, while another paid out what looked like a thick hempen rope that had been fastened somehow to the bridge's base.

His imp niggled at him, and he cupped his hands around his mouth. "Ho! What are you men doing there?"

The man with the rope in his hands looked up. "Stringing a barrier, sir," he called back. "Tis the season for the new men to arrive, y'see, and some of them take a fancy to slip past the barrier and ride over t'weir. Eccles up at Folly Bridge loses more punts that way, sir."

"I see." Rueful, Eddy thought back to his own university days and some of the scrapes he and his friends had indulged in out of youthful folly and boredom. In retrospect, it was astounding that they hadn't snapped their necks or died in some ignominious fashion. "Well, then, good luck with your nets."

Both men nodded, turning back to their task.

Following the bank, Eddy found himself on a towpath leading towards another neighborhood of working-class homes. He realized his mistake when he entered a tiny, dingy square, anchored by a squalid-looking pub. The people here looked more like the poor he remembered from Richmond, the bulk of them malnourished and dull-eyed with drink or depression. There was an occasional flash of color, not to mention cunning calculation, from women whose low-cut bodices, garish toilette and swaggering walks proclaimed their profession.

One of them approached him now, flicking a dyed red lock of hair over a shoulder that hadn't seen soap or water in a number of days. "'Ello, duck," she crooned. "Fancy a bit of fun? There's a crib right 'round the corner if you want a bed, or a knee-trembler's a shilling."

He drew back, bemused by the woman's effrontery. "I seem to have made a wrong turn. My apologies."

"Don't apologize, duck. You ain't done nothing wrong. Yet," she guffawed. With a swift motion, she thrust her arm around his, holding it tight. "Go on. A gentlemen like you, I'll give a good ride, I will."

With some difficulty, he extracted his arm from the whore's practiced clutch. "As I said, madam, I made a wrong turn—"

"I ain't no madam, I work for a living," she said, grabbing for his coat sleeve again. "Come on, then—"

He yanked it out of her grip. "Don't touch me!"

"Oy!" A tall, stony-faced bruiser in a loud waistcoat and brown frock coat that had seen better days appeared at the whore's side. "You giving my Maisie a bit of bother?"

Undoubtedly the man was Maisie's pimp. "No, not at all," Eddy insisted. "I simply—"

"You trying to run out on her or something?"

"He thinks he's too good for the likes of me," Maisie sneered.

"Maybe he needs a lesson in manners, then," the pimp growled, flicking open his waistcoat. Inside, something sharp gleamed silver. Eddy stepped back, gripping the handle of his walking stick.

"What's all this, then?"

The pimp drew his coat shut, glaring over Eddy's shoulder. He risked a quick glance back and withered when he spotted Constable Furnow and four young men, including Dodgson.

"I believe I asked you a question, sir," Furnow said politely.

"You're off your patch, peeler," the pimp murmured, grinning with yellowed teeth. "This ain't university property, so you got no right to be here."

"I'm afraid that's not quite correct, sir," Furnow said. "The Oxford University Police are responsible for keeping order in the city between sundown and sunup. What a pity if we have to start patrolling this patch, as you put it, on a regular basis."

The pimp's triumphant sneer dimmed. "That would be a shame," he muttered, pulling Maisie to his side. "But I see you gentlemen have better things to do than talk to a local, so my girl and me will be on our way."

"Capital idea," Furnow commented, watching until the pimp and whore had slunk around a corner. Only then did he turn to Eddy. "You do wind up in the most remarkable situations, Mr. Poe."

"I got lost," Eddy said, glaring at the undergraduates at Furnow's side. "While I do appreciate your assistance, I have to wonder what you're doing here?"

"Following you, of course," the constable said mildly. "Mr. Venables was kind enough to pass along your proposed whereabouts to this young man here," he nodded at Dodgson, "and I simply tagged along. We spotted you coming out of the Billings household and trailed along in your wake."

Dodgson had the good grace to look embarrassed. "I th-thought we might d-discuss," he swallowed hard, "my poems. That I told you about earlier."

Apparently the young man's distaste for falsehoods was wearing off. "Oh. Of course." Eddy flashed a thin smile at him. "I would be more than delighted to do just that, Dodgson, as soon as I wrap up my business with the constable." He turned back to Furnow. "Which is…"

The constable was unflappable. "Your pen knife, sir. The coroner confirmed that it was not the kind used on Miss Billings."

Hope bubbled up. "Does that mean that I can continue on

my tour?"

Furnow shrugged. "I'm afraid not, Mr. Poe. Our investigation is not yet concluded, and such a confirmation does not guarantee that you don't own a second knife better suited to butchery. While our enquiries are continuing, I would be happy to escort you and," he glanced at Dodgson and the other students, "your young friends back to the Mitre."

Eddy's hope vanished. Gritting his teeth, he followed his captors out of the dingy square.

CHAPTER ELEVEN

Charles winced when he saw the fury in Poe's face after Furnow deposited them at the entrance to the Mitre. "What precisely were you doing tonight, Mr. Dodgson?" the American snapped. "I believe I said that I would summon you if I required your help."

O'Donnell began to reply but Charles held up a hand. "I thought you message might have gone astray." Well, it wasn't impossible, he reasoned. "I apologize for bringing Mr. Furnow with me, but he heard me speaking to the man at the front desk, and I didn't know h-how to evade him." He decided to throw his own jibe. "I was also under the i-impression that you were assisting them, only to find out that in fact you're under suspicion of c-committing this murder."

Poe's jaw worked at that. "Unfortunately, my reputation as a storyteller of the macabre worked against me, and the local police asked me to remain in Oxford until they found the murderer," he finally said. "As I am on a lecture tour, I cannot afford to waste time cooling my heels here while they search for this maniac, so I set out to find him myself."

Charles hated being so rude, especially to an older man, but he was tired, hungry, and not in the mood to play word games. "You told me you were helping the constabulary."

"I am, as I already said," Poe said truculently. "I also did not kill Jane Billings, as you and your friend here can attest to."

O'Donnell started at that. "We can?"

"Indeed. As both of you know, I was at the Saddler's Arms with my publisher's man last night. By the time I returned to the Mitre, poor Jane was already dead."

"And how do you know that, Mr. Poe?" Charles pressed.

The American glared at all of them, mustache twitching. "Gentlemen, do I have your word, your most *solemn* word, that what I am about to say will not be relayed elsewhere?"

Charles didn't like the idea of giving his word to someone so careless with the truth, but his friends quickly agreed. Reluctantly, he also nodded.

Poe nodded back. "When I returned to the Mitre, I was in my cups. I'm ashamed to admit it, but it's true. As a result, I went into the wrong room. Thinking it was mine, I climbed into bed still dressed and went to sleep. Before I drifted off, however, I noticed the smell of blood. My late wife was consumptive—it's an odor that's acutely familiar to me." He rubbed at his mouth, stilling a tremble. "When I awoke, I found Jane's body at the foot of the bed. I immediately returned to my room and remained there until the police came to question me."

Reade and O'Donnell were horrified, Hebron grim. To his regret, Charles could picture the events; the drunken Poe stumbling through the hotel's hallway, barging into a room he thought was his own and collapsing on the bed, only to receive a bloody surprise in the morning. "That's how you f-found the message."

"What message?" O'Donnell demanded.

"The murderer left an anagram on the chambermaid's body in Ancient G-greek. When unscrambled and translated into English, it read, 'Catch me if you can.'"

O'Donnell turned to the American. "Did you take the note? If you show us the paper, we might be able to recognize the handwriting, or where the paper might have been sold—"

"It wasn't a note," Poe said shortly. "The letters had been carved into Jane's skin."

Charles flinched. "You d-d-d—" He struggled for control of his tongue. "Didn't t-tell me that."

"And why would I? So that we would both have nightmares?" Poe shook his head. "I freely admit that I am not the best of men, but I don't enjoy the pain of others, and I most certainly don't enjoy inflicting it upon them. You're still so young, Dodgson. You don't need to know how cruel the world can be."

He knew the American meant well, but the overly paternal response still rankled. "I'm no stranger to death, and I'm familiar with the cruelties inflicted by the strong on the weak," he snapped. His time at Rugby and the indignities he had endured while at the boarding school had made sure of that. "My speech may be hesitant at t-times, but I would appreciate it if you didn't t-treat me as a child."

Poe stared at him for a moment, then sighed. "You're quite correct, Mr. Dodgson. For all your youth, you're a man, and a good one. Far better than I am, in any case."

That mollified him slightly. "Thank you. Now, we n-need to tell the police what we learned about the message. If you are not, in fact, working with them—"

"I am," Poe insisted. "They simply aren't aware of it. They already have Jane's body, which means the local coroner would have seen the letters by now. If I go to Furnow and tell him what we unraveled from that anagram, I'll have to admit how I found the message in the first place. I believe we can all grasp how incriminating that would be."

They all fell silent for a moment. "What about an anonymous note to the bulldogs?" Hebron suggested. "It keeps Mr. Poe out of it, and it passes along the information."

"That won't work," Reade pointed out. "Either they'll ignore it as a prank, or they'll hunt down the author to find out how he knew about the letters in the first place."

Poe's head rose, as if coming out of a deep sleep. "True. But we don't need to give our message to the police in order for them to receive it."

The older man's words seemed nonsensical. "To whom do we send it, then?" Charles asked.

Now the American smiled. "To the newspapers, my dear Dodgson."

Eddy leaned back from the table, replete. The public house to which he and his new acquaintances had repaired wasn't the Saddler's Arms, for which he was grateful. Instead, it appeared to be a favorite gathering spot for students, judging by the rowing oars, college scarves, and framed Oxford paraphernalia arranged on the walls.

He was also grateful that Dodgson's friends had grasped the sense in his words. "The story of the murder has undoubtedly appeared in your local newspapers today, and may well be in *The Times* by tomorrow," he'd explained. "The goal of a newspaper editor is to sell copies of the paper—macabre as it may sound, any new information about the murder will tempt people to buy. If we send one of your local papers an anonymous letter 'from a concerned bystander' detailing the symbols on the dead girl's stomach and Dodgson's translation, I can guarantee you that it'll be printed tomorrow and in the hands of the police within an hour of publication."

The four had agreed to his scheme, Dodgson with some reluctance and O'Donnell with a glee that bordered on devilish, and accompanied him to his room to raid his cache of paper, envelopes, and stamps. Once the letter had been composed and posted to the offices of *Jackson's Oxford Journal*, O'Donnell had led them around the corner to a pub called the King's Arms which featured a back room with darkly varnished tables and chairs, far from the drinkers in the front area. After the rather intense young man had magnanimously announced that he was paying the bill and they were to eat whatever they liked, Eddy had indulged himself in sliced beef, vegetables, and roasted potatoes.

The others ate as heartily, washing down their repasts with a local beer. With only a hint of regret, he had ordered a glass of lemonade instead. "Thank you, gentlemen," he said after wiping his mouth with a napkin. "You've been a great help to me in a difficult time."

O'Donnell snorted. "We didn't do anything, really. It was all Dodgson and his enormous brain. Three cheers for his translation skills!"

The others took up their glasses, chanting hip-hip-hoorah while Dodgson blushed. "It w-was nothing," the young man insisted.

"It was not nothing," Eddy insisted. "You were the one who suggested that the message might be in code."

"B-but you were the one who realized it was an anagram," Dodgson pointed out. "Once I had that piece of information, it was simple enough to unscramble the words and translate them."

"And you were the one with the skill to translate Ancient Greek. You don't give yourself enough credit, Dodgson. When this murderer is found, it will be thanks in part to you."

Dodgson seemed uncomfortable with the praise, but O'Donnell beamed. "Now that we've informed the bulldogs,

Mr. Poe, will you continue to search for the murderer?"

"I don't see where I have a choice," he admitted. "If I leave the investigation to the local police, I could still be here in a month's time. I need to find this man, and as soon as humanly possible."

O'Donnell slapped his hand against the table, making the pint glasses and plates rattle. "Then we are at your service, sirrah! We shall help you find this dastard and bring him to justice!"

The other three gave their friend a long-suffering look. "And just how do you intend to do that?" Hebron rumbled. "Your Greek is terrible and you don't have Dodgson's touch with puzzles."

"Don't chop logic with me after I've eaten, Hebron. It gives me wind." O'Donnell tapped the table again. "Between the four of us, we're intelligent, capable, diligent—"

Reade snorted.

"Fine. Dodgson's intelligent, Hebron's capable, you're diligent, and I'm charming yet ruthless. If we combine our talents, surely we can be of some assistance to Mr. Poe."

Eddy swallowed a sigh. It was bad enough when he had only one eager young man to worry about. *Then again, it's not as if you have anyone else in your corner.* Four Oxford undergraduates were certainly better than nothing. "I often need a sounding board when I try to work out a story. I suspect I may require the same assistance for ratiocination."

O'Donnell's brows came down at that. "Ratiocination?"

"F-rom the Latin, 'to compute, to calculate, to reason,'" Dodgson murmured.

"Oh, well, Latin." O'Donnell waved airily. "I suppose it has some use in day to day life, but dashed if I could ever find it."

Eddy hurried on. "Ratiocination is used by my fictional detective Dupin to solve crimes. It struck me that I could use the same technique to track down this murderer. So far, I've determined that he walks a great deal and has enough money to have his shoes mended regularly."

The four young men exchanged glances. "You do realize that you've just described the bulk of the university, yes?" Reade said. "And probably a significant proportion of town, as well."

At least his own supposition was grounded in fact. "I've had less than a day at my efforts, Mr. Reade. I also know that before her death, Jane Billings had me sign a book of poetry to a paramour, but this young man seems to be unknown to her family. She also had another admirer who didn't seem very happy over this association."

Hebron leaned forward, interested. "Could it have been a crime of passion?"

"Strange as it may sound, I hope it was," Eddy replied. "Otherwise, it means that our killer gutted an innocent young woman in cold blood."

Armed with the fragments of information he had conveyed, the young men began talking animatedly, coming up with theories and destroying them as ruthlessly as an infant knocking over wooden blocks. The only one who didn't spout possible motives was Dodgson. He was quiet, considering his friends' words and offering the occasional rebuttal or support.

Eddy found himself warming to the young man. While his primness could be annoying, Dodgson was clearly intelligent and had a keen grasp of logic as well as languages. Furthermore, he offered resources that Eddy would need in order to clear his name and bring the murderer to justice. *It seems that Fate knows what I need better than I do.*

A loud crash sounded from the front of the pub, followed by raised voices. He leaned backwards to get a better view of the commotion and spotted Stiles arguing with the bartender.

"I want another drink, damn your eyes!" the young nobleman shouted, flushed cheeks indicating that he'd already been at the bottle. "I have money, and I want to be served!"

"You won't be served here," the bartender said, folding thick arms across this chest. "And if you don't get out now, I'll call in the bulldogs."

Stiles bared his teeth but retreated. As he headed for the door, his gaze found Eddy's and locked for an instant. The nobleman's face was contorted in anger and petulance, but there was also something else there; grief, combined with a flash of naked fear.

Stiles was at the Mitre this morning demanding to speak with Jane, and now he's staggering around Oxford drunk and distraught. And didn't Dodgson say that his first name is Philip? Philip Stiles—PRS?

With a grimace Stiles tore his attention away and plunged out the door. But Eddy was suddenly sure that he knew who had fathered Jane's poor babe.

CHAPTER TWELVE

After Dodgson and his friends, who had puckishly described themselves as the Four Horsemen, escorted Eddy back to the Mitre, he went to his room and fell gratefully into bed—his own room's bed this time, wearing proper nightclothes like a civilized person. But sleep proved unsurprisingly elusive. After two years of marriage, he'd grown used to the warm presence of Elmira next to him at night.

How my life has changed. He turned over, punching the pillow into a more comfortable shape, and burrowed back in as the memories began to flow. The year after his beloved Sissy's death had been a black whirlwind of a time. He'd drunk far more alcohol than was good for his precarious health, behaved in ways that left the remainder of his reputation in tatters, and courted a number of noted *femmes de lettres* more out of panic than any real ardor. When he found himself torn between the noted poetess Sarah Helen Whitman and a woman named Nancy Richmond, he'd even swallowed laudanum in a feeble suicide attempt, hoping that Miss Richmond would fulfill her promise to visit his deathbed.

You couldn't even do that right. He had planned to take half the dose with the intention of taking the other half after he'd mailed a letter summoning Miss Richmond. But that half dose made him severely dizzy; he'd vomited and passed out in his room, waking up hours later covered in crusted stomach contents and awash in self-disgust. Loveless, jobless, penniless, and utterly alone, all he had to look forward to was the hope of a quick death in some gutter.

And then a friend gave him the news that would change his life forever.

As a young man, he had fallen in love with a beautiful blue-eyed brunette named Elmira Royster. Their relationship had blossomed during the long, sultry summer before he left for the University of Virginia, and Elmira had entranced him with her aristocratic beauty and sweet smile. The evening before his departure for Charlottesville he had asked her to marry him, confident that he would make her his wife at the end of the school year.

That confidence had been shaken to the core when he wrote her letter after letter from his rooms at the university, never receiving a response. Increasingly in debt from John Allan's insufficient allowance and the gambling he'd been forced to engage in to raise funds for books and lodging, he had finally accepted Elmira's silence as a rupture of their betrothal. After that betrayal he had left the university, determining to enroll in the Army and make peace with the fact that she was lost to him forever.

But the good Lord took pity on you for once, didn't he? It was years later when, upon recovering from his suicide attempt, Eddy had learned that Elmira Royster Shelton was now a widow. Moreover, they both lived in the same city. It had taken him a full week to drum up the courage to go to the address provided. Ten minutes after the maid had admitted him, a handsome blue-eyed brunette in widow's weeds swept into the sitting room. Eddy found himself face to face with his beautiful, beloved Elmira, who had accepted his proposal of marriage so many years ago before he left for the University of Virginia, and who now stared at him as if a ghost had entered her sitting room.

There had been tears at that first meeting, and much talk, and he'd held her hand as she revealed what her father had done. Mr. Royster, feeling that an orphaned and penniless writer was an unworthy choice for his daughter's hand, had put a stop to their budding romance by the simple expedient of intercepting and destroying Eddy's letters, something she herself had learned only after her marriage to Alexander Shelton, a wealthy businessman.

But Shelton had died some years ago, leaving Elmira a wealthy widow and a clear path for Eddy.

He turned over in bed again, staring at the inky ceiling. *My poor sweetheart.* He had been so terrified of losing her again that he'd pushed his suit beyond all the bounds of propriety, begging Elmira for a solid two weeks to become his wife.

She'd finally said yes, but insisted that he take a vow of temperance at the local hall first. He'd trooped down there with gratitude and determination, vowing publicly to avoid all liquor from that moment onwards, and privately to make Elmira proud of her decision to become his wife. His former excesses had been caused by intolerable pressures, he told himself; trying to support his family on the spotty pay of a writer, a mingled sense of pride and desperation that led him into a regrettable *affaire de coeur* with the noted poetess Frances Sargent Osgood, and finally watching Sissy succumb to consumption. He had felt certain that these pressures would not be repeated with Elmira at his side.

And I was right, wasn't I? Satisfied by Elmira's pride and trust in him, he'd avoided alcohol in all forms from that day at the Temperance Hall until that damned night at the Saddler's Arms. Guilt washed over him yet again, causing his eyes to grow damp with unshed tears. *I'm so sorry, my angel. You deserve someone far better than me.*

His incipient in-laws had certainly agreed with that. Elmira's children Ann and Southall had been against the marriage, and her brothers George, James and Alexander Royster had looked on Eddy as a womanizing drunkard, a parasite trying to drain their sister of her inheritance from her late husband. Eddy had hoped to convince them of his pledge to be a good and sober husband once he'd returned from a trip to New York to edit a local writer's work.

Two years later and thousands of miles away, he still broke out in a cold sweat at what had happened next. The Royster brothers had followed him onto the train, cornering him at the United States Hotel in Philadelphia. To his horror, the brothers informed him in no uncertain terms that he would not be marrying their sister. If he possessed an ounce of sense, a grim George Royster had told him, he would continue on to New York and never return to Richmond or Elmira ever again. If he did try to come back, steps would be taken to make sure that he didn't live long enough to marry into the Royster family.

Terrified by the Roysters' death threats, he had spent the next few days on the run. He hid with friends such as George Lippard, cutting off his distinctive mustache and even exchanging his fine suit of clothing and polished boots for the dirty, mismatched clothes of a working man. These desperate measures were all for one goal; to elude the Royster brothers and return to Elmira as soon as possible. He had felt sure that she could be persuaded to speed up the wedding schedule and cleave her life to his. Once that was done, her brothers could go hang.

And so Eddy had crept onto a train heading south in his workman's clothes, arriving in Baltimore on October 1, 1849. At the station, he'd discovered that he had missed the connecting train to Richmond, and had to make a choice. Was it wiser to remain in the crowds at the station, where the Roysters would hopefully be reluctant to take any sort of public action, or to retrieve his trunk full of valuable manuscripts and annotated books from the station's luggage room and hide out at a local hotel until the next Richmond train was ready to leave?

The second option had appealed to him greatly; he felt filthy and exhausted from his days on the run, and wished for nothing more than the chance to wash and rest before catching the next train to Richmond. But even as he went to the luggage room to withdraw his trunk, something made him change his mind. He never knew if it had been his imp or the angel of his better nature, but in the end he'd decided that it was wiser to remain in the safety of the station's milling crowds.

His decision had been vindicated when he spotted Alexander Royster skulking along the outskirts of the people streaming in and out of the station. Now he just had to get on the next Richmond train without them spotting him.

Thank God you have a creative turn of mind. After a few words with one of the station employees and an exchange of his paltry remaining funds, he found himself in the possession of a signalman's jacket and peaked cap. Redressed, he had headed to a third-class carriage without incident, even walking right past Alexander Royster as the tall man studied the well-dressed members of the crowd. It had been bitterly amusing that the Roysters, the scions of Richmond society, would never think to look twice at a lowly railroad employee.

Once back in Richmond, he went straight to Elmira's house and threw himself on her mercy. Once again, luck was on his side; his fiancée, already upset by the fact that her father had separated them years ago, had been braced by her brothers over her upcoming nuptials and was furious at this final attempt at interference. With gratifying speed, she'd summoned a Reverend Gordon from the nearby Presbyterian church and became Sarah Elmira Poe that afternoon with her sullen children in attendance.

When the Royster brothers had arrived at the Shelton house, irate over the loss of their quarry, Elmira introduced them to her new husband and informed them in no uncertain terms that they would welcome Eddy as their brother-in-law or face her enmity. She had been considered a beauty as a young woman, but as she grew older her family had discovered that a spine of steel lay underneath the soft, feminine exterior. With the marriage signed and sealed, there was nothing the brothers could do that wouldn't also damage their sister's reputation.

And so the Roysters had grudgingly acceded to Elmira's wishes, and Eddy found himself with a wife who was exactly what he needed; a helpmeet who would tolerate nothing less than the best from him, and who would in return serve as his rock in an uncertain and storm-tossed world.

For the last two years their marriage had been successful, so much so that Ann and Southall had finally warmed to him. His writing output had doubled, with his poem "Annabel Lee" winning him accolades from even the snobbish New England literary cliques, and his Gothic tales and further adventures of the detective C. Auguste Dupin had enthralled audiences across the country. He had even felt secure enough to launch *The Stylus*, his longed-for literary magazine.

Eddy turned over again, tugging at the covers until they were comfortable. *Damn it all, The Stylus* should *have been a rousing success.* The magazine had done quite well at first, with critical reviews from such literary luminaries as Henry Wadsworth Longfellow and Rufus Griswold. But the magazine's financial outlay began to outstrip its intake, and Eddy found himself under threat of having to sell it to investors or shut it down completely.

At least his previous experience in the publishing profession had served him well. Taking a leaf from a former business partner, he had made contact with Ponsonby, proposing a lecture tour of the British Isles where he could also stump up funds for the ailing *Stylus*. To his relief, Ponsonby had thought it was a capital idea to send the author of "The Raven" and "Annabel Lee" out on tour, and made the bulk of the arrangements that had led him here to Oxford.

Where I promptly broke my solemn pledge of temperance to Elmira, and landed myself in a deadly contretemps as a result. More tears rose at the thought, and he swiped at the warm salt water on his cheeks. *I can't live without her. It's not even the money or the home—she completes me, acts as a counterweight to my cursed imp, and soothes my soul.* If she were to leave him, he would die just as surely as he should have died that night back in 1849.

There was no hope for sleep now. Throwing back the covers, he struggled out of bed and got onto his knees next to the mattress. Clasping his hands together, he began to pray to a god he wasn't sure existed, but who might be his only hope of keeping Elmira. *I love her so much. I beg of you, dear God, if you can hear me, please help me.*

Please.

CHAPTER THIRTEEN

"You were right," Dodgson said the next morning, holding up a folded broadsheet. "They published the information about the murderer's message on the front page."

"I thought as much." Eddy plucked the newspaper from the young man's hand and scanned the story that took up a full column. "I'm only surprised they weren't able to get someone into the morgue to sketch the message itself. It would make a fascinating engraving."

Dodgson visibly shuddered. He had showed up at the hotel the next morning, the newest issue of *Jackson's Oxford Journal* in hand. Even so, he hadn't been Eddy's first visitor that morning; that honor had gone to Tomlinson, who had arrived to deliver an additional per diem and assure him that his continued residence at the Mitre would be covered by Ponsonby's. "You might want to think about writing a short piece about this sad occurrence," the publisher's man had said, tapping the side of his long nose. "I can assure you, sir, your audiences in other cities shall be rapt if you include it in your lecture."

Eddy dutifully agreed, although he had to wonder how enthusiastic the British reading audience would be about the real-life death of a young woman. Stomach now rumbling, he invited Dodgson to join him for breakfast, and the two men were soon seated at a small table in the corner of the Mitre's dining room.

"I *am* s-sorry about bringing Furnow with me yesterday," Dodgson said, sounding more contrite than he had the day before. "I came here thinking to talk to you about, well," he glanced around the cozy room, with its occupants applying themselves to steaming pots of Oolong and plates of kippers and other breakfast dishes, "your situation, and I'm afraid Mr. Furnow caught me asking the m-man at the front desk about you."

"Don't fret about it. Furnow wanted me to know that he's keeping an eye on me. I'm sure he would have passed along that message one way or the other." He gave the younger man a sardonic look. "And your quick thinking about my giving you a literary critique was rather impressive. A pity you don't actually write. You seem to have a knack for tall tales."

Dodgson flushed. "Well, as a matter of fact, I d-do write—little stories, mainly, and the occasional p-poem—"

"Now, about the Billings family," Eddy continued, eager to head off yet another request for a critique from an unpublished writer, "it seems that Mr. Billings was quite sure that Jane had no suitors, and yet we know for a fact that Jane gave my book to a paramour. I also learned that Mrs. Billings had lofty marital aspirations for her daughters." He forked up a mouthful of kipper. "I do wish I'd had more time to speak with Mrs. Billings," he said after swallowing. "I suspect she knew more about Jane's romantic attachments than she wanted to say in front of her husband. And I found it very curious that your Mr. Stiles came barging in here yesterday, demanding to speak with her."

Dodgson choked a bit on his tea. "Stiles?" he managed after a cough. "Are you implying that Philip Stiles was having s-some sort of an *affair de coeur* with a chambermaid?"

"You sound surprised."

"Not s-surprised—absolutely astounded. Stiles is one of that unfortunate breed of Christ Church men who seems to think that he was b-blessed by the Almighty. His uncle is an earl with no children, and now that his father has passed Stiles is to inherit everything. He barely deigns to converse with ladies of his own class because they're not rarefied enough for him. To think that he'd court a working-class girl is simply absurd."

Eddy wondered if his new friend was truly that naïve. "I doubt he was courting her, Dodgson. I presume that his designs had a much more, er, straightforward goal."

"Oh." Dodgson grimaced. "Which makes his actions even more despicable—to take advantage of a girl from a lesser station is most unw-worthy of a good Christian gentleman."

Yes, definitely naïve. Sighing, Eddy reached for the teapot when he spotted Maggie entering the tearoom. Shyly, she approached their table.

"Excuse me, Mr. Poe," she said softly, "but I wanted—that is, I thought—"

She blushed a deep pink and seemed on the verge of fleeing until Dodgson leaned forward, giving her a cheerful smile. "Hello, young miss. And what's your name?"

The girl blushed even harder. "Maggie, sir. Maggie Billings."

"Jane's younger sister," Eddy explained *sotto voce*.

"Ah." A look of sympathy crossed the younger man's face. "Would you care for some toast and jam, Miss Billings?"

Before the girl could answer, one of the servers bustled up with a face like thunder. "You know you're not to come in here, girl," the woman scolded. "Now off with you and go back to your pots."

"But we've invited her to dine with us," Eddy said quickly, giving the woman his most charming smile. "Can't she stay?"

Flustered, the server glared down at Maggie, then around the dining room as if hoping someone would swoop in and save her from having to decide between disciplining the staff and insulting a guest. “It’s not right, sir,” she said gruffly. “Staff ain’t supposed to dine with guests.”

“I know, but the child just lost her sister.” Eddy dropped his voice to a persuasive murmur. “Really, would one piece of toast do any harm?”

“And a cup of tea?” Maggie said hopefully.

“Of course, dear girl. What good is toast without a cup of tea to wash it down, after all?”

“Well, I suppose,” the woman allowed. “But just one cup, mind, then you,” she nodded at Maggie, “get back to your work.”

Maggie nodded back, and the woman trundled off with a parting sniff. To Eddy’s surprise, Dodgson stood up and pulled out a chair for the little girl as if seating a tiny duchess. “Miss Billings, would you be so kind as to join us?” he said formally.

She sat down, giving him a hesitant smile as he poured her a cup of tea with a healthy dollop of cream and two lumps of sugar. “And I think a fresh biscuit would be more pleasant than toast,” he said judiciously, selecting a round floury item studded with raisins. Placing it on a plate, he slid the treat in front of her.

She reached for the biscuit, then hesitated, looking at the table for something. “Mamma says proper ladies always use a napkin when they eat.”

“Indeed they do,” Eddy agreed. “As we are currently short of extra napkins, please accept mine.” He handed over the untouched square of linen.

“Thank you.” She smoothed the napkin in a square on her lap, only then taking a bite from the biscuit. “Jane said that you had come all the way from America for a lecture.”

"Very true. It's how I met my new friend Mr. Dodgson."

Maggie gave Dodgson a hesitant smile, then turned her attention back to Eddy. "Jane read me some of your poems from a magazine," she said solemnly. "Some were scary, but I thought others were very pretty."

Well, he couldn't expect literary criticism from a child. "I'm glad you found them pretty," he said magnanimously. "But I don't think you braved the dragon at the door to discuss my poetry."

The girl shook her head. "Mamma said that you offered to sign something for Jane, but she didn't know what," she admitted. "Jane didn't want her to know about it, or Pa."

Dodgson leaned forward. "Know about what, Miss Billings?"

"That she had a book for her sweetheart."

"Did Jane have a sweetheart, then?" Eddy asked carefully.

The girl nodded. "Jane said he was very nice to her, and that someday they would get married," she said, taking another bite of the biscuit.

"D-do you know the name of Jane's sweetheart, by any chance?" Dodgson asked.

Frowning, she shook her head. "Jane told me it was a secret, but that Mamma would be ever so happy and Pa would understand. She showed me his handkerchief—she said he gave it to her as a m … mento. It was white linen, with letters stitched in blue silk on it."

A memento. Eddy pounced on the clue. "Do you remember what the letters were?"

She nodded. "PRS. She kept it under her pillow, and would take it out at night and kiss it."

PRS—the same as in her book. "Did Jane give you any idea of when they might be married?"

"No, but she said I would have a new dress when it

happened." The light left her eyes, and she pushed her biscuit away. "But now it won't happen at all. Mamma and Pa said Jane had an accident on the stairs and that's how she died. But she never stumbled, sir, not once—she could walk up and down stairs with a full basket of laundry and not miss a step, not even after she got sick."

"She was sick?" Eddy asked.

"Yes, sir, for the last two weeks. She started keeping a bowl under her bed, and every morning she'd heave up into it, and have to carry it out back to the dunny and wash it afterwards. She made me promise not to tell Mamma or Pa, that she'd feel better soon." The girl's eyes filled with tears. "Is that why she fell on the stairs, sir? Because she was sick? Should I have told Mamma?"

Dodgson laid his hand over Maggie's small one. "She didn't fall because she was sick," the younger man said kindly. "And you mustn't b-blame yourself for keeping your sister's secret. That was right and proper. As for Jane, she's with our Lord in Heaven, now, where she'll be well and happy forever. In fact, it w-wouldn't surprise me at all if she became your guardian angel, keeping watch over you."

It was the right thing to say, judging by the relaxation in the girl's shoulders. "My dear girl, I would very much like to see Jane's handkerchief, if it's at all possible," Eddy said carefully. "If I could use it to work out who her sweetheart is, I could fulfill her last request. Do you think you could bring the handkerchief here to the hotel and show it to me?"

She bit her lip, eyes downcast. "I think so," she admitted. "But you mustn't tell Mamma or Pa. Or Mr. Venables."

"On my honor as a gentleman, I will protect your sister's secret."

"We both will," Dodgson added, earning another hesitant

smile from the girl. "Now, we need to discuss certain grownup matters, which wouldn't be very interesting to you. Perhaps you should take another biscuit and head back to the kitchens, and come back tomorrow with the handkerchief?"

"Yes, sir." She hopped off the chair, accepting another biscuit in return for her napkin. "If you find Jane's sweetheart, Mr. Poe, will you tell him that she liked him very much?"

His heart ached at the innocence in her words. "I will, my dear."

She nodded and left. He waited until she had disappeared through the dining room door before leaning back in his chair with a sigh. "You're quite good with children, Dodgson."

The undergraduate shrugged. "I'm the eldest of nine, with six younger sisters. I've had some practice in the art of k-keeping little girls happy."

"I'd say you're an expert. And thanks to young Miss Billings, we now have another piece of the puzzle," Eddy said. "A handkerchief embroidered with PRS—I don't suppose you happen to know what our Mr. Stiles's middle name is?"

Dodgson frowned. "If I remember correctly, it's Robert. Named for his uncle the marquis, as he liked to trumpet when proclaiming the brightness of his future. What interests me m-more, however, is the news of Jane's illness."

"Mm. We may want to continue this in private." He glanced at the other residents of the dining room. "Nothing blunts the appetite quite so much as the discussion of murder."

CHAPTER FOURTEEN

Charles followed his host from the dining room to the staircase. As they climbed to the first floor, he studied the doors lining the hallway. "Do you know how many people are currently staying in the hotel?"

"Ten, including myself, and four of them are on this floor," Poe explained, opening his door and ushering him inside. "Which means that there are three rooms on this floor alone where Jane's killer could have waited in ambush for her."

He felt slightly green when he glanced at the hotel room door opposite Poe's, knowing what had happened behind it. "How can you bear to stay here, knowing what happened?" he asked, taking a seat under the window.

"One does what one must," Poe said philosophically. "You don't believe in ghosts, do you?"

"Of course not. The spirits of the departed go to Heaven or Hell." He frowned. "However, it does make me worry about poor Jane. Would it have been possible for her to ascend to the arms of our Lord in her condition?"

The writer stared at him, then shook his head. "I suspect the Lord is understanding, particularly where babies are concerned. Our question now is, was Stiles the father?"

"The evidence does point in that direction," Charles admitted. "But as much as I dislike the man, I can't see him bbutchering his paramour."

"Neither do I." Poe began to pace, one finger stroking his mustache as he stalked the length of the room. To Charles's eye the man was a bundle of nervous energy, all sharp elbows and jerky movements. "Quite apart from the fact that I doubt he has the stomach for such violence, men like him don't like to get their hands dirty. And to complicate matters, it seems that Stiles wasn't the only man who had romantic inclinations towards Jane."

He straightened at that. "What do you mean?"

Poe recounted what the desk clerk had said and his reaction to the idea of Stiles seducing the chambermaid. "Which leaves us with the question of whether Jane was killed in order to prevent her from revealing Stiles's folly, or out of jealousy that she was carrying another man's child."

Charles immediately saw the flaw in that line of reasoning. "Do you think this Venables chap knew Ancient Greek?"

"I doubt it."

"Then the message you f-found on her body would seem to exculpate him from this crime. Which brings us back to Stiles, or someone associated with Stiles."

Poe stopped suddenly. "How do you think Stiles's uncle would react to the knowledge that he had an illegitimate cadet branch on the way?"

Charles considered the question. "I've only heard tales of the Marquis of Wells, but he's supposedly a very proud man. I suspect he would not be pleased at this turn of events."

"Would he disown his nephew if Stiles should get an inappropriate female in the family way?" Poe pressed.

"I couldn't say." The idea of such an event made him deeply uncomfortable. He had been raised to respect the feminine sex, and the activities that led to childbirth were to take place within the boundaries of marriage or not at all. "However, it's much more likely that the unfortunate young woman and her child would receive some sort of p-payment and be encouraged to remove themselves from the locality." It was easy enough to imagine—the arrogant peer, careful to shepherd his legacy in the form of his nephew. Should the nephew be foolish enough to have illegitimate offspring, it would be vital to have mother and child sent far, far away.

"Assuming that the young woman would accept such a proposal," Poe pointed out, pacing again. "From everything I've heard so far, Jane was an intelligent and strong-willed young woman, backed by a mother who desperately wanted her to improve her station in society. I don't think that combination made for a young lady who would disappear gracefully into the mists of time with her little bastard."

He flinched at the word. "Poe!"

"Well, it is the correct terminology," the writer said, unrepentant. "Hear me out, Dodgson. This whole situation smacks of more than a poor chambermaid being ruined by a rich nobleman. Even her death makes that clear. Why not simply strangle her on the way home and leave her body next to a hedge? It would certainly be easier for the murderer. Why kill her in such a gruesome and memorable way, and then pose her body so that it would be discovered and guaranteed to become a seven-day's-wonder?"

He tried to follow Poe's train of logic. "Humiliation, perhaps?"

"Perhaps. Her manner of demise will haunt her family, that's a guarantee. But I also think it was meant to be a warning."

Charles found himself swept along with Poe's extravagant theory weaving. "To whom?"

"To someone who wanted more for Jane than some money

and banishment from Oxford, perhaps? What if Mrs. Billings was aware of her daughter's condition, and was blackmailing Stiles to make her child legitimate? And that unfortunate blackmail led to Jane's death?"

As Charles pondered the lurid possibility a knock sounded at the door. "W-were you expecting company?"

"No. It's probably Furnow, here to intimidate me into a confession," Poe grumbled, going to the door.

Opening it, however, revealed a frantic Tomlinson bouncing on the balls of his feet in agitation. "Mr. Poe, I've just received a most peculiar visit from a Mr. Collin of the Oxford City Watch," the publishing manager said breathlessly.

With a sigh, Poe gestured for him to come in. "I see. And what did the stalwart constable tell you?"

"He has informed me that you are not permitted to leave Oxford—" Tomlinson spotted Charles and gawped. "Oh. I do beg your pardon."

Poe waved off the manager's discomfort. "Dodgson is already aware of the situation, so you may speak freely in front of him. And as for your question, yes, I am indeed trapped in your fair city until Furnow and his compatriots at the Oxford University Police find the girl's killer. I can assure you that I was not responsible for her death, but my proximity to the room where she died has raised the constabulary's suspicions." He pulled a face. "And I suspect the darker of my literary works hasn't helped in their opinion of me."

"Oh, dear." Tomlinson pulled out a handkerchief and mopped his brow. "Mr. Ponsonby will not like this at all, sir. It was my understanding that you were assisting the police, not being investigated by them. And you were supposed to be on the train to Coventry in less than an hour, so now we'll have to telegram ahead to the organizers and cancel tonight's lecture.

Oh, this is a muddle of horrendous proportions!"

To Charles's astonishment Poe clasped a hand to his breast, donning an expression of what could only be called tragic determination. "Believe me when I say that I'm not delighted about this in the least, Tomlinson," he intoned. "But what I told you about assisting them was the truth. My young friend and I have already collected a number of clues about the identity of the killer and I firmly believe that we'll have the fiend cornered within a day or two. In fact, I've already started working on a lecture that will explain how we achieved this feat—something, I may add, that wouldn't have happened without Mr. Ponsonby's patronage."

Charles had strong doubts that they were anywhere close to identifying the murderer, but Tomlinson seemed willing to cling to the tissue of lies Poe was so expertly spinning. "I see," he finally said, wiping at his face again. "Well, if you do find the murderer, that will of course reflect well upon Mr. Ponsonby and his company. But if that wasn't enough, we have yet another complication." The manager patted at his coat, fishing out an envelope. "You've been invited to a soirée at Sir Richard Middleton's home this evening."

Charles recognized the name. "Sir Richard's a Christ Church man. Q-quite the patron of the arts."

"Indeed, and his niece attended your lecture, Mr. Poe," Tomlinson said. "She sent an invitation to my office first thing this morning. I had assumed that you would be leaving for Coventry so was about to send your regrets, but—"

"I would be delighted to come," Poe said instantly. "And of course I would enthusiastically promote my Ponsonby collection during my attendance." He glanced down at his frock coat and trousers. "Er, what does one wear to a soirée here?"

"Lord, I hadn't thought of that. Something a bit more

elaborate than what you're wearing, I'm afraid," Tomlinson admitted, eyeing the writer's small, spare frame. "I take it the rest of your garments are similar to what you're currently wearing?"

"They are."

"Hm. My nephew may have something that would suit you. He's similar in height, although slightly rounder in circumference. We'll have to throw ourselves on the mercy of my tailor and see what he can do."

"Excellent, excellent." Poe turned an ingenuous face to Charles. "Now, what about young Dodgson here?"

He blinked. "M-me?"

"Of course. You yourself said that this Sir Richard is a Christ Church man, so I'm sure that members of your college are welcome at his parties." Poe's voice was full of high good humor, but his eyes were pleading. "If I'm to attend tonight, I would feel more comfortable knowing that I had such a steadfast young companion at my side."

"Oh, I do think that's an excellent idea," Tomlinson agreed, to Charles's chagrin. "Do you have the necessary clothes, Dodgson?"

The last thing he wanted to do was attend a society soirée. *But someone needs to keep Poe out of yet more trouble, and Tomlinson clearly can't be trusted.* "I do."

"Wonderful. I'll have a copy of the invitation delivered to your rooms, then." Tomlinson rubbed his hands together. "Well, gentlemen, let's see if we can't make a silk purse out of a sow's ear, eh?"

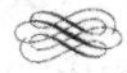

Elizabeth Billings sat in her front garden, grateful for a moment away from her well-meaning in-laws and neighbors. They'd buzzed around her like helpful honeybees since the news about Jane spread around up and down their street. *"Would you like a cup of tea, Lizzie?" "Where do you keep your linens, Lizzie?" "Would you like us to use this dress for Jane?"*

She stared at the patch of turf at her feet. It was simply too much, all of this outpouring of emotion. Even after all these years of marriage to Michael, she still felt uncomfortable with the easier ways of his working-class family. Michael himself was still stunned at the news and sat in the parlor next to Jane's still-empty coffin, while Margaret was in her (now solely owned) bedroom, crying.

Meanwhile, she was left to deal with the actual business of burying her eldest child. Elizabeth crossed her arms tightly across her chest, trying to sort her thoughts. *I should be sobbing my heart out. My daughter was killed in cold blood. I should be mourning with my family.*

But she couldn't. She passed a perfectly steady hand across her forehead. *Father always said I took after Grandfather—his little girl soldier. Grandfather faced down a charge by French forces and didn't blink once. That same blood flows in my veins.*

I don't have time for grief, not now. There's still Margaret's future to play for. Once that's secure, I can mourn for Jane.

Spine stiffening, she stood and went back into the house, just in time to have her sister-in-law Mary step into her path. "You should sit with Michael for awhile, dearie," Mary advised, covering Elizabeth's hand with her own red, work-roughened one. "He needs you now."

Elizabeth gave her sister-in-law a tight smile. "I just need to run an errand first, and then I'll sit with him. Until then, if you could take my place—"

"O' course I will," Mary said, squeezing Elizabeth's hand again. "I'm so sorry about all this, Lizzie. Jane was an angel, she was. To think of what that cruel beast did to her—"

"I can't talk about it," Elizabeth forced out, relieved when she saw a look of shame in her sister-in-law's eyes. "I'll be back straightaway."

Mary went back into the parlor, and she hurried upstairs to the small bedroom she shared with her husband. A pot of ink and a quill pen were unearthed from her dresser drawer, along with a single piece of cheap notepaper. Taking the implements to the small table by the window, she wrote a short note, underlining certain words to drive her point home.

Margaret would be married well, she vowed. Or Philip Stiles would be held accountable.

CHAPTER FIFTEEN

It was early evening when the hansom cab pulled up in front of a graceful town house, its elegant array of mullioned windows glowing with light. Tomlinson climbed out of the cab first, thrusting some coins at the cabbie as Eddy joined him on the pavement. "We'll have to find Sir Richard straightaway, of course," the publishing manager said. "He's quite eager to meet you. And if he asks, would you be willing to do a recitation or two? He does enjoy hearing an author or poet's work from their own mouth."

"It would be my honor," Eddy said, bemused by the irony. Yesterday, he had begun the day with a foul hangover and a corpse at the end of his bed. Tonight, he was at a literary salon being feted by noble patrons. *If I wrote it down as a story, no publisher would ever buy it, claiming it to be too fantastic for belief.*

At least he looked ready for a literary soirée. After a quick stop at the Ponsonby warehouse to send off the necessary telegrams, he had accompanied Tomlinson to the man's tailor for an afternoon of modifications to the borrowed frock coat, waistcoat, and trousers. The manager's faith in his tailor had been justified, and the lustrous black fabric of Eddy's new clothing now fit him like a second skin. *Ah, Elmira, if only you were here to see this.*

Tomlinson pulled out his pocket watch, checking it. "Now, we should decide what you should say if anyone asks you about your involvement with the murder—"

"I've already been thinking about that," Eddy said smoothly. "As my room was directly across the hallway, it's logical that your local constabulary would wish to speak with me. My detention is an unfortunate but unavoidable side effect of their investigation, but it hardly indicates guilt—after all, if Constable Furnow or Officer Collin had proof that I had committed the murder, I would be in your local jail, yes?"

"I would certainly think so," Tomlinson agreed.

"Indeed. And in return for enjoying the hospitality of Oxford, I feel that it's my duty to help the police with their efforts and search for the murderer, details of which will be explained in my future lectures under Mr. Ponsonby's aegis." He spread his hands. "Assuming that he still wishes to work with me after all this."

Tomlinson gave him a reluctant smile. "Notoriety is one of the world's best salesmen, Mr. Poe. If you help the police catch this killer, I can assure you that Mr. Ponsonby will be more than happy to work with you."

"Well, then. Shall we go in?"

A liveried servant greeted them at the entrance, ushering them into the grand foyer where clusters of people stood and chatted. "If you would be so kind as to wait here, I'll locate our host," Tomlinson said, heading off.

Alone, Eddy studied the attendees, noting that British feminine fashions in evening wear were quite similar to what he'd seen at his last dinner party in Richmond. The majority of the women wore a relatively low-cut bodice, exposing a pleasing amount of their neck and shoulders in a style Elmira called the 'bertha.' Naturally modest, his wife usually wore her evening dresses with a filmy lace shawl covering her exposed shoulders.

From what he could see of the soirée's female attendees, however, not all of them had felt the need for such protection of their charms.

The fabric saved on the top half of the dress had been utilized at the bottom, with skirts belling out in a graceful dome of silk from their wearer's waist. He stepped back hastily, allowing a lady to sweep by him like a ship under full sail. *They must be a damned nuisance to handle, particularly in close quarters.*

The men were dressed on the whole much like he was; a dark frock coat and matching trousers, waistcoat, white linen shirt and cravat. A few of the younger men had apparently decided to cut a dash and were wearing brightly colored and patterned waistcoats that skimmed the edges of good taste. After a moment, he spotted Dodgson in a group of young men and waved to catch his attention.

Dodgson detached himself from the cluster and came over. "I see you m-made it," the younger man said, glancing at Eddy's new clothes. Blessedly, the undergraduate had decided to skip the eye-watering sartorial choices of his peers and was wearing a slightly more formal version of his outfit from earlier that day. "Tomlinson's tailor should be commended. You look quite splendid."

"Thank you, although glancing at your compatriots I wonder if I should have asked for a waistcoat striped in mauve and peacock blue."

The younger man grimaced. "The things that are done in the name of fashion," he muttered. "The servants are making the rounds with refreshments. I found the punch to be a bit strong, but that may be more to your taste." He paused, abashed. "Or perhaps not."

"I believe it would be in my best interest to abstain from alcoholic beverages tonight," Eddy agreed. "If there is some sort of fruit juice or other non-potent drink available, I'll stick to that."

Just then Tomlinson emerged from the crowd, looking triumphant. "Ah, there you are, Mr. Poe. I've found Sir Richard and I'm to bring you straightaway."

Eddy gave Dodgson a wry look. "Duty calls. In the meantime, you may want to circulate and see what the hoi polloi are discussing this evening."

The undergraduate nodded in understanding and wandered off.

Sir Richard Middleton turned out to be a tall, spare man of later age, with a thick, leonine crop of yellow hair only now going to silver and sharp blue eyes half-hidden behind a pair of spectacles. He was chatting with a young woman wearing what was, even to Eddy's untrained eye, an extremely expensive dress. Unlike the rest of the female attendees who tended towards mild pastels in their toilette, she was gowned in a white and aqua striped chiffon with knife-pleated aqua fabric setting off her neckline and sleeves, serving as the female counterpart of the fashion-forward young bucks in the entrance hallway.

"Sir Richard," Tomlinson said, beetling forward, "may I present Edgar Allan Poe."

"Ah, Mr. Poe!" Sir Richard said, giving him an affable nod. "Splendid of you to come tonight. I do enjoy meeting members of the literati, particularly ones who can wield such a dark pen with your skill, eh?"

"I was honored by your invitation, sir," Eddy said, nodding back. "It's as much a pleasure for me to meet those who enjoy the art of poetry."

"Ah, well, enough of those in Oxford, I'd be bound," Sir Richard said, turning to the young lady at his side. "Gentlemen, let me introduce my niece, Lady Georgiana Gardner."

Lady Georgiana was a short, slender blonde with eyes that matched the teal stripes in her gown and a nose that could best be described as Roman. Eddy bowed over her gloved hand, which bore a ring in the form of a golden dragon clutching an opal egg. The parsimonious part of his brain estimated that the exotic bauble could have paid for a year's lodging during Sissy's final illness. "A pleasure, Lady Georgiana," he said, doing his best to sound charmed.

"The pleasure is mine, sir," the woman replied in a pleasantly husky voice. "When Uncle Richard told me that you had accepted our invitation, I was absolutely delighted. I find your poetry to be quite chimerical, speaking to both the light and the dark half of human nature."

The young woman's intuitive observation impressed him. "Few people realize that, and even fewer can phrase it so elegantly. May I ask if you are yourself a poetess?"

Instead of blushing or demurring, she calmly gazed into his eyes. "Hardly in your caliber, Mr. Poe, but I do enjoy the art of wordsmithing. I find it's one of the few freedoms that those of my gender are allowed."

"Oh, dear," Sir Richard sighed. "Georgiana, my dear, this is neither the time nor the place for your modern views."

She patted her uncle's hand. "Mr. Poe is not one of your stuffy friends from the House of Lords, Uncle Dicky. I hardly think he'll glower at me in disapproval."

"I would never dare," Eddy said gallantly. "Instead, I find myself slain by your wit and logic, and must lay my heart at your feet as spoils of the joust."

"And so I will claim it, sir, and return it to you with my thanks," she said with a charming smile. "Uncle Dicky, I believe I see Mrs. Murchinson and her dreadful offspring. I should head her off before young Pursley or Desmond try to set fire to the footman again."

"Please do, my dear," Sir Richard said, watching fondly as she headed towards a thin matron shepherding twin redheads already tugging at maternal hands. "That girl will be a handful for some lucky man, mark my words. I believe you're already wed, Mr. Poe?"

"Indeed, sir."

"Probably for the best. I'm afraid she'd run roughshod over you within a fortnight." Sir Richard's small smile indicated he wasn't quite as exasperated with his niece's forthright nature as he seemed. "Until I find someone with the intestinal fortitude to stand up to her, at least I'll have a capable hostess for events such as tonight. Now, Mr. Poe, we should fetch you a refreshment." He gestured with a crooked finger at one of the servants, who materialized at Eddy's elbow with a silver platter of punch cups.

The delicious scent of rum wafted up from the deep red liquor, and Eddy saw Tomlinson blanch in panic. The sight was humorous enough that he was able to ignore his imp's wheedling. "Thank you, Sir Richard, but health reasons force me to stay away from alcoholic beverages. If there is a non-potent version of the punch, however, I would be glad for a cup of it."

"Of course, of course," Sir Richard said. "Braidwood, fetch a cup from the Diana punchbowl." Once the servant was gone, he leaned closer and murmured, "Virgin punch, you see. Frankly, I can't stomach spirits anymore, either. Does horrendous things to my digestion, eh? I do miss a good glass of wine now and then, however."

"Yes," Eddy agreed wistfully, "but unfortunately one must do what's necessary for one's health. Now, If I may be so bold, Sir Richard, in what area of the literary arts do your own interests lie?"

Charles lifted a punch cup from the proffered tray, nodding his thanks and sipping carefully at the ruby liquid. The bite of rum was stronger than he'd expected, and he winced at the sting.

"Braidwood does tend to have a rather heavy hand on the rum bottle when mixing the punch," a female voice said. He turned to the speaker, swallowing hard when he realized it was the young lady in the brightly striped gown he'd seen earlier. "I've spoken to him about it, but he keeps saying that it's the recipe he learned while he was in the West Indies, and to change it now would be a travesty."

"W-well, I wouldn't c-c-call it a t-t-t—" He bit his tongue, mentally cursing his stammer. It was rarely present when he was amusing his younger sisters or their friends, made the occasional appearance when he was called upon to read in church or speak in class, and roared into humiliating life whenever he was nervous, upset or surprised, as he was by a strange female coming up and speaking to him so boldly. "It's not b-bad," he managed, feeling his cheeks sting with blood.

The lady studied her own cup with a dubious look. "I'm afraid you're being entirely too kind to Braidwood, Mr...."

There was no help for it. "D-d-dodgson. Charles Dodgson, of Christ C-church," he said, giving her a small, jerky bow.

"Oh, like Uncle Dicky—how delightful! I'm Lady Georgiana Gardner," she said, offering her hand. He took it hesitantly. "I don't believe I've seen you at one of Uncle Dicky's soirées before, Mr. Dodgson. Do you not care for the arts?"

He blinked, surreptitiously glancing around the room for one of the Horsemen. They had arrived together, but O'Donnell immediately peeled off to head after a gaggle of young ladies, and Hebron and Reade had been drawn to the buffet like flies to honey. He couldn't even see Poe, drat it all. "I appreciate the arts as well as any other educated m-man, I suppose. But if truth be told, my interests lie more in the fields of mathematics and logic."

To his surprise, she didn't seem bored by his admission. "Then you prefer the cold, clear surety of things that must be proven," she said. "Surely you must appreciate Bach's fugues, then, with their mathematical precision."

"Er, I'm afraid I'm not much for music," he said, scanning the room again.

"The works of Jan Vermeer?"

"Who?"

"Oh, dear." Lady Georgiana touched her fan to her lips lightly. "You are a very single-minded man, aren't you, Mr. Dodgson? At least tell me that there's room for faith in your regimented world view?"

"C-certainly," he said with some heat. "If your uncle was a member of the House, then you must know that it is hardly a place for those without faith."

Some of the amusement left the young woman's face, and she nodded soberly now. "Well said, Mr. Dodgson, and you have my apologies if I offended you. In truth, I'm impressed that you have a turn of mind that can navigate the intricacies of higher mathematics. It is a skill that fascinates me."

Suddenly abashed at his overreaction, he stared at the floor in embarrassment. "Oh. In which case, I d-do apologize for the h-harshness of my words. Have you ever s-studied algebra or other branches of mathematics?"

"My tutors were quite convinced that my head was stuffed with cotton when it came to facts and figures," Lady Georgiana said with a rueful laugh. "As for logic, Mr. Grossmith said it was a blessing that I was a woman, since logical behavior would never be expected from me."

That was a common enough belief, and one that he had never agreed with. "That seems rather sh-short-sighted of Mr. Grossmith. My sisters all comprehended the basic c-concepts of logic when I explained it to them, and th-they were much younger than you." Granted, his sisters hadn't been as fascinated as he had been, but they had picked up the principles well enough.

Her face lit up at his statement. "Really? How did you teach them?"

"W-well, we started with word games such as sorites."

"Sorites?"

"It means 'the fallacy of the heap' in Ancient Greek," he said, warming to the topic. "It's a group of p-propositions chained together, where the predicate of each proposition is the subject of the next premise, and the conclusion unites the subject of the first proposition with the predicate of the last. I would create such a chain, then scramble the propositions and have the girls work them out in order, testing the result with symbolic logic. The challenge with sorites is to make sure that you're not led astray by false logic, such as the statement that a cat has four legs, and the animal that draws a carriage has four legs, thus carriages are drawn by cats."

Lady Georgiana's eyes crinkled, and she muffled a chuckle. "I just had an image of our tabbies in harness, poor things. But I see your point about false logic."

"If it's of any consolation, my sisters tended to have the same reaction to that particular polysyllogism," he admitted. "If it would be of interest to you, we could play a round of sorites, and I could explain the rules as we go along."

Before she could reply, a tall man who had to be Sir Richard strode into the room, Poe in tow. "Honored guests, I crave your indulgence and ask you to gather 'round," he announced.

The crowd, alert for entertainment, formed a genteel circle around their host. "As you know, I am something of a literary follower, and I am delighted to announce that we have a most distinguished poet with us tonight, all the way from America," he continued. "Furthermore, he has kindly consented to give us a reading of one of his masterpieces, 'The Raven.' Ladies and gentlemen, I give you Edgar Allan Poe."

The audience clapped as Poe stepped into the center of their circle. "May I ask that the lights be dimmed? I have found that this enhances the effect of my work," he said. The servants bustled to the candelabras, snuffing most of the wicks until only a dim glow illuminated the room.

"Thank you." The American took a moment to sweep his gaze around the waiting audience. Charles assumed the man knew full well the effect of candlelight on his large, grey eyes and broad, well-formed forehead. *He may be something of a scoundrel, but he certainly knows how to hold an audience.*

Taking a pose, Poe began.

CHAPTER SIXTEEN

The killer stared at the note, taking a moment to ensure that the sealing wax hadn't been cracked before reading the simple message. *As I expected. She simply couldn't leave enough alone, could she?*

The message contained a demand to meet, as well as a threat to go to the police if the meeting did not occur. He wondered what she had planned. Yet another blackmail attempt? Or was it something more arcane?

It would be quite entertaining to find out. *For me, at least.* He was sure she wouldn't find it entertaining at all.

Humming to himself, he stood and tossed the note into the fire, watching the flames turn the cheap paper to char and ash before slipping on his greatcoat. He paused, making sure that the contents of his inner breast pocket were still there, then headed into the October night, an anticipatory smile on his face.

Once upon a midnight dreary, while I pondered weak and weary,
Over many a quaint and curious volume of forgotten lore,
While I nodded, nearly napping, suddenly there came a tapping,
As of some one gently rapping, rapping at my chamber door.
''Tis some visitor,' I muttered, 'tapping at my chamber door -
Only this, and nothing more.'

Ah, distinctly I remember it was in the bleak December,
And each separate dying ember wrought its ghost upon the floor.
Eagerly I wished the morrow; - vainly I had sought to borrow
From my books surcease of sorrow - sorrow for the lost Lenore -
For the rare and radiant maiden whom the angels named Lenore -
Nameless here for evermore.

And the silken sad uncertain rustling of each purple curtain
Thrilled me - filled me with fantastic terrors never felt before;
So that now, to still the beating of my heart, I stood repeating
''Tis some visitor entreating entrance at my chamber door -
Some late visitor entreating entrance at my chamber door; -
This it is, and nothing more,'

Near one of Oxford's many canals, a small park and its trees offered a taste of peace and solitude to the residents of the area. Busy during the day with perambulating visitors, nannies and their charges, the park became quiet after dark, offering a haven of a different sort to those who needed it.

Elizabeth Billings paced anxiously near an elaborate yew topiary, wondering where he could be. She knew he'd received the message; she dropped it off herself, giving the underling a sixpence to guarantee delivery.

A shape materialized at the other end of the topiary. "Mrs. Billings?" a low voice said.

She clutched the shawl tighter around her shoulders. "You gave me a fright!" she hissed.

"No more than the fright you gave me with your letter," the man said, approaching. "But I'm here, as you demanded. Now what do you want?"

My daughter back, you fool. But that was an impossibility. "I want justice."

He raised his hands, spreading them. "Then go to the police. Surely they are the dispensers of justice, no? Whereas I am merely a messenger."

She wanted to scream, to strike at him, vent some of the rage that had burned in her breast since the moment Michael had staggered through the door with the news of Jane. But she couldn't, not while there was still a chance for Margaret. "I have another daughter," she bit out. "I am willing to forget what I know about Jane's condition, and why it led to her murder, if Margaret is married in her place."

Presently my soul grew stronger; hesitating then no longer,
'Sir,' said I, 'or Madam, truly your forgiveness I implore;
But the fact is I was napping, and so gently you came rapping,
And so faintly you came tapping, tapping at my chamber door,
That I scarce was sure I heard you' - here I opened wide the door; -
Darkness there, and nothing more.

Deep into that darkness peering, long I stood there wondering, fearing,
Doubting, dreaming dreams no mortal ever dared to dream before
But the silence was unbroken, and the darkness gave no token,
And the only word there spoken was the whispered word, 'Lenore!'
This I whispered, and an echo murmured back the word, 'Lenore!'
Merely this and nothing more.

Back into the chamber turning, all my soul within me burning,
Soon again I heard a tapping somewhat louder than before.
'Surely,' said I, 'surely that is something at my window lattice;
Let me see then, what thereat is, and this mystery explore -
Let my heart be still a moment and this mystery explore; -

'Tis the wind and nothing more!'

"And what do you know about Jane's murder?" the man said, sounding curious.

"Who ordered it, for one thing," she snapped. "An accusation of murder would taint Lord Dunford's honor, and it would certainly scupper any chances of his nephew marrying."

The glow of a distant streetlamp threw a hazy nimbus around the man's head as it tilted to the side. "I see. I do wonder, however, why you would lay this act at Lord Dunford's feet. You don't think it could have been his nephew?"

She laughed once, a harsh sound on the chill night. "Philip Stiles is too much of a craven fool to do such a thing."

"And yet you still want to link little Margaret to him in holy matrimony." His chuckle was as bleak as hers. "Are you that desperate to regain your lost social standing?"

Mrs. Billings ignored the angry tears rising in her eyes. "I am desperate to make sure that my—" she stumbled over the word *daughters*, "—my daughter is not forced to lead the life I've lived. My father was a barrister, and my grandfather fought with Cornwallis. Margaret is not some pitiful drab come up from the gutter, despite our current situation. If Lord Dunford makes this marriage happen, my lips will remain sealed about Jane."

Open here I flung the shutter, when, with many a flirt and flutter,
In there stepped a stately raven of the saintly days of yore.
Not the least obeisance made he; not a minute stopped or stayed he;
But, with mien of lord or lady, perched above my chamber door -
Perched upon a bust of Pallas just above my chamber door -

Perched, and sat, and nothing more.

Then this ebony bird beguiling my sad fancy into smiling,
By the grave and stern decorum of the countenance it wore,
'Though thy crest be shorn and shaven, thou,' I said, 'art sure no craven.
Ghastly grim and ancient raven wandering from the nightly shore -
Tell me what thy lordly name is on the Night's Plutonian shore!'
Quoth the raven, 'Nevermore.'

Much I marvelled this ungainly fowl to hear discourse so plainly,
Though its answer little meaning - little relevancy bore;
For we cannot help agreeing that no living human being
Ever yet was blessed with seeing bird above his chamber door -
Bird or beast above the sculptured bust above his chamber door,
With such name as 'Nevermore.'

There was silence for a long moment, broken only by the rattle of the wind through the trees overhead. Finally, the man sighed. "I regret to inform you that Lord Dunford already has plans for his nephew's bride, and they do not include your daughter. I will return to him with this demand, if you wish, but I can already tell you that he'll refuse."

She shook her head. "Then I shall go to the constabulary with what I know. And I believe his lordship will find that it will not be an easy road with them. Nor will you, if you had any involvement in my daughter's death." She shrank back when the figure stepped forward. "Come any closer and I'll scream."

The man paused, then gave her a small bow, hands out to the sides. "Well, we can't have that, can we?" he said.

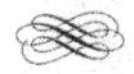

But the raven, sitting lonely on the placid bust, spoke only,
That one word, as if his soul in that one word he did outpour.
Nothing further then he uttered - not a feather then he fluttered -
Till I scarcely more than muttered 'Other friends have flown before -
On the morrow he will leave me, as my hopes have flown before.'
Then the bird said, 'Nevermore.'

Startled at the stillness broken by reply so aptly spoken,
'Doubtless,' said I, 'what it utters is its only stock and store,
Caught from some unhappy master whom unmerciful disaster
Followed fast and followed faster till his songs one burden bore -
Till the dirges of his hope that melancholy burden bore
Of "Nevermore."'

But the raven still beguiling all my sad soul into smiling,
Straight I wheeled a cushioned seat in front of bird and bust and door;
Then, upon the velvet sinking, I betook myself to linking
Fancy unto fancy, thinking what this ominous bird of yore -
What this grim, ungainly, ghastly, gaunt, and ominous bird of yore
Meant in croaking 'Nevermore.'

Before she could move he leapt forward, slamming into her and knocking her to the ground, then scrambling up so that he knelt astride her waist. She tried to gasp, breathless from the impact, only to find strong hands ringing her throat, choking off her air. She struggled in terror, clawing against his arms, but the grip was inexorable. Red and black flowers burst in from the edges of her vision, and she knew with a dreadful finality that she'd overplayed her hand.

Her murderer leaned closer, staring into her eyes. "Goodbye, Mrs. Billings," he whispered. "Say hello to Jane for me."

Before she died, she finally recognized the odd tone in his voice. It was joy.

This I sat engaged in guessing, but no syllable expressing
To the fowl whose fiery eyes now burned into my bosom's core;
This and more I sat divining, with my head at ease reclining
On the cushion's velvet lining that the lamp-light gloated o'er,
But whose velvet violet lining with the lamp-light gloating o'er,
She shall press, ah, nevermore!

Then, methought, the air grew denser, perfumed from an unseen censer
Swung by Seraphim whose foot-falls tinkled on the tufted floor.
'Wretch,' I cried, 'thy God hath lent thee - by these angels he has sent thee
Respite - respite and nepenthe from thy memories of Lenore!
Quaff, oh quaff this kind nepenthe, and forget this lost Lenore!'
Quoth the raven, 'Nevermore.'

'Prophet!' said I, 'thing of evil! - prophet still, if bird or devil! -
Whether tempter sent, or whether tempest tossed thee here ashore,
Desolate yet all undaunted, on this desert land enchanted -
On this home by horror haunted - tell me truly, I implore -
Is there - is there balm in Gilead? - tell me - tell me, I implore!'
Quoth the raven, 'Nevermore.'

The killer waited for a moment longer, fragile bones crackling under his grip, then released the dead woman's throat. Her head thumped gently onto the loam, a thin trickle of spittle at the corner of her mouth gleaming silver in the moonlight.

"What an ignorant cow you are, Mrs. Billings," he whispered.

And to offer Margaret in Jane's stead, as if Dunford would agree to such nonsense. Leaning back, he studied the dead woman's glazed countenance as it stared into the twilight sky. Simply strangling her didn't seem ... enough, somehow.

Reaching into his jacket, he brought out his knife. His only regret was that the ignorant cow was already dead. Listening to her squeals would have been delightful.

Well, she did threaten blackmail. It's only appropriate that I take the organ that offered such offense. He stuck his fingers into her half-opened mouth, wrenching the jaw open until he heard a wet cracking noise. *This should make a pretty puzzle. I do hope Mr. Poe gets to see my new note.*

Humming to himself, he began to slice.

'Prophet!' said I, 'thing of evil! - prophet still, if bird or devil!
By that Heaven that bends above us - by that God we both adore -
Tell this soul with sorrow laden if, within the distant Aidenn,
It shall clasp a sainted maiden whom the angels named Lenore -
Clasp a rare and radiant maiden, whom the angels named Lenore?'
Quoth the raven, 'Nevermore.'

'Be that word our sign of parting, bird or fiend!' I shrieked upstarting -
'Get thee back into the tempest and the Night's Plutonian shore!
Leave no black plume as a token of that lie thy soul hath spoken!
Leave my loneliness unbroken! - quit the bust above my door!
Take thy beak from out my heart, and take thy form from off my door!'

Quoth the raven, 'Nevermore.'

And the raven, never flitting, still is sitting, still is sitting
On the pallid bust of Pallas just above my chamber door;
And his eyes have all the seeming of a demon's that is dreaming,
And the lamp-light o'er him streaming throws his shadow on the floor;
And my soul from out that shadow that lies floating on the floor
Shall be lifted - nevermore!

CHAPTER SEVENTEEN

There was nothing quite like the approbation of an appreciative crowd for the poetic ego, Eddy thought, even if all one had to drink was virgin punch. The reaction to his reading of "The Raven" had been thoroughly gratifying and reminded him of Anne Lynch's famous parties back in New York. A wide array of creative types would gather at Lynchie's modest home and sip tea or broth (alcohol being strictly forbidden from her soirées) while a writer recited his or her latest work, or a musician played a new composition. Some of the finest creative works in America had enjoyed their first public outing at Lynchie's, including his "Raven."

A sudden flash of memory overcame him, of the poetess Fanny Osgood sitting and listening to his first recitation of "The Raven," tears in her glorious eyes at the heart-rending impact of his verse. He considered the silver cup in his hand, his sense of satisfaction fading. Fanny was beyond the veil now, her pen stilled forever, taken like so many women he'd loved by the ghostly grasp of consumption. *And for all I know, Elmira is in a strange bed somewhere in Bath at this very moment, with God only knows what disease coursing through her veins. Dear sweet Jesu, have an ounce of pity on me for once in my miserable life. I cannot lose her as well—I* cannot.

Sir Richard appeared at his side, startling him out of his

gloomy thoughts. “Stupendous work, Mr. Poe. Now I understand why you’re the toast of London,” he said, gesturing through the throng to a spot in the corner where a tall gentleman waited, punch cup in hand. “If you’d be so kind, there’s someone to whom I’d like to introduce you.”

With a start, Eddy recognized his fellow passenger from the train. The man’s iron-grey hair was neatly brushed back from a broad, powerful forehead, and two rather cold blue eyes topped what could only be called a British nose.

“I see you’ve found yourself a poet who isn’t mired in all that Romantic froth and fuss,” the man drawled now, taking a sip from his own cup.

Sir Richard chuckled. “Mr. Poe, allow me to introduce my good friend Lord Robert Dunford, the Marquis of Wells. Dunford, this is Edgar Poe, the American poet I’d mentioned.”

Eddy gave the nobleman a brief, respectful bow, getting a slow nod in return. “While I happen to admire the Romantic school of poetry, I find myself more drawn to the Gothic movement when it comes to imagery and inspiration,” he said impulsively, wondering how the nobleman would take it.

“I see. Death and the Maiden, and an ever-present psychopomp to remind us of what we have lost and can never have again,” Dunford said. “I prefer more realistic topics in my poetry—the diligence due to a bastard child, for example, or a saga about battle. I do have to wonder who you’ve lost, Mr. Poe, that you must immortalize them so in poetry.”

The marquis’s dismissive manner reminded him unpleasantly of his foster father John Allan, the no-nonsense Scottish businessman who had disowned him after his foster mother’s death. “I assure you, sir, that they’re worthy of such immortalizing,” he said, not wanting to discuss Sissy, Fanny Allan, or his mother with this stranger. “One of the goals of poetry is to celebrate emotion, after all, and the premature loss we suffer with a loved one's death naturally inspires the poet to memorialize that emotion in the form of verse."

Dunford's smile turned sardonic. "Hm. Quite fascinating to see behind the curtain, so to speak, and examine the inner workings of a poet's mind."

The man's tone suggested that he wasn't impressed with what he found. "Equally fascinating, to see a traveling companion in the mellow glow of a soirée's candlelight," Eddy said, manufacturing a pleasant smile. "We traveled up from London together three days ago, did we not?"

Those cold blue eyes didn't so much as blink. "Ah. I didn't recognize you. I'm afraid my mind was on other matters during that trip."

Sir Richard cleared his throat. "Yes, I was wondering, will young Stiles be attending tonight? I'm sure Georgiana would be happy to spend some time with him."

Stiles? "Are you speaking of Philip Stiles?" Eddy said, striving to sound casual.

Now something flickered in Dunford's gaze. "I am. Do you know my nephew?"

Not personally, but I know of his excesses. "Only by reputation."

A second throat clearing from Sir Richard, this one louder than the first. "As a matter of fact, Dunford, Poe here is another aficionado of word puzzles and cryptograms," he said quickly. "It's my understanding that he has quite the reputation for solving even the most fiendishly difficult conundrums."

The glitter in the marquis's eyes turned to one of challenge. "Really, now," he said softly. "Is this true, Mr. Poe?"

Eddy nodded warily. "It is, indeed. I have challenged all comers in a wide variety of locales to try and stump me with their most difficult word puzzles," he said, not without pride.

"To date, I have never been defeated."

"Well, then. I wager that we would have quite the merry battle over some of the puzzles I've collected over the years," Dunford purred. "My nephew's also an aficionado of cryptograms, one of the few things we actually have in common. I'm rather tempted to have you over to Pennyworth House at some point and introduce you to my collection."

"I would consider it an honor," Eddy said, hiding his excitement. Receiving an invitation to what would eventually become young Stiles's estate might be useful, indeed. "In fact, it would be intriguing to pit my skills against those of your nephew, as well."

"I'm sure," the marquis said, looking around. "Where is that young scoundrel? I sent Walton after him hours ago. They should have arrived by now."

"Ah, you know what young men are like," Sir Richard said. "I'm sure Philip will be here straightaway. In the meantime, how about another cup of punch?" He waved over a servant, who provided them with full cups.

Eddy's mouth flooded with saliva at the smell of the rum in the punch. "Er, Sir Richard—"

"Now that I think of it, Mr. Poe, I believe I will have you over to Pennyworth House, after all," Dunford said. "Middleton here and his young hoyden are coming for luncheon with myself and Philip tomorrow. Dine with us, and afterwards we'll have a ramble through my collection and see what we can find. In fact, why don't you come up with a challenging puzzle yourself tonight, and put me to work?"

Grateful for the distraction, Eddy lowered the luring cup. Dining with the forbidding noble promised to be problematic, especially if Dunford insisted on cryptographic challenges. But Sir Richard looked relieved at Eddy's inclusion in the luncheon party, and keeping a potential patron happy was always a good idea. *And if Stiles is present, I may be able to get him off to the side and ask some pointed questions about Jane Billings and the night she died.*

"Thank you for the invitation, my lord," he said, saluting the peers with his cup. A passing servant gave him the opportunity to put it and the temptation it contained on a silver tray. "I believe I can come up with a puzzle that would challenge you sufficiently."

Charles stared at the list of propositions he'd scrawled on a scavenged piece of paper, torn between aggravation and a grudging admiration. It was bad enough that he'd been trapped by a strange young woman and his own vanity into demonstrating how to play sorites, but it was quite unfair that Lady Georgiana turned out to be so devilishly good at it.

"I thought you said your tutor despaired of you learning logic," he muttered as she waited with her own, already completed list.

Her demure smile didn't hide the amusement in her eyes. "He did. Of course, I was eight at the time. I've studied somewhat since then." The bright cheer in her face suddenly vanished. "Oh, poo. There's Philip Stiles. How tedious."

Glancing around, Charles spotted his classmate lurking near the sitting room door. Dealing with the arrogant nobleman was unappealing to say the least, but desperate times called for desperate measures. "I fear I m-must take your leave, Lady Georgiana," he said, handing his incomplete list to her. "I need to speak with Stiles on an urgent matter."

"I have no idea why anyone would wish to speak with him willingly, but if you must, you must," she said, laying down their pencils and papers on a side table. "I'm sure I can find you again once your talk is complete."

"Er, yes." Trying to put the inscrutable mysteries of the female from his mind, Charles hurried over to Stiles. The young nobleman seemed drunker than usual, swigging sloppily from his punch cup. Next to him stood a grim-looking fellow in unrestrained black, touching Stiles's sleeve as he murmured something in his ear. Stiles pulled his arm away violently, shaking his head; the man gave him a hard look, but finally nodded and left.

Charles hesitated, remembering the innumerable times when Stiles had poked fun at his stammer. *That doesn't matter now. He ruined Jane, and he's involved with her murder somehow. I need to speak with him.*

He stepped forward and nodded. "Stiles."

The blond man looked up, blearily trying to focus. When he managed it, a clownish grin wreathed his face. "Dodo!" he crowed. "Good Lord, man, do you mean to tell me that something actually lured you away from those dusty tomes? And you're even dressed like a gentleman—ha!"

Charles tried not to stiffen. "I decided to accept Sir Richard's invitation to the House," he said slowly, working not to stutter. "As Mr. Poe was also invited, I looked forward to hearing more of his work."

"The American is here?" Stiles wheeled around, as if he expected Poe to pop out of the woodwork. "Bless my soul, I should seek him out and congratulate him on his flimflammery. I delivered his cursed little book to the uncle—I dare say it cracked his cheeks a bit, heh."

Stiles staggered slightly, reaching out, and Charles grabbed his arm. "Are you all right?"

The nobleman gave him a wide, loose-lipped grin. "Never

better, Dodo, never better. My future stretches out before me like a winding bolt of cloth-of-gold, and all is as it should be." He tipped the punch cup up, his tongue coming out to catch the last crimson droplets, then lowered it with a moue. "I need another drink. I need another three drinks, in fact."

"Perhaps you've had enough," Charles said cautiously.

"Never. Never enough, Dodo. It would take a river of punch, a veritable Amazon, to quench my thirst tonight." Stiles's slack lips contracted, and a glassy sheen covered his eyes. "Pity it wouldn't work on the stains on my soul, eh?"

Charles glanced around quickly. No one was close enough to overhear. "What do you mean?"

Stiles shook his head like a soaked dog trying to dry itself. "The things I've done, Dodo, things no man in my position should ever be required to do. Denial of myself, of her. But Uncle insisted, you see, when he found out—"

The grim-faced man reappeared, this time taking Stiles's other arm. "Sir, your uncle wishes to speak with you," he said in a flat northern accent.

"Ah, yes. The founder of the family, the font from whom all privilege flows. He but snaps his fingers, and I come to heel." For a moment, the hectic hilarity left Stiles's face, and he looked lost. Then he jerked his arms out of both their grips. "I'm not a child, to be led around by nannies," he blurted. "Tell me where Uncle is, Walton. Let's get this over with."

Walton nodded and guided a stumbling Stiles off to meet with his relative. Charles watched them go, the blond man's words tumbling through his mind.

Pity it wouldn't work on the stains on my soul.

The things I've done, things no man in my position should ever be required to do.

But Uncle insisted, you see—

There was a confession here, he felt sure of it. But a confession to what? Was Stiles admitting to the ruination of an innocent girl, or to her murder? And what exactly had the Marquis of Wells insisted on?

He had to find Poe.

CHAPTER EIGHTEEN

"What a marvelous poem, Mr. Poe," a brunette matron in a stylish grey gown gushed. Next to her, a man Eddy assumed was her husband nodded as if his head was on a string. "So dark and passionate, the very epitome of the Gothic movement. Head and shoulders above those horrible "penny dreadfuls" in the popular magazines, don't you know?" She fluttered her fan and preened. "Tell me, have you ever read any of the works of Horace Walpole?"

"I have indeed read Mr. Walpole's *The Castle of Otranto*," Eddy replied courteously, "as well as Mrs. Radcliffe's works." He deliberately glossed over the fact that some of his own fictional works had been classified as penny dreadfuls. "Ultimately, I believe that if you look long enough into the darkling mirror of the soul, you will see terrors and wonders that far outstrip any shambling monster or blood drinker in a penny dreadful. In fact, one of the things I strive to do with my own magazine is to promote the works of poets who are like-minded to Shelly and Keats, not to mention magazinists who follow in the footsteps of Polidori and Mrs. Shelly."

The lady sighed in pleasure. "That is my thought to the very letter, Mr. Poe. How refreshing it is to find someone of the same mind!"

He was amused by his own cynicism. He would have argued

the opposite point just as enthusiastically if it might win him a subscription or a book sale. "It is just as refreshing to me as well, madam. There are those in other areas of my native land who do not have the same kind of resonance for works that reach into the darkest parts of the soul, and I'm afraid they've made my work as both poet and publisher quite difficult at times." He leaned forward, cheered when the couple copied his gesture. "I have been informed by some of these perfidious people that since my poetry and fiction does not trumpet morality above all, that I must be utterly without morals, as well."

"How unfair," the matron declared. "Particularly since you are quite obviously a man of principle. This magazine of yours—"

"*The Stylus*," Eddy interjected helpfully.

"What an excellent name. Is it possible for those of us on this side of the Atlantic to subscribe to it?"

He gave her his best humble look. "Of course, madam, for the comparatively low price of £4 a year." He decided a slight markup was necessary for transatlantic shipping.

"That seems quite reasonable to me," the matron said, tapping her husband on the shoulder with her fan. "Reginald, be so kind as to give Mr. Poe the cost of his subscription and our details."

As her husband patted his pockets, a smiling Tomlinson bustled up. "You've made quite the splash, Mr. Poe," he whispered into the writer's ear. "I've collected twelve subscriptions already."

"Thirteen," Eddy whispered back before turning back to the couple. "My dear madam, I'm afraid Mr. Tomlinson here informs me that my presence has been requested by our host, but he will be happy to assist you with your subscription. If you'll excuse me?"

At the woman's fluttering agreement, Tomlinson pulled out a small notebook and pencil. "Now, your preferred postal address is...."

Walking away, Eddy allowed himself a relieved smile. Thirteen subscriptions, plus the five from the first night's signing, exceeded the quota he'd privately established for Oxford. At least some good had come out of this dreadful situation.

Yes, a situation where a young woman has been gutted, and where the police still suspect you of her murder.

Ignoring the abrupt craving for a drink, he headed off in search of the servant with the tray of virgin punch. In the process he spotted an unsteady Stiles being led away by a grim man in servant's black. He was tempted to follow them in the hopes that Stiles might say something incriminating while in his cups. *Except that his uncle's manservant will make sure that doesn't happen. You'll be meeting the young rascal again soon enough. Concentrate on the audience and behave as the poet they came to see.*

With some regret he turned away from the pair, smiling at an approaching group.

Charles made his way through the chatting guests in search of Poe. The rooms were growing warmer with the increasing number of bodies, and he could hear music in the distance. When a hand touched his sleeve, he turned, expecting to see the short American.

Instead, Lady Georgiana stood there surrounded by O'Donnell, Hebron, and Reade, as well as an older man. "Mr. Dodgson—and here I thought I would have to send out a search party for you," she said with good humor. "Uncle Dicky, this is

Charles Dodgson. He's in the House."

"Ah." Sir Richard gave him an appraising look. "I remember my time at Christ Church fondly. Quite the roisterer I was—didn't settle down until my third year, of course. The Dean never did figure out who left the goat in his bedroom, heh." He frowned, spotting someone across the room. "Speak of the devil—there's the Dean. Face like thunder, too. Georgiana, dear, keep our young men entertained, won't you?"

"Of course, Uncle Dicky," Georgiana said, moving to cut Charles off before he could make his escape. "Were you able to have your talk with Mr. Stiles?"

"Stiles?" O'Donnell's expression sharpened. "And what does our very own Falstaff have to say for himself?"

He couldn't mention Stiles's strange quasi-confession in front of Lady Georgiana. "N-not much. His uncle's servant came looking for him before we could speak."

Lady Georgiana's lips pursed. "Not a great loss, then," she said, the distaste in her voice palpable.

"I take it you know the ineffable Stiles, Lady Georgiana?" O'Donnell asked.

"Since childhood. He was a fat, annoying little boy who constantly harassed my pug, and he hasn't improved much in the intervening years. I believe the marquis had inquired after my hand for him when I turned sixteen. I told Uncle Dicky that I would rather join a convent and stitch tapestries or whatever it is that Romish nuns do these days. Uncle Dicky wasn't pleased, but he finally saw my point after Philip was almost sent down from Harrow for throwing a private soirée in his rooms with some of his closest friends." She made a face. "It was also rumored that Philip had engaged some female entertainment for the evening. They must have been absolutely dreadful performers, judging from Uncle Dicky's reaction."

O'Donnell choked in mid-sip of his punch, and both Reade and Hebron looked as if they were about to burst into laughter. Annoyed at their indelicacy, Charles said, "Do you think that the marquis is still set on winning your hand for Stiles?"

"It wouldn't surprise me at all. The marquis arrived in Oxford three days ago and came straight here to closet himself with Uncle Dicky. I suspect he was requesting a match yet again." The delicate muscles of her jaw firmed. "And my answer is still the same. I will not be shackled to that boor for the rest of my life. I'll take the veil if I must."

"Here, here!" O'Donnell toasted her with his cup. "Let some milksop heiress be saddled with Stiles. You, my lady, have years ahead of you in which to revel amongst your crowd of adoring beaux."

She tapped his arm with her fan. "Oh, hush, Mr. O'Donnell. I'm quite happy taking care of Uncle Dicky and acting as his hostess. I feel no driving need to rush to the altar with anyone, and certainly not Philip Stiles. Especially if it means I would have to spend time with that horrible Walton—the man gives me the absolute shivers."

"Walton?" Charles asked.

"The marquis's valet. Walton also served as his batman during their time in India. Supposedly he learned vicious fighting skills from the Thugees and other native tribes. When the marquis finally returned home, Walton came along, but rumor has it that he also runs any unpleasant errands that the marquis might have."

"How interesting," Charles said faintly. If the marquis and his servant were in town before the chambermaid's murder, that added new potential suspects to the hunt. "Will you please excuse me, Lady Georgina? I need to speak with Mr. Poe."

"Well, I believe he's been waylaid by his admirers in the Blue

Room." She nodded at an adjoining room that matched the mentioned hue. "But—"

"Thank you." He gave her an abbreviated bow and hurried off.

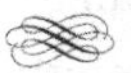

As Eddy extricated himself from the group of well-wishers, a footman came up to him. "Mr. Poe, there's someone at the door who wishes to speak with you on a matter of greatest urgency."

His relief disappeared like smoke. There were only three people in Oxford who might want to speak with him, and two of them were already at the party. "Well, then, I suppose I should meet with the gentleman."

A look of disapproval creased the footman's face. "Hardly a gentleman, sir, and his type should know better than to come to the front door. The servant's entrance is good enough for them."

That clinched his suspicions. With a heavy heart, he followed the doorman to the foyer, where Furnow was waiting with a grim look on his face. "Mr. Poe," the constable said briefly. "Just the man I've been looking for. Might I have a word?"

Eddy glanced over his shoulder. No one from the party had noticed their discussion. "Could we possibly do this somewhere else?" he said, his voice low. "I don't wish Sir Richard to get the impression that I'm regularly hounded by the police."

"As you wish, sir." Furnow nodded towards a side room.

Back stiff, Eddy joined him. "What new reason have you found to harass me tonight, Mr. Furnow? Perhaps a raven feather was found in the girl's hair, or ink smudges on her fingertips from turning the pages of one of my collections?"

Furnow gave him a flat look. "If you wish to file a complaint about my conduct, sir, you may speak to my superior. In the meantime, I'm not here about Jane Billings. I'm here about Mrs. Elizabeth Billings."

Surely she hadn't objected to his visit. "What of her?"

"May I ask what exactly you discussed with her when you were at her residence, sir?"

Eddy lifted his chin. "Why in the world would you need to know that? Did she register some kind of complaint?"

"No, sir." The constable's expression grew colder. "In fact, she won't be complaining about anything, anymore."

His gut chilled at the implication. "What do you mean?"

Just then Dodgson hurried into the room, rocking to a stop when he saw Furnow. "Oh, d-dear."

"Mr. Dodgson," the bulldog rumbled in disapproval. "You do keep odd company these days, don't you, sir?"

"I-it's the company I prefer," Dodgson said bravely.

"Hrm." The stolid gaze fell on Eddy again. "Will you tell me what you discussed with Mrs. Billings, sir?"

His throat tightened. "I offered her my condolences on the death of her daughter and offered to sign a copy of my work."

"And you didn't have harsh words with the lady at all?"

"Of course not."

This time, the stolid look had something of the hunting cat in it. "And your whereabouts at dusk today?"

The chill grew, making him want to shiver. "I was at Mr. Tomlinson's tailor, being fitted for this suit. What does this have to do with Mrs. Billings?"

"Did you leave the tailor's premises at any time?" Collin said, ignoring his question.

"Good God, man, I was in my undergarments. How could I leave?" Eddy asked. "If you want an exact recounting of my whereabouts, I breakfasted with Mr. Dodgson this morning, then we retired to my room to discuss writing matters and this muddle I currently find myself in." There, it wasn't a complete lie and hopefully Dodgson would stop looking so guilty. "Sometime around noon, Mr. Tomlinson arrived and told me that I had been invited to this soirée. We repaired to his office to send off some business telegrams and take luncheon, after which we went to his tailor's shop where I was fitted for this suit, the tailoring of which took the bulk of the afternoon." He gestured at the garment. "Once that was done, Tomlinson escorted me here. I assure you, I have not been out of anyone's presence all afternoon and evening."

"I'll speak to Mr. Tomlinson and his tailor for confirmation." Furnow turned to Dodgson. "You can confirm that Mr. Poe was with you this morning, Mr. Dodgson?"

The younger man paled a bit, but nodded "Until noon or so, yes, at which point he and Tomlinson departed together. Mr. Furnow, please, what has happened?"

The constable studied them. "I think perhaps you'd both best come with me."

Eddy bristled. "Are we under arrest?"

"Think of it as assisting the constabulary with their enquiries, sir."

That wasn't the no he wanted, and poor Dodgson looked as unhappy as he felt. Whatever was so important that it caused the bulldog to crash Sir Richard Middleton's soirée and fetch them promised to be grim, indeed. "I'll get my coat."

CHAPTER NINETEEN

Outside Sir Richard's residence, a rather decrepit black wagon waited for them at the curb. Another bulldog, a younger one with acne scars and a sizable Adam's apple, sat in the driver's seat, the reins loosely held in one hand. "Don't suggest you ride in back, sirs. Hasn't been sluiced down since our last roundups of the pubs," he said, nodding for them to climb into the narrow passenger area behind him.

"What a relief," Eddy muttered as they took their seats on the hard wooden bench. "May I at least ask where we're going, constable?"

Furnow had climbed up to join the driver. He glanced over his shoulder now. "Castle Mill Park."

It didn't sound familiar at all. Eddy leaned close to Dodgson. "Is that a university property?"

"I d-don't believe so," Dodgson whispered back. "But the University Constabulary has the right to investigate any crime committed within three miles of a university building, which essentially means the entire town center and much of the surrounding environs."

"I see."

The ride was somewhat jouncy but mercifully short, and the wagon pulled up in front of a small park. "Follow me," Furnow said peremptorily, climbing down.

Eddy felt the gooseflesh rise on his skin when he smelled the meaty, coppery odor underneath the crispness of the October air. "Blood," he muttered involuntarily.

Furnow paused. "And how did you know that, Mr. Poe?"

He glared at the constable. "My first wife was a consumptive. She once burst a blood vessel in her throat while singing for some company and bled horribly, and her last days were spent coughing it up in great quantities. Blood and I are old companions, Mr. Furnow."

The constable nodded at that and led them into the park. A number of other bowler-hatted men were patrolling the grounds, poking desultorily at the bushes, while an older portly gentleman wearing an elaborate chain around his neck spoke in hushed terms with a tall, distinguished man in a black top hat. "The mayor," Furnow said, jerking his head at the bechained man. "Came running when he heard the fuss."

"And the other man?" Eddy asked, before feeling Dodgson's elbow rapidly jab his ribs. The undergraduate gave a short shake of his head, causing Furnow to bark once in humorless laughter.

"That, Mr. Poe, is my superior, Mr. William Lievesley," the constable said. "He is not a very happy man tonight, and when he's unhappy he makes those around him unhappy, so I would strongly suggest you assist us to the best of your abilities before he takes a mind to introduce you to the inside of our local gaol for the crime of annoying him."

Dodgson looked terrified. *And with good reason.* "I will certainly do whatever I can to assist you," Eddy said.

"This way, then." Furnow led the both of them to a clump of bushes near a carefully trimmed topiary. "A pair of Magdalene men found her and fetched us. Mind the vomit—one of them lost his supper."

Skirting the odorous puddle, Eddy spotted the body stuffed underneath the bushes, blood-smeared face turned to the path as if searching for assistance that was far too late. With a dull horror, he recognized it as Mrs. Billings. His gaze immediately went to her exposed chest, one slack nipple peeping over the edge of a wrenched-open bodice, and the dark letters carved there. Above them were two dark smudges directly over her throat.

"My God," he breathed. Behind him, he could hear Dodgson praying softly.

"Do you recognize the victim, Mr. Poe?" Furnow asked.

He nodded, feeling disconnected from the scene. *A dream within a dream. Or simply a nightmare.* "It's Jane Billings's mother."

"Indeed," the constable agreed. "We believe she was killed sometime after sunset. Strange, how women in this family have been dying since you arrived in Oxford."

Ignoring Furnow's jibe, he stepped closer, studying the pathetic corpse. Blood had trickled out of her mouth, streaking her cheek with what appeared to be black gore in the dim streetlight. Reluctantly he leaned down, trying to memorize the ancient Greek glyphs the killer had carved into her chest.

Furnow, mistaking his intention, dropped into a creaky crouch, gently prying open Mrs. Billings's chin. The congealed blood flaked away at his touch, and he peered inside her mouth. "This is where things take an unpleasant turn," he said, leaning back to reveal what lay inside.

Eddy looked, then recoiled, unwilling to believe what he was seeing. "Oh, Christ," he muttered. "Her tongue is gone."

Behind them, Dodgson gagged, then hurried away. The sound of retching was quickly followed by a splash.

"Indeed," Furnow agreed. "Now you understand why I wanted to know where you were around dusk today."

The strange detachment began to evaporate, replaced by anger. "As I've already told you, I had nothing do to with Jane's death, nor did I hold down this poor woman and slice out her tongue," he ground out. "For pity's sake, Furnow, use your head—you can verify my whereabouts for the entire day with Dodgson, Tomlinson, and his tailor."

The constable shrugged. "A man in a fitting has to be alone for a bit while he's changing and such. If you claimed a touch of stomach trouble, nobody would think twice about your absence, even if it was prolonged."

Eddy's ire eased as he understood what Furnow was doing. The constable was a good man, as horrified by these murders as anyone else, and was determined to find the killer. And that meant wringing the last details out of a suspect, no matter how uncomfortable or embarrassing the process might be, in order to confirm that they were, indeed, innocent.

"The tailor shop is on Cornmarket, near the High Street," he pointed out. "Even if I had been able to slip out of the tailor's unseen, there's no way that I could have raced across an unfamiliar city, lured Mrs. Billings to this park, murdered her in such a foul manner, then returned to the tailor shop without anyone noticing. For goodness's sake, look at the gouts of blood on the poor woman's face. In slicing out her tongue, the killer would undoubtedly have caught at least some blood on his shirtfront or sleeves. You are more than welcome to return to the tailor's shop and examine my clothes there for traces of blood."

Something shifted in the constable's bearing, a lowering of the shoulders. Furnow sighed heavily. "Are you sure enough to testify to all of this in court, Mr. Poe?"

"If I must."

Dodgson returned, corpse-pale in the moonlight and wiping at his mouth with a handkerchief. "My apologies. I've n-n-never...." He swallowed hard, trailing off.

The bulldog's gaze swung between the two of them. Finally, he shook his head. "Lucky for you, Mr. Poe, that you've found such good friends during your sojourn here. But that still leaves a murderer wandering the streets."

He fell silent as Lievesley walked up. The head of the constabulary was a tall man with bull-like shoulders that were barely constrained by the tailoring of his jacket. Silvering hair, a broad, bluff face and heavy brows over dark, thoughtful eyes gave him an air of unmistakable authority. "Furnow, I'm sure you can explain why these two gentlemen are here," he said in a calm tone.

"I can, sir," Furnow said, nodding at Eddy. "This gentleman here is a guest at the Mitre. He has a hotel room on the same floor where we found the dead chambermaid."

"Really?" The dark eyes turned to him. "Mr. Poe, I believe, from America?"

Eddy blinked in surprise. "I am indeed, sir."

"My wife came to your lecture at Christ Church. She found it quite edifying," Lievesley said. "I also heard about the altercation afterwards. Some men have no sense of propriety."

He wasn't sure if the chief constable was referring to Stiles, him, or both. "An unpleasant occurrence, but one that I trust will not happen again."

"Mm." Lievesley turned back to the bulldog. "And you brought a distinguished poet to a crime scene for what purpose, Furnow?"

The constable braced under the scrutiny. "Mr. Poe met with Mrs. Billings yesterday afternoon at her home. I found it odd that he was connected with both women and wished to question him further."

"At the scene of a murder," Lievesley observed. "Which is not where we usually question people. How many people were also staying on the same floor where the chambermaid was killed, Furnow?"

"Three, sir."

"Did any of them visit Mrs. Billings?"

"No, sir."

"Jane had asked me to sign a book for her," Eddy interjected. "I wanted to honor her last wish and pay my respects to her parents, hence my appearance at the Billings home."

"How kind of you," Lievesley murmured. "So, because Mr. Poe had a room on the same floor where Miss Billings was murdered and had the good grace to visit her family and pay his condolences, you decided to go to Sir Richard Middleton's house, enter a private soirée, and extract a guest so that you could bring him to a particularly bloody murder scene." His voice never rose above a pleasant speaking tone, but every syllable was still a whipcrack. "Do I have your reasoning correct, Furnow?"

The constable took a deep breath. "I thought it was worth following up, sir."

"And so you did. Tell me, did Mr. Poe confess to the murders?"

"No, sir."

"Ah. Was he in the vicinity when this poor woman was slaughtered?"

"No, sir. He was across town at a tailor's shop, sir."

Lievesley gave his underling a wintry smile. "Being fitted for a suit, I presume? Well, then. I believe we can safely exclude him from our circle of suspects for this crime, don't you?"

"Yes, sir," Furnow said stolidly.

"Capital. Why don't you run Mr. Poe and his friend—" The

chief constable's eyebrows went up in silent enquiry.

"Ch-charles D-Dodgson, of Christ Church," Dodgson said miserably.

Lievesley gave him a brief nod. "Mr. Dodgson, back to whence they came, then return here for further study of the scene. Perhaps we can yet winkle out who could have committed such a monstrous crime, eh?"

Eddy's attention was drawn back to Mrs. Billings's body and the turf surrounding it. An image popped into his mind. "He's left-handed."

That dark gaze left Furnow and fixed on him. "Mr. Poe?"

He withered slightly under the chief constable's attention. "I just realized the murderer is left-handed."

"And how would you know that, Mr. Poe?"

"If I may ask your indulgence, study the grass." He gestured for them to step back. Their footprints were clearly visible in the park turf, now damp with evening dew. "There's no sign of struggle anywhere else, otherwise we would see crushed blades of grass and disturbed areas of dew. He set upon her here, directly next to the bushes, probably so that they could serve as a screen for his actions, and when he was done he shoved her under them."

He pointed to the depression he'd spotted. "Moreover, the bushes are to Mrs. Billings's right, while on her left side is a small depression that's much too short for a footprint. I take it the constables didn't move her in any way?"

Lievesley looked to Furnow, who shook his head.

"Well, then. Imagine yourselves, gentlemen, performing some sort of physical labor that requires you to be on your knees and sawing at an object." He leaned forward, spreading his left hand out and slicing at an imaginary object with his right hand. "You rest one knee on the object if possible for added leverage while you saw, and the other on the ground. If the ground is soft enough, the pressure can form a shallow depression. I believe your killer knocked Mrs. Billings to the ground, strangled her, then knelt over her to perform his butchery." He gestured at the looming yew hedge. "But there's no room for him to have done this in her current position, not if he was using his right hand to cut. The only way he could have left a depression in this particular position," he mimed shifting his imaginary weapon to his other hand, "is if he were left-handed."

"Your rationale is impeccable, Mr. Poe," the chief constable concurred. "Is there anything else you can tell us about this man?"

"He appears to be something of a collector."

"And how do you arrive at that conclusion?"

Eddy grimaced. *That was a foolish slip-up.* "Mrs. Billings's tongue is missing, and I read the article in the news about her daughter. Judging from the description of the body, I suspect he may have liberated a souvenir from her, as well."

The chief constable let out a slow, measured breath. "Hm. I congratulate you on your powers of observation, Mr. Poe." One shaggy eyebrow arched. "Or should I say, Monsieur Dupin?"

He had been wondering when someone would trot that out. "I see you've heard of my deductive tales, Mr. Lievesley. I wish I was half as astute as my literary creation." He gestured to the body. "And Monsieur Dupin has the great advantage that his creator knows the murderer's identity ahead of time. In this case, I am as puzzled about his identity and motive as you are."

"Nonetheless, your observations seem to be of merit, and will be taken under consideration," Lievesley said. "In the meantime, Constable Furnow, please have these men returned to their destination. Ideally in a vehicle less conspicuous than a police wagon."

If they returned to Middleton's now, they would have to explain what had happened and why they'd been taken to the scene of a murder. It was hardly the impression he wanted to leave on the literati of Oxford. "I believe Sir Richard's soiree would be almost over by this point," he said. "If the constable could be so kind as to return us to the Mitre instead?"

At Lievesley's nod, Furnow rumbled, "This way, gentlemen."

CHAPTER TWENTY

A hansom hailed by Furnow deposited Eddy and a silent Dodgson in front of the Mitre. "I'm sure we'll be in contact again, Mr. Poe," the constable said gruffly before telling the driver to take them back to the hotel.

Eddy watched the cab roll away, wondering if he was free to leave Oxford or not. "By a route obscure and lonely, haunted by ill angels only, where an Eidolon, named NIGHT, on a black throne reigns upright," he intoned, half to himself. "I have reached these lands but newly from an ultimate dim Thule, from a wild clime that lieth, sublime, out of space, out of time."

"Very nice," Dodgson observed, "but what does that have to do with this new situation?"

"It means, my dear Dodgson, that there is a fallen angel stalking the streets of your city." He turned his face to the soft golden glow of the Mitre's lanterns, cherishing their faint warmth. "And apparently he is not finished with his game."

"He certainly is not, considering what he wrote on that poor woman's chest."

He relaxed. "Good. You saw the letters. I was afraid I'd have to recall them from memory, which is not at its best tonight. Have you puzzled out our murderous friend's latest anagram?"

"On the ride back, yes." Dodgson's brow furrowed. "I believe the translation is, 'Death to traitors.'"

Which begged the question; who exactly was Mrs. Billings a traitor *to*? "How very curious," Eddy said softly.

"Curiouser and curiouser, even." Dodgson suddenly yawned, covering his mouth. "Dreadfully sorry," he mumbled. "It's been a very long day."

"Yes, it has." He considered his young friend with some sympathy. "I doubt there's much more we can do tonight, and I suspect our bloodthirsty friend's appetite is slaked for now. I suggest you return to your rooms, and we'll resume this on the morrow—if you're still up for it, that is."

The undergraduate's chin came up at that. "I'm with you until the bitter end, Mr. Poe."

"Excellent. Then I bid you good night."

With a nod and another yawn, Dodgson turned and trudged off down the street. Alone, Eddy entered the hotel, his thoughts on the murdered women and their killer.

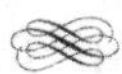

Charles barely had time to close the door to his room before a thundering knocking sounded. Afraid that his neighbors along the hallway would be awakened, he opened it again.

And was pushed aside as the Horsemen crowded into his room. "Where did you go, man?" O'Donnell demanded. "We spent a good half hour searching the entire house for you until one of the servants told us you'd left with Poe."

"Lady Georgiana was quite put out that you left without saying goodnight," Reade added. "I'd suggest sending flowers or something else appropriate for an apology."

Concern for Lady Georgiana's feelings didn't hold a high place in his concern at the moment. "There's been another murder," he said, taking a seat in his favorite chair. "The police came to collect Poe, and asked me to come as well."

"God's blood." O'Donnell dropped into a nearby chair, while Reade and Hebron dragged up others. "Who was it?"

"The mother of the murdered chambermaid." The memory of her gaping mouth left him sick. "The poor woman had her tongue cut out."

O'Donnell cursed softly under his breath, while Hebron leaned forward. "Do they think Poe did it?" the Mancunian asked.

"I believe they s-suspected him, but it seems she was killed sometime around dusk. Poe was at the tailor's with Mr. Tomlinson at that point, and then they both went straight to Sir Richard's. It would have been impossible for him to kill Mrs. Billings—the timing s-simply doesn't work." He shuddered at the memory of the gruesome glyphs on Mrs. Billings's bosom. "She had Greek letters cut into her skin, as well, which suggests that whoever killed her daughter was also responsible for her death."

O'Donnell slammed a hand on his armrest. "Gentlemen, we clearly have a madman in our midst. And if the police can't find him, then it's up to us to stop him before another innocent woman dies."

Hebron gave their friend a flat look. "That's all well and good, but do you have any idea who this madman might be?"

The words left Charles's mouth before he could stop them: "I think it may be Stiles."

The other Horsemen stared at him in surprise. "Steady on, Dodgson," Reade said. "I can't say I'm fond of the blighter at all, but that's a dangerous accusation to make. What are your grounds?"

"P-poe said that Jane had asked him to sign one of his books for a paramour. That p-paramour's initials were PRS, which also happen to be Stiles's initials. It also s-seems that he may have gotten the young lady into an unfortunate condition."

O'Donnell clicked his tongue. "Unsurprising, knowing that lout. But it doesn't explain why you think Stiles killed both her and her mother, and in such a gory manner."

He forced his weary brain into action. "At the beginning of the term, Stiles b-boasted about how he'd butchered one of his whelping bitches in order to gain her puppies. The same thing was done to the chambermaid, more or l-less. And the message left on Mrs. Billings was 'Death to traitors.' Moreover, both messages were left as anagrams in Ancient Greek. Wh-whoever the killer is, he has at least a basic grasp of anatomy and a better one of Ancient Greek, as well as a love of puzzles, which does seem to fit Stiles. And if M-miss Billings was indeed in an unfortunate condition, then her mother might have pressed Stiles for some form of reparations—a stipend, perhaps."

"Or a wedding," Reade said, tugging thoughtfully at his lower lip. "Which would have been out of the question for Stiles—his uncle will want him to marry a noblewoman."

"Such as Lady Georgiana," O'Donnell added. "She's beautiful, wealthy, and quite the catch for someone with the appropriate pedigree. But if the chambermaid's mother threatened to make her daughter's condition a matter of public knowledge...."

Charles considered that scenario. If Lady Georgiana caught wind of Stiles's situation, her refusal to marry him would undoubtedly become adamantine. *How badly did the marquis want the match? And how far would Stiles go to protect his gilded future?*

"What we think doesn't matter," Hebron said firmly, interrupting his thoughts. "We can't go to the police with theories—we need proof. Did any of you see Stiles before the soirée?"

"I saw him there, but not until after Dodgson had left with

Mr. Poe," Reade said. "I must admit, Stiles seemed far more maudlin than offensive, not to mention drunk as the proverbial lord."

"He was," Charles agreed, repeating what Stiles had said to him. "It's another reason why I s-suspect him."

The Mancunian frowned. "We still need proof. A knife, bloodstained clothing, a hanky that belonged to Mrs. Billings—"

"Her tongue."

Reade choked a bit, and even O'Donnell turned pale. "You really think he kept it?" the smaller man asked.

"It wasn't in the park, according to the constables. P-perhaps he took it as some sort of horrible keepsake."

Hebron nodded at that. "We need to search his rooms. If we can find evidence there, we can take it to Furnow."

Charles wasn't sure of the legality of such an action, but his friends' enthusiasm for the idea was contagious. "D-do you know where Stiles is now?"

"He was with Lady Georgiana when we left, poor lady," O'Donnell said. "Judging from the way he was banging on about hunting, I suspect he's still there."

Charles felt a flicker of compassion for the noblewoman. "His rooms are on the ground floor. We could try the door, I suppose."

"Capital." O'Donnell donned a cunning expression. "Shall we, gentlemen?"

A few minutes later they stood outside Stiles's rooms, O'Donnell peering shiftily up and down the corridor for any witnesses. Satisfied that they were alone, he tried the handle. "Drat. It's locked."

Relief mixed with regret bubbled up in Charles's breast. "Well, that's that—"

"Hang on." The smaller man hurried off. Charles waited with

the other two Horsemen, feeling increasingly exposed as the moments passed.

Just as he was about to suggest that they return to his room, O'Donnell appeared. Grinning, he held up a key.

"Where did you get that?" Reade demanded.

"I bribed one of the scouts, of course. Our classmate isn't exactly what you would call favored below stairs." O'Donnell winked at them. "Shall we?"

Charles followed his friends through the now-opened door. As expected, Stiles's rooms were richly furnished with expensive furniture including an ornately carved wardrobe, as well as gilt-framed hunting prints and deep gold curtains. An empty wine bottle and discarded glass stood on a low table, silent testimony to their owner's current condition. A sudden prickle of jealousy poked at him, annoyance that someone as tawdry and unworthy as Stiles could enjoy such luxury. *Your room is warm and comfortable, far better than some can ever hope for. Be grateful for the gifts the Lord has given you and don't wish for what you cannot have.*

"Start looking in drawers, boxes, anywhere that something can be hidden," Hebron ordered, going straight to the fireplace. Grabbing a fire iron, he started poking at the ashes.

O'Donnell went to the bedroom, while Reade began examining containers in the sitting room. Uncomfortable, Charles went to the bookcases. Unlike the ones in his room, these were leanly stocked, with a handful of textbooks outnumbered by penny dreadfuls and cheap-looking books. He picked one up and started leafing through it, then gasped.

"What is it?" Hebron demanded.

Charles felt his cheeks burning. "Nothing," he muttered, shoving the erotic volume back onto the shelf. Another book, newer looking, caught his eye. Gingerly, he opened it to the frontispiece, and recognized it as Poe's collection of poems.

On the flyleaf was an inscription in a manly hand to PRS. Beneath that, written in paler ink and a more delicate hand, were the words, "For my love. Carry this book with you, and know that my heart is yours, always. J."

He stared at the words, struck by the depth of feeling in them. No matter how inappropriate their liaison might have been, it was clear that Jane Billings had truly loved Stiles and had hoped that her feelings would be returned.

"Hst!"

He turned. Hebron was staring at the door, and now Charles could hear a scraping sound on the wood. The Mancunian lunged, grabbing him by the arm and shoving him unceremoniously into the wardrobe. The odor of mothballs and cedar filled his nose, and he had to pinch his nostrils shut to ward off a sneeze.

Then O'Donnell and Reade were shoved in beside him, crammed together further as Hebron wormed his way in before closing the door. They all waited silently in the darkness, trying to control their panting breath and listening.

The sound of a door opening, then closing. Next they heard heavy footsteps across the floor, barely muffled by the carpet, and then a low, sodden chuckle. "Ah, Georgiana. I must correct that holier-than-thou attitude of yours once we're married," Stiles mumbled. "Perhaps a few swats from a birch would do the trick, eh?"

A soft crackle sounded in the wardrobe. To his surprise, Charles realized he'd clenched his fists so tightly his knuckles had popped. Someone grasped his lower arm, squeezing a warning.

Stiles continued to burble drunkenly to himself, calling down imprecations on his uncle, Walton, Blakeney, and Sir Richard. "To hell with all of you," he concluded, hiccuping. "Once I'm marquis, I'll do as I like. And I'll *bed* whomever I like." Another hiccup turned into a raspy sob, and the footsteps approached the wardrobe. Charles could feel his friends tensing, waiting for the wooden door to be thrown open and their hiding place revealed.

And then the footsteps changed course, growing softer. He assumed Stiles had stumbled into his bedroom, and his guess was proved correct when another door slammed. What followed felt like an infinity until they heard the sound of distant snoring.

Silently, Hebron opened the wardrobe and ushered them out, hurrying them towards the exit. Once the door was locked behind them, he said, "O'Donnell, take that key back to wherever you found it. *Now*. Once you're done, meet us in Dodgson's room."

A pale O'Donnell didn't have a humorous comment for once and rushed off. Silently, Charles led the others back to his room. "Well, th-that was an adventure," he tried to joke once they were safely inside.

"That was far too close," Hebron said tersely. "Reade, did you find anything?"

"Apart from a collection of rather startling etchings, no," Reade admitted.

"I was afraid of that. There wasn't anything suspicious in his grate, either."

A soft rapping sounded at the door, and Charles admitted O'Donnell. When Hebron questioned him, he confessed that he hadn't found anything identifying Stiles as the murderer. "So what do we do now?" he asked.

"It's too risky to go back to the room," Hebron decided. "Bribed or not, the scout might talk, and I will not be sent down because of Philip Stiles. We need to follow him, see if we can locate evidence that way."

"Or catch him in the act," Reade said darkly.

Charles's stomach twisted at the words. "D-do you really think he'll kill again?"

"If he thinks it's the only way to save his own neck from the noose, yes," Hebron said flatly. "And we don't know who else the chambermaid told about their *affaire de coeur*."

A memory from that morning burst into his mind—young Maggie sitting at the dining table at the Mitre and telling Poe all she knew about Jane's secret suitor. "She has—had—a younger sister. Maggie knew about their affair."

Hebron's expression grew even grimmer. "Then that child may well be in mortal danger."

In a room lit by a single candle, the killer soaked his shirt in a tin washing up bowl full of cold water. He swished the fabric in the water, studying the fading stain critically, then resumed scrubbing at it with a yellowed cake of soap and a small brush. The waistcoat had already been washed and was currently hung over the back of a chair placed in front of the fire. He'd only found a drop or two on his frock coat, simple enough to rinse away, and nothing at all on his trousers except dew and some grass stains.

It would be easier to strip off the blood-soaked garments and throw them on the fire, but that was too dangerous. If the constables, idiots that they were, decided to come calling and poked through his ashes, he would be hard-pressed to explain why he burnt a perfectly good set of clothes. Besides, he rather fancied the idea of wearing the shirt right under their noses, a badge of his achievements.

He lifted the shirt from the now-pink-tinged water, rinsing it with clean water from a pitcher. *Good enough for now. I'll look at it again in the daylight and see if it needs another scrub.* Twisting the fabric to wring out as much water as possible, he draped the shirt over another chair to dry.

The water went out the window, poured discreetly into the bushes below. Satisfied that all outward signs of his activities had been safely erased, he disrobed and prepared for bed. His souvenirs were safely locked in a trunk under his bed, drying out in a box filled with coarse salt. *I wonder if Poe and his little toady will be able to unlock my message. I have to admit, watching them scramble though my leavings has been more entertaining than I'd thought.*

After blowing out the candle, he smiled into the darkness, imagining people throughout the city turning disquietly in their beds at the idea of a monster in their midst.

CHAPTER TWENTY-ONE

The next morning, Eddy's appetite was non-existent, but he forced himself to go down to the Mitre's dining room and pick at a plate of food, his thoughts returning over and over to the mutilated body of Mrs. Billings. *Her daughter's unborn child was removed, and she lost her tongue. They could be taken as warnings, yes, but what if they're something more? What if someone is playing some kind of foul game here?*

While he chewed on a morsel of egg, he studied his fellow guests. In the bow window was a family of four—father, mother and two sons—working their way through breakfast, the mother importuning her rambunctious offspring to eat like gentlemen. He recognized two other men from the previous morning's breakfast, engaged in quiet conversation, and wondered if Furnow had been as diligent with them. *Does their continued presence at the Mitre indicate that they're also trapped in Oxford until the killer is found? Or is that honor reserved for me?*

To his surprise, a rather weary-looking Dodgson entered the room. Eddy waved him to the table. "Forgive me for saying so, but you look like you haven't slept a wink," he said. "Should I have the waiter fetch you some coffee or tea?"

"Thank you, but n-no. Unfortunately, sleep was rather elusive last night," the undergraduate admitted. "I came over here to tell you of what we found after I returned to the House."

Eddy listened in increasing amazement as Dodgson recounted his tale of breaking into Stiles's rooms and searching for evidence. "I found a book of your poems that you inscribed to PRS, with an additional inscription by Jane. I m-must have shoved it in my pocket when we heard him," the undergraduate concluded, sliding the book across the table. "I wish we'd found something m-more concrete."

"I assure you, Dodgson, you and your friends have performed yeoman service for me," Eddy disagreed, taking a moment to read Jane's last declaration of love before tucking the book into his coat pocket. "We now have incontrovertible proof that Stiles was connected to Miss Billings. If nothing else, this might persuade Furnow and his superiors to turn their attentions to our young nobleman and his whereabouts for the past few days. And I might be allowed to continue my tour, belated as it is."

Dodgson grimaced. "Yes, but how are you going to explain coming into possession of the book? I doubt what we did last night was lawful. We could even be s-sent down for entering another undergraduate's room without permission."

What about my freedom, you young fool? With an effort, he controlled his irritation. Frustrating as it was, he couldn't blame Dodgson for not wanting to destroy his academic career, not to mention his hopes for the future. "I won't bring this to Furnow unless I absolutely must. Besides, this afternoon I've been invited to luncheon with the Marquis, Sir Richard, Lady Georgiana and young Stiles. It could prove to be quite informative."

"Better you than m-me," Dodgson said, smothering a yawn. "Oh, by the way, there are some members of the Fourth Estate waiting for you at the front desk."

"Newspapermen?"

"Yes. It s-seems your presence at the scene last night was

leaked to the press. And apparently one of the reporters writes for *The Times*, so you may want to be careful in what you say."

"I should think so," Eddy replied, reviewing his options. On the one hand, being associated with two murders was hardly a good thing. On the other hand, if he used the fact of his Dupin stories to explain his presence at the scene as support for the police investigation, it could prompt further interest in the stories, and possibly even open British markets for new tales. "Thank you for the advance warning, my friend," he said, wiping his mouth and standing. "Can you return later this afternoon? We may have some more investigative work to do."

Dodgson nodded with weary enthusiasm. "I c-could be here by five o'clock."

"Excellent. I'll meet you in the lobby." He pulled out his pocket watch and consulted it. "In the meantime, you'd best hie yourself off to class. One of us should maintain a good reputation, at least."

"Indeed. I'll see you this afternoon, Mr. Poe."

After Dodgson left, Eddy did a quick check to make sure his clothes were neat and crumb-free, then headed into the lobby where a small group of men in brown checked suits and derby hats were gathered. "Gentlemen," he said, letting his drawl hang in the air, "I am Edgar Allan Poe. I believe you wished to speak with me?"

The reporters surged forward, eager for the hunt. "Mr. Poe, what is your connection to these murders?" one man asked.

"Is it true that the university constabulary has requested your help?" another said.

"Did you know the chambermaid's family?"

"Are you a suspect, Mr. Poe?" This from a burly redhead with a neatly trimmed mustache and an uncomfortably sharp gleam in his eye. Eddy suspected the man was the *Times* reporter.

He held up his hands. "One at a time, gentlemen, please," he said, keeping his voice pleasant. "My connection to these murders is merely that I was resident in the hotel when Miss Jane Billings met her unfortunate fate. I had spoken with her upon my arrival when she requested my autograph in one of my collections. After her death, I went to offer my condolences to her family, which is the limits of my connection with the deceased."

"What about her mother's death last night? We know the police brought you to the scene," the *Times* reporter said.

Eddy gave the man a sad smile. "I was asked to view the scene by a Constable Furnow of the Oxford University Police and offer my commentary, which I did. As for whether I am a suspect in these crimes, I rather doubt that I would still be a free man if I were."

"So you're helping the constabulary with their enquiries?" the second reporter asked. "Like your character Monsewer Dupeen? You're helping them detect clues and such?"

He had to swallow a smile at the mangling of the French honorific and name. "Monsieur Dupin is a brilliant detective. I am merely a writer and poet. If my poor powers of observation can be of any use to the constabulary, however, I am at their service…"

Academic robes flapping behind him like limp bat wings, Charles kept one hand clapped to his mortarboard as he dashed up the grey stone stairs to Mr. Sisson's rooms. Like other dons' rooms, it sported two doors at the entrance; an inner door that could be closed to prevent drafts and distracting noises from affecting the parties inside, and an outer door made of polished oak that could be closed for complete privacy. When a don was in the middle of a class or didn't want to be interrupted, he would close the outside door, known as 'sporting the oak.' An undergraduate late to class often found himself facing this oak door, which would bring words from the don later.

To his relief, only the inner door of Sisson's rooms was closed. He slipped inside, taking the first empty chair he could find and fishing out the correct textbook. As fate would have it, Blakeney was in the seat next to him and gave him a dubious look as Sisson entered the room, textbook in hand.

"Gentlemen," he began, shutting the outer and inner door before opening the book in his hand and leisurely licking a finger to flip the pages, "much of what is deemed 'higher mathematics' could best be described as a series of techniques used to reduce problems to what might be deemed 'mundane mathematics.'"

As Sisson continued his lecture, Blakeney leaned over to Charles. "I heard about the murder in Castle Mill Park last night," he whispered. "It's all over Oxford by now. Were you really taken up by the bulldogs right out of Sir Richard's home?"

Charles wished he knew how to curse effectively. Oxford ran on gossip like a horse ran on hay; it was impossible that someone wouldn't have heard about Furnow arriving at Sir Richard Middleton's house and put two and two together. "It's c-complicated," he whispered back. "They wanted Mr. Poe to view the scene, and I was swept along, rather."

The sallow undergraduate grimaced. "You couldn't get me to look at a murdered woman for all the tea in China. Do the bulldogs think this Poe fellow did it?"

Why did everyone seem to think that Poe was some sort of heartless murderer? "C-certainly not. He was with myself or his publisher all of yesterday afternoon. Besides, that sort of bestial behavior is quite beyond Poe."

Blakeney shrugged. "From what I heard, he was quite the wastrel even two years ago. And his stories—brr! 'The Pit and the Pendulum' kept me up with nightmares for a week. Someone who could write such gruesome tales can't be completely right in the head—"

"Mr. Blakeney," Sisson boomed, interrupting their whispered conversation, "I presume you're discussing the topic of linearization with Mr. Dodgson."

Charles and Blakeney both flinched, straightening up guiltily. "Er, yes, sir," Blakeney said.

"Splendid, splendid. Then I'm sure you'd be happy to provide us with a definition of linearization."

Blakeney bit his lip. "To be honest, sir, I didn't quite understand the definition, so I was asking Dodgson to explain it to me."

Sisson's gimlet gaze turned to Charles. "How kind of you to help your fellow classmates, Mr. Dodgson. As you appear to understand the concept more fully than Mr. Blakeney, would you be so kind as to provide us with a definition of linearization?"

Charles cleared his throat, even as his gut tightened. For him, understanding the definition was far easier than reciting it. "Linearization is the technique of using a t-tangent line to estimate values of a f-function, sir."

"Very good, Dodgson. And how would one use this technique to estimate the value of a function? Do feel free to demonstrate your knowledge on the chalkboard."

The other men in the class nudged each other, expecting him to admit defeat and be excoriated with Sisson's wit. Instead, he rose and went to the ancient chalkboard mounted on the far wall of the room, sketching out the axes and points of a graph and writing out the appropriate formulae as he haltingly explained what he was scribing on the slate.

The class was silent. As a whole, they turned to Sisson, who studied the board as if it held instructions on how to locate the Holy Grail. Finally, he nodded. "I see that you haven't been wasting all of your time at upper-class literary salons, Dodgson," he harrumphed. "Let's move on to the topic of differentials, shall we?"

Sitting down, Charles gave the cowed Blakeney a brief, forgiving nod, then bent his head over his book. But a niggling voice at the back of his mind wondered if people were starting to tar him with the same brush used to paint Poe as a potential madman. Turning over the inscribed book of poems had seemed like the logical thing to do that morning, but now he had to wonder if he'd done the right thing.

At the end of the class, he filed out with the other men. "Dodgson," Blakeney called.

He paused, letting Blakeney catch up with him. "I'm sorry about that," the undergraduate said quickly. "I knew you could recite the definition from heart, and I was completely at sea."

"I-it's all right."

He turned to leave, but Blakeney kept pace with him. "I didn't mean to insult Mr. Poe, by the way," he said quickly. "I know how unfair it is to be labeled something you aren't, simply because of your circumstances. If I offended you, I apologize."

Apparently he was to be burdened with Blakeney's company. "There's no need. I don't know the m-man well, I must admit, but I cannot see him as a murderer. His excursions into darkness are all fictional."

"Of course, of course." Blakeney looked around furtively. "May I ask you an odd question? It's something that came up in my Philosophy lecture."

He wondered what made Blakeney think he knew anything about philosophy. "G-go ahead."

"If you knew someone had committed a crime, but informing the authorities would result in the ruination of your own life, what would you do about it?"

He stopped, staring at the other man. "What kind of crime?"

A reddish flush suffused Blakeney's sallow cheeks. "A serious one."

"Murder?"

Now Blakeney looked away. "I—well, yes, murder if you like. Would you turn the person into the authorities, knowing that in doing so every hope of a better life for yourself would be taken away and you would be turned out onto the street? Or would you hold your tongue and let the criminal go free in order to maintain your own security?"

Clearly Blakeney was talking about Stiles. "I've always believed that it is every Englishman's duty to s-support the law and defeat the criminal element," Charles said carefully. "And I would argue that a good Christian should not suffer a murderer to roam free. Is there some way that the authorities could be informed anonymously? By a letter, perhaps, or a telegram?"

"According to the terms of the query, no." Blakeney smiled weakly. "Quite a philosophical conundrum, eh? To do what is right, but ruin your own life in the process. A good man would do it without hesitation, of course, but what if one isn't strong enough to do such a thing?"

He knew what his answer should be; to pray for strength and bring the criminal to justice, no matter the personal consequences. *But what if that is precisely what Blakeney is trying to do this very moment?*

After hesitating, he lowered his voice. "Perhaps he could ask for help from s-someone who is familiar with the circumstances.

They might be able to find a way to inform the authorities without endangering his own position."

For a moment Blakeney seemed hopeful, but then he shook his head. "If only that could happen. It would certainly be a balm to the individual." He sighed. "Thank you, Dodgson. You've given me much to chew on before the next lecture. I'll see you at Hall later."

He hurried off, leaving Charles to wonder what exactly Blakeney knew about the murders of Jane and Elizabeth Billings.

CHAPTER TWENTY-TWO

Once the reporters had been persuaded to leave, Eddy detoured to the front desk. Mr. Venables was behind it, his face pale and strained. "Good morning, Mr. Poe."

"Ah, good morning, Mr. Venables. I'm afraid I may have to extend my stay here one more night."

He was surprised to see a flash of anger in the other man's eyes. "Of course, sir," Venables said shortly. "Your stay can be extended. I presume the bill should be sent to Mr. Ponsonby?"

"As arranged, yes." It was hardly surprising if the hotel keeper was tired of the intermittent police presence and its cause. Apologetically, he continued, "Also, I need to speak with William about some things. Is he available?"

Venables ducked his head, staring fixedly at the mahogany counter. "William's not here," he muttered. "I sent him to Bath."

"Oh. Well, when he returns—"

"He won't be, not for a while. He needs to get away for a bit, to get his mind off things."

Eddy wanted to curse at the news. *Damn it all, why couldn't he wait until we'd found the killer?* "Well, I can certainly see the value in that," he forced himself to say. "In which case, I suppose my questions will have to wait."

Now Venables did look up at him, skin mottled with emotion.

"William is a good lad, Mr. Poe," he said passionately. "He wouldn't harm a fly, not a fly. What that Furnow bloke said—well, it was horrible."

He's not angry with me—he's angry with the police. That was even more worrying. "Furnow was here?"

"This morning, with his cronies. Asked to see William's room—I said why, and he just smarmed, 'Constabulary business, my good man.'" Venables's hands clenched on the counter, his knuckles whitening. "They have no right to stick their noses into the business of townsfolk. But I had to let them in, didn't I? It wasn't five minutes later when Furnow came steaming out, demanding to know where William was. I told him he was in Bath for a few days, and the hound took off in a ferocious lather. I won't have aught said against my boy, Mr. Poe—he's a good lad, I tell you."

"I'm sure he is," Eddy soothed. But was that the truth? Granted, William had been near the bottom of his list of potential suspects, but the clerk's sudden decampment to Bath moved him up somewhat. "Er, I have some errands to run, and a luncheon appointment. If anyone wishes to speak with me, would you be so kind as to tell them that I shall return at five o'clock?"

"Of course, sir." Venables was staring at the desk again, a furious father trying to defend his absent son. Not without sympathy, Eddy nodded at him and left.

Outside the hotel, he hailed a hansom and gave the name of the park. The driver, a thin little man with a shock of carroty hair and bulging blue eyes, turned in his seat and winked. "Off to see the murder scene, eh? You're not the first passenger I've picked up who wanted to see it, sir."

Eddy groaned inwardly at the news. Bad enough that the constabulary had tromped all over the park last night; if the cabbie was right and it had become a one-day wonder for Oxford's braver inhabitants, it was unlikely that any traces of the killer could still be found.

And indeed as the hansom pulled up in front of the park, it was already awash with curiosity seekers, eager to gawk at the spot where a woman was brutally slain and mutilated. A few bulldogs and watchmen patrolled here and there, but the bulk of them seemed more interested in flirting with young, giggling maidservants and nannies out on their half day than keeping an eye out for a potential killer. Undergraduates free from classes poked at various bushes, and even a couple of well-dressed elderly gentlemen could be seen studying the surroundings as they strolled.

After paying the cabbie, Eddy wandered around the park. The spot where Mrs. Billings's body had been found was marked off with a rope and some hastily erected posts, and a pair of women walked by it chatting excitedly about the murder and wondering if the park would now be haunted. The writing part of his brain perked up; *a vengeful ghost mother seeking retribution for herself and her daughter might make an interesting story—*

His thoughts were interrupted by a tall man in a plain grey suit skulking along the outskirts of the crowd. Something about him seemed strangely familiar. Eddy set off through the crowd, trying to get a closer view. Unlike the other curiosity seekers, the lurker didn't appear to be searching for the spot where Mrs. Billings had been murdered. In fact, his head turned from side to side as he scanned the other people in the park, looking for someone.

Belatedly, Eddy recognized the man as William Venables. *Bath, eh? It must have been a deucedly short trip.* He threaded through the people around him with more vigor and was almost within reaching distance of the clerk when he felt a tap on his arm.

Turning in irritation, he found Lady Georgiana Gardner beaming at him. Today she was dressed in an eye-catching gown of blue-green silk, topped with a warm woolen jacket in a darker shade of the color, and her bonnet sported a riot of lace and artificial flowers. Next to her, a short, plump, dark haired woman in a serviceable brown visiting dress appeared to be a little wren next to a glorious peacock.

"Mr. Poe! I suppose I shouldn't be surprised to find you here," the young noblewoman said. "I'm so very sorry that I didn't have the chance to say goodbye yesterday to you and your young friend. Uncle Dicky told me about the bulldogs and their summons."

Eddy glanced behind himself hastily, but William had already disappeared. Forcing a polite smile, he bowed to the young woman. "Yes, well, as Mr. Furnow would undoubtedly put it, solving a murder and stopping a criminal takes precedence over personal pleasure. I do hope your uncle wasn't angered by my abrupt departure."

"Not at all," she reassured him. "Uncle Dicky knows what the bulldogs are like from personal experience. I do hope they didn't inconvenience you." She leaned closer. "The news has gone all around town, you see. It's been said that you were brought in to examine the scene and see if you could spot any elusive clues as to the identity of the murderer."

Thank you, Dupin. "One might say that I offered some salient information to the constables," he said, keeping the nature of the information deliberately vague. "What they do with it, of course, is out of my hands, but I have the fullest confidence in their capabilities."

"The bulldogs?" the woman at Lady Georgiana's side observed. "If they're looking for a clutch of Keble men who have made off with a don's furniture as a prank, perhaps, but I doubt they could find much else."

Lady Georgiana gave the woman a fond but exasperated look. "Mr. Poe, this is Miss Gray, my former governess and current companion."

He gave the woman a bow and received a curtsey in return. "Introducing me as her former governess is her way of explaining why I appear to speak out of turn," Miss Gray said, unrepentant. "And mark my words, the constables will need to bring up one of those police detectives from Scotland Yard if they want to stop this murderer."

"I suspect a crime of this nature is somewhat out of their purview," Eddy allowed. "Still, Mr. Furnow seems a dogged sort, if you'll excuse the pun, and I found Mr. Lievesley to be a most perspicacious man indeed."

"I suppose," Lady Georgiana added, looking around for someone. "I take it that your professorial young friend isn't with you this morning?"

It took Eddy a moment to realize she was referring to Dodgson. "Ah, no. I'm afraid academic pursuits required his attendance elsewhere."

She frowned. "Oh. A shame—we were having a marvelous discussion about logic and sorites last night, and I was hoping that he would continue his instruction," she said, ignoring the dry look she received from Miss Gray as she glanced around the park. "On further thought, this locale is far too crowded for my taste, and we're due at the Deanery in an hour to prepare for the luncheon with Lord Dunford. I suppose we should return home, Gray."

"You're dining with the marquis, as well?" Eddy asked. "I've also been invited, and I'm wondering if I should shop around for some armor before I set off."

Lady Georgiana laughed. "The marquis is a dour sort, isn't

he? But I'm glad you're joining us today, Mr. Poe. Apparently I'm to be used as a sop to cheer up Philip about his removal from Christ Church." She made a face. "He's being pulled out by the marquis for the rest of the year. Something about a health problem, I believe."

The hairs on the back of Eddy's neck prickled at the news. The sudden arrival of the marquis in town, the death of the pregnant chambermaid followed by her mother's demise, and now Philip Stiles was to be removed from his classes at Christ Church. If Dunford was aware of his nephew's proclivities, he certainly wouldn't be above using the perquisites of rank and wealth to remove him from the attention of the law.

If Stiles was the murderer, after all, and not William Venables. Or someone else, blast it all.

"—with the marquis."

His attention returned to Lady Georgiana. "My apologies—you were saying?"

"I said, you should be careful with the marquis," Lady Georgiana repeated. "He prides himself on his intellectual pursuits, particularly his skill with word puzzles and cryptograms, and he doesn't like to lose. If you should set him at a puzzle that he can't solve, well, the outcome could be extremely unpleasant."

Eddy wondered if she was warning him about the marquis—or his grim-visaged valet. "While I am not as familiar with the perquisites of rank as a native-born Briton would be, I did spend my childhood here in boarding school, and I have some familiarity with the sense of privilege that can afflict certain members of the peerage," he assured her. "I have devised a particularly challenging cryptogram, but if the marquis is as clever as he claims to be, he should be able to solve it."

Lady Georgiana gave him a relieved smile. "In which case,

this may be a pleasant meal, after all. To be truthful, I suspect Uncle Dicky will appreciate the distraction—he attends these luncheons more out of duty than any true cordiality." Her smiled widened even further. "Oh, I've just had the most splendid idea. If you would care to escort us home, we can all travel to luncheon together."

"Lady Georgiana!" Miss Gray said, giving her charge a stern look. "You cannot be offering invitations to Sir Richard's home willy-nilly."

"Nonsense, Gray," Lady Georgiana scoffed. "Mr. Poe was an invited guest last night, and his presence will greatly improve the character of our ride to Lord Dunford's home. Besides, I for one would appreciate some company that wasn't constantly twittering at me about my behavior or my unladylike tendency to read books."

Trying not to smile, Eddy privately agreed with Sir Richard that whoever married this small blonde whirlwind would indeed have his hands full. And what with William Venables gone and the crowds trampling over any evidence that the killer might have left, there was no longer any reason to remain at the park. "It would be my honor to escort you and your companion home, Lady Georgiana," he said, offering his arm.

"See, Grey? I told you it would all work out." She took his arm with a dimpled smile, her companion falling into disapproving step behind them as they left the park. "Now, tell me more about Mr. Dodgson," she purred.

CHAPTER TWENTY-THREE

From his vantage point across the street, William Venables waited until the American writer was safely away with the two ladies before leaving the park. He'd gotten up early as usual that morning to make sure that the fires were stoked, the ostlers were at work in the small stable behind the inn, and that the kitchen staff were in progress with the breakfast foods. When Cook had complained that a batch of eggs were bad, he'd offered to run to the farmer's market and see if any more were available.

He'd had a basket of brown and white eggs over his arm and was headed back to the Mitre when one of the ostlers appeared and stopped him. "Your pa said not to come back right now," the young man had said, swiping a hand across his sweaty brow as if he'd run all the way. "The hounds are after you."

William's mouth had gone dry at the news. "Me? Why do they want me?"

"Dunno. Your pa said they tossed your room and found summat. He said you're to clear out to your Aunt Tillie's in Bath for a few days."

"But Aunt Tillie—" He'd broken off, understanding his father's message. Aunt Matilda lived in Tunbridge Wells; if Mr. Venables was afraid to give her true location to one of their own employees, it was for fear that the bulldogs would winkle it out of him and come after William. Which could only mean one thing.

They'd found his portraits.

He knew it had been foolish to put them up in his room, tacked to the wall over his desk, but he loved to draw. And sketching Jane had been one of his greatest joys. Capturing the flicker of sunlight on her hair or the gleam of humor in her smile filled him with pleasure, and she'd always been flattered by his requests to sit for a drawing. He realized that he was in love with her during the third sketch and had snapped his charcoal in sheer surprise.

Not that she felt that way towards him. He was no fool; they'd walked out a few times, but in the end she saw him as a friend and nothing more. In a way, he was impressed; what with the Mitre being a success and him in line to inherit it in time, he was considered to be something of a catch among the local girls. But that didn't matter to Jane, and she had been kind but firm about her refusal. He wasn't one to press his attentions where they weren't wanted, so he accepted it and was content to remain her friend.

And then she'd fallen for that puffed-up blowhard Stiles, who'd promptly gotten her in the family way. She'd confessed it to William not a week ago after he found her pale and vomiting in the dunny. "Promise me you won't say anything, Will," she'd begged, clutching a hand to her belly. "He's going to marry me, he said so."

All he could do was agree, even though what he really wanted to do was go 'round to Stiles's college and thrash the bugger. A few days later she was dead, and he cursed himself for passing up the opportunity to beat seven hells out of Philip Stiles. *If he killed you, Jane, I swear I won't let him get away with it. I'll throttle him myself.*

Unfortunately, the police weren't even considering Stiles as a suspect. It was much easier to look at the lovesick hotel clerk who kept secret portraits of the dead girl in his room. William left the city center, keeping his shoulders hunched as he forced himself to walk at a brisk but unremarkable clip. He had gone for a long walk the previous evening, as well, which now meant that no one could vouch for him during the time when Mrs. Billings had been murdered. If the constables thought he'd killed Jane, they would undoubtedly assume that he'd killed her mother, as well.

There was no hope for it. He'd have to leave Oxford, at least for some time. But that would force him to miss Jane's funeral. William's heart clenched painfully as he thought of the coroner's men carrying her small, sheet-draped body out of the hotel as if she was something to be thrown on a trash heap. *I can't leave without telling her goodbye.*

Keeping his head down, he threaded the residential streets north of the city's center until he reached the Billings's semi-detached house, pounding on the red side's door. It was opened by a tear-stained Maggie, her eyes widening when she saw him. "Oh, Will!" she wailed, throwing herself at him.

He gently pushed her inside the door, closing it behind him, then knelt and took the girl in his arms. "Hush, now, Maggie," he whispered. "I'm so sorry, sweetheart, so sorry."

"But they're gone," she sobbed, rubbing at her eyes with an already wet hand. "And they won't let Pa see Mamma, and they only let us have Jane this morning, and Aunt Sally and Emma had to work ever so long to lay her out, and they made me stay upstairs, and it doesn't look like her, William, it doesn't!"

"Death changes people, sweetheart," he said softly, giving her a reassuring squeeze. "But Jane and your ma are safe with the angels, now, and we can take comfort in that. Now, where's your pa?"

"In the parlor, with—with—" She burst into a fresh round of tears, her thin frame shaking as she sobbed. Getting to his feet, William kept one arm around her shoulders as he guided them down the narrow hallway to the front parlor.

Inside, a plain pine coffin stood on two trestles, tall candelabras at either end with genuine beeswax candles burning cleanly. The room was full of flowers, urns and vases with blooms placed on every available flat surface. Between the candles and the almost overwhelming floral scent of the assorted bouquets, any other unpleasant odors would be covered.

Somberly clad people clustered here and there in the parlor, but as it was a workday it was still mostly empty. A straight back chair had been set up near the coffin, and Mr. Billings sat on it, eyes dry but lost and empty as they stared at the floor.

William approached, careful not to brush any of the floral tributes and send them crashing to the floor. "Mr. Billings," he said quietly. "You have my condolences, sir."

Billings's head slowly came up as if it was on a string operated by a puppeteer. "Thank you," he said hollowly, before focusing on the man in front of him. "Ah, William. You're a good man to come and pay your respects." His smile was carved from pain and grief. "Our Jane was right fond of you. I would have been proud if…." He broke off, his throat working.

Seeing the older man struggle not to cry made it harder to hold back his own tears. "I know, sir. It just wasn't meant to be. But she'll always be in my heart."

Reluctantly, he glanced at the coffin behind Billings. Inside it, Jane was laid out in her best amber-colored gown, a small bouquet of posies in her hands. Her aunts had washed her carefully, drying her hair and brushing it neatly into mahogany curls around her face. Someone had dabbed the tiniest bit of rouge onto her cheeks and lips, trying to relieve the pallor of her skin. To William, the artificial blush simply reinforced the fact that she was dead.

He stepped past Billings, to the side of the coffin. For the moment, he was alone with Jane. It was now or never. "I would have taken care of you, lass," he whispered softly, sliding a hand into his trouser pocket and pulling out a plain silver ring, the same one that had sat on his mother's left hand for all of her married life. "No matter what, I would've loved you and your babe."

Moving so that his actions were blocked from the rest of the room, he lifted her left hand and pushed the ring onto her third finger, ignoring the clammy texture of her skin. "There," he whispered. "Show that to St. Peter and tell him that you were loved by a good man. They'll let you and your little one in, I'm sure of it."

Replacing her hand on the small bouquet, he felt Maggie move next to him. The girl stared up at him with wide, questioning eyes. "You knew?" she asked in a whisper.

He glanced over his shoulder at Mr. Billings, but the older man was deaf to anything but his own grief. "Aye, I did. And I would've married her, as well."

She took his hand, the living warmth of her a sad comparison to Jane's cold fingers. "I wish you had. Then she'd be here with us now, instead of with Mamma and the angels."

The simple words brought tears to his eyes, and he looked up at the low, patched ceiling to keep them from overflowing. "I wish that, too," he said roughly.

Behind them, someone cleared his throat softly. William turned, expecting to see one of the Billingses or a neighbor waiting to view the corpse. Instead, it was the constable from the University police, bleakly resolute.

"Hello, Mr. Venables," the man said. "Might I have a word

with you outside, in private?"

Dumbly, William nodded, following the constable out of the parlor without a word. Maggie still clung to his hand as he walked, her gaze shifting nervously between the two men. "What's wrong, Will?"

"Nothing, sweetheart." He paused at the door, glancing back at the parlor and its funereal display. "Be a good girl and go back stay with your pa. He'll need you, now."

Her lower lip trembled, but she obeyed. With a sigh, William followed Furnow out of the house into the front garden. Two more constables were waiting there, grim guardians in their black suits and bowler hats. "Thank you."

Furnow frowned. "For what?"

"For not arresting me in front of Maggie and Mr. Billings."

The bulldog's mouth pursed in thought. "And why should I arrest you for anything, Mr. Venables?"

"Because you think I killed Jane."

"Did you?" Furnow asked softly.

"No, but you won't believe me, will you?" Grief threatened to overwhelm him, and he didn't care when the tears began to fall. "It doesn't matter. She's dead, now, and I'll never see her again."

Furnow straightened, his attitude becoming one of professional detachment. "We found numerous portraits of Miss Billings on the walls of your room, Mr. Venables. We also spoke to employees of the hotel who informed us that you had romantic feelings for the young woman. Furthermore, your father said that you had asked Miss Billings to marry you at one time, and she refused. I suspect her mother was against such a marriage, preferring a union with a man of better social standing for her daughter. Were you angry at Mrs. Billings for interfering in such a way?"

It sounded horrible, put like that. "Of course not. Jane didn't love me, that's all. Said she was fond of me, but no more." His mouth was so dry.

"Where were you between the hours of nine o'clock and midnight on October the eleventh?"

"I was at the hotel, in my room."

"Can anyone confirm this?"

"No."

Another nod from Furnow. "Did you lure Jane Billings into an empty guest room on the first floor and murder her?"

He wanted to vomit. "No."

"Where were you yesterday between the hours of five and seven o'clock yesterday evening?"

"Out for a walk. I like to walk, and Pa thought it would get my mind off of things."

"Did you lure Mrs. Billings to Castle Mill Park and murder her?"

His fists clenched. "No."

"Can you prove this? Was anyone with you during those hours?"

"I told you, I was out walking. Didn't go anywhere near that park."

"But can you prove this?"

He shook his head. *It was Stiles, damn you. I know it was.* But if he said that, he would have to confess that Stiles had stolen Jane's virtue, and he wouldn't do that for all the devils in hell.

The constable jerked his chin at his compatriots, and they approached. "Mr. William Venables, I am placing you under arrest for the murder of Miss Jane Billings and Mrs. Elizabeth Billings," he said, as each bulldog placed a hand on William's shoulders. "Come along quietly so that we don't disturb the family."

Moving like a sleepwalker, William allowed himself to be guided to the police wagon waiting at the curb, and unceremoniously loaded into the back. Sliding to the floor, he curled into a ball of silent misery as the wagon lurched forward.

CHAPTER TWENTY-FOUR

As the sun reached its zenith, a brisk wind began to blow in from the west, picking up moisture as it streamed across the Oxfordshire countryside. Clouds butted together, forming puffy clumps over the dreaming spires, and servants moved down the long tables in Christ Church's Great Hall lighting candles to better illuminate the midday repast.

Charles had gathered with Hebron and Reade at their usual table, still wondering about Blakeney's strange question and ignoring his friends' usual grumbling about the food. "Am I forgetting the joys of real food already, or is hollandaise sauce supposed to be this color?" he heard Hebron say as the Horseman poked at the unmistakably pink sauce that coated his baked cod.

"I'm fairly sure that hollandaise is supposed to be a rather pale yellow," Reade replied, tasting it. "Ah. It seems the cooks have found a way to use up the tomatoes that were left over from breakfast."

Charles sighed and began scraping the sauce off his cod with a butter knife. "I had the s-strangest conversation with Blakeney this m-morning. He claimed it was a philosophical question, but he wanted to know what I'd do if turning in a c-criminal meant ruining my own life."

Hebron straightened up. "Do you think he meant Stiles?"

"W-well, I don't know who else he could have meant, do you?"

A breathless O'Donnell jogged in. "Got caught by Plesic—wanted to quiz me on my Greek noun declensions," he said, nudging Hebron. "Move over, you know that's my spot."

Hebron sighed but did as asked, and O'Donnell took his seat at the left end of the table. "Have you heard the news about Stiles?"

Charles stopped poking at his cod. "W-what news?"

"He's being taken out by his uncle for the rest of term," O'Donnell said. "The good marquis is claiming that the environment of Oxford isn't healthy for his only heir and wants him back at their country estate until the start of Hilary term."

The four of them exchanged worried looks, the memory of the previous night's adventure still fresh in mind. "When is he leaving?" Reade asked.

"He's left. I saw a pair of scouts cleaning out his rooms on my way here." O'Donnell lowered his voice. "If the bulldogs find out that he was mixed up with that chambermaid, that could explain much. The marquis wouldn't want him involved in a scandal."

"Not that there's much risk of that now," Reade said. "Just before I got here, I heard that the hounds had picked up the son of the hotel keeper as the killer. Apparently his room was littered with portraits of her."

Charles froze. "A-a-are they sure?"

His table mates glanced at him. "Well, they seemed sure enough to arrest him," Reade said. "From what I'd heard, he actually went to the girl's house to pay his respects. That's where the hounds grabbed him."

O'Donnell shook his head. "Stiles should consider himself damned lucky that the bulldogs weren't looking at him. Well, at least we'll be rid of him until Hilary term. Now if he could only take his lickspittle with him, we might enjoy our meals more."

"Enough of that," Reade commanded. "Dodgson, you were saying something about Blakeney—"

But Dodgson's chair was empty.

Charles fished his pocket watch out of his waistcoat as he jogged down the stairs of the Great Hall, peering at the time. *Almost one o'clock.* He would miss Classics, which he hated to do, but this was far more important.

Passing the ancient oak door with NO PEEL burned into it, he rushed out onto Tom Quad, his mind on O'Donnell and Reade's news. With William Venables in custody, the bulldogs wouldn't bother to look any further for murder suspects. Even if the clerk could prove his innocence, Stiles was safely in the marquis's custody and effectively beyond the reach of the authorities.

And if William couldn't prove his innocence, Stiles would walk away a free man and the wrong man could be sent to the scaffold. Charles knew enough of the university constabulary to understand that they couldn't leave an event such as Mrs. Billings's murder unsolved; the townspeople were already unhappy that they possessed the legal power that they did. *If they don't find the killer, it could knock the underpinnings of their authority out from under them.* And if Stiles was safely in the country somewhere, serving out his removal from Michaelmas term, well, then, why not convict the hotel-keeper's son, who appeared to have motive, means and a location for the murder?

Except that William Venables doesn't read or write Ancient Greek, so there's no way he could have left those letters on Jane or Mrs. Billings. He had been willing to protect Poe as long as no one else was endangered as a result, but that time was now past. Poe had to tell the bulldogs what had happened the morning of the twelfth, and how they'd sent the note explaining the translation of the symbols. And if it meant that he himself would be sent down for his role in the matter, then so be it. *I suppose I have an answer for Blakeney's philosophy question now.*

Oh, dear—Blakeney. He wanted to groan. As if convincing Poe to speak with the constables wasn't bad enough, he also had to persuade Blakeney to tell them his suspicions about Stiles. Leaving the path that led to the college exit, he headed instead for the residential quarters, hunting for Blakeney's room.

His fellow undergraduate was in his shirtsleeves when he answered Charles's knock. "Dodgson? What are you doing here?"

"I n-need to speak with you—" Reluctantly, Charles pushed into the man's room.

And stopped. The room was much like his, except that any personal effects had been removed and packed into a small crate. A trunk sat open on the bed, half-filled with clothing. "W-where are you going?"

"Oh, you didn't hear the news? Stiles is being pulled out for the term." Blakeney returned to his task of packing.

"B-but … what does that have to do with you?"

The sallow man shrugged. "I'm being punished. I was supposed to keep Stiles on the narrow path, and I didn't. If I'm very, very lucky, I might be allowed to return for Hilary term." His voice lowered. "But I don't feel very lucky at the moment."

Confused, Charles moved until he could look Blakeney in the face. "I don't understand. Why are you being sent down for Stiles's behavior?"

Blakeney sighed. "I'm not being sent down. Lord Dunford

paid for me to attend Christ Church as Stiles's companion. My family is poor, and he knew there was no way I would ever be able to attend any university, much less Oxford, unless I had a sponsor. He paid for my enrollment, and in return I was to serve as his nephew's shadow and keep him from the worst of his excesses. But I failed, thus I have to leave with Stiles."

His earlier "philosophical question" burned through Charles's mind. "How exactly did you fail?" he asked carefully.

But Blakeney only shook his head. "It doesn't matter now. Lord Dunford is displeased with me, and that is all there is to it. A pity—I really did hope to try for the Gibbs award." He tried to smile, but it made him look even more hangdog. "I'm afraid I have to ask you to leave. Two of Dunford's servants are arriving very soon to take my things, and I need to finish packing before they arrive."

Charles found himself ushered back to the door. Gripping the frame, he tried again. "Blakeney, if you know something that needs to be conveyed to the authorities, I'll help you do it. My father may not be a marquis, but he does have friends in the House who will help protect you, if you need it."

He hoped Blakeney would confess everything then and there, but the other man shook his head. "Thank you, Dodgson, truly. But you don't want to cross Lord Dunford. People who do that wind up regretting it."

With the greatest of care, he urged Charles out into the hallway, then closed the door. There was a soft sound of the lock clicking.

Charles wanted to pound on the door, demand that Blakeney open it, tell the truth about Stiles. But the man was clearly too frightened of his benefactor. Frustrated, he left, hurrying out of the college and making for the Mitre.

At the hotel, a young woman in a somewhat rumpled gown

was now staffing the front desk. "May I help you, sir?" she asked.

"Y-yes, I'm looking for o-o-one of your guests, a Mr. Edgar P-poe," he said, trying to bull his way through his stutter. "I w-was wondering if he'd returned."

"I'm sorry, sir, I'm not familiar with the gentleman."

He gritted his teeth. "Is Mr. V-v-venables available? He m-may know."

The young woman's expression changed, turning reluctant. "Mr. Venables isn't available, sir. If you'd like to leave a message for our guest, I'll be happy to give it to him when he returns."

He had no other choice. "Yes, I'll d-do that," he said through his teeth.

She pushed a piece of paper across the desk. Charles dipped the desk's quill pen into the ink pot, trying to marshal his thoughts into a coherent message, but was distracted when a young boy dashed into the lobby.

"Letter for a guest," the boy piped.

"Give it over, then," the young woman said, holding out her hand.

The boy clutched the folded note to his chest. "The nob said I'd get sixpence for delivering it."

She scoffed. "He'd have paid you before sending you off. Now hand over the note or I'll take the back of my hand to you."

Scowling, the boy threw the note onto the desk and scurried to the door, pausing only to give a rude gesture before disappearing out into the street. The young woman—a senior chambermaid, Charles thought, or perhaps a server drafted for her ability to read and do sums—shook her head as she picked up the folded paper, glancing at the writing on it. "Hmph. You're not the only one leaving messages for Mr. Poe, it seems."

Charles stared at the note. Regular post came in an envelope with a stamp, but a folded piece of paper would have to come from somewhere in Oxford. *So who's sending Poe notes?*

He had a dark suspicion he knew. *I need to see it—but how? What would Poe do if he were in my shoes?*

The thought of the American's glib falsehoods spawned an idea. He leaned on the desktop, assuming a furtive look. "I heard that William Venables was taken up for the murder of Jane Billings. I've run into him a few times, and he never struck me as the type to do such a thing."

The lure of gossip worked. Glancing around, the desk girl leaned in as well. "The constables said William killed Jane," she whispered. "But that can't be true, sir. He loved Jane, I know he did, and he's a good, kind man. It wasn't his fault she didn't fancy him. If I'd been in her shoes, I would have accepted his proposal and been off to Gretna Green like a shot."

He nodded in pretended understanding. "Is Mr. Venables trying to get him out?"

"Yes, sir. Poor man, he's half out of his mind with worry. He has to find a barrister who will take William's case, and it's all horribly wrong." She shook her head. "It was that American writer, it had to be. He came in drunk as a lord the night before Jane was killed, and he writes all those horrible stories and poems about death. The constables should have arrested him instead of poor William. Or that other bloke, the one Jane's fancy man knew. He gave me goosebumps, he did, with the way he stared at her."

The other bloke. Could that be Walton? The grim valet would have been enough to frighten any woman. "Do you know this man's name?"

The chambermaid shook her head. "Used to see him sometimes with Jane's lad. He was polite enough when His Nibs was paying attention, but his eyes were hard as stone, sir. Jane said she'd asked her lad to send him away, but he wouldn't. Said he felt safer with the bloke about—"

A grey-haired woman in a flour-dusted vest poked her head into the lobby. "Anna! Cook says the veal chops are off and she needs more for tomorrow. You're to go to the market right now."

"Yes, Mrs. McCarthy." With an apologetic roll of the eyes for Charles, Anna hurried after the older woman.

Leaving the letter on the desk. *Well, at least I won't have to tell a falsehood to see it.* He picked it up, studying it closely. The paper was of top quality, the same kind sold at his favorite stationers on St. Aldate's. Someone had written Poe's name in peacock blue ink, and the oddly elegant scrawl seemed familiar, somehow.

Glancing around guiltily, he slipped the note into his pocket, then ducked out the front door of the hotel, waiting until he was safely around the corner before unfolding it. If it was some sort of business information from the publisher or a personal communication from a friend, he would simply replace it on the front desk, no harm done—

The page held yet another anagram, written in the same blue ink and handwriting as Poe's name. But instead of Ancient Greek symbols, this one was done in familiar Latin letters.

Charles sucked in a breath. This would be easier with pen and paper, but time was of the essence. He stared at the letters, burning them into his memory, then closed his eyes and pictured the letters in his mind, rearranging them over and over again.

To his frustration, words stubbornly refused to appear. *Wait—Latin letters? Perhaps that's a hint.*

He tried rearranging the letters again until he finally had a sentence in Latin, then translated it.

His eyes popped open in horror. *To the devil with propriety—I must get to Pennyworth House now.*

CHAPTER TWENTY-FIVE

The killer opened the tradesman's door to the mansion, slipping the key back into his pocket. He knew the servants' routine well enough by now to avoid them; the footmen would be busy with their assigned duties, and the maids were cleaning the public rooms at this time of day. The kitchen staff would be enjoying the break between meals, and the ostlers were busy tending his lordship's horses in the stable.

Moving quietly through the cool, hushed hallways, he reached Dunford's private office and knocked. The familiar gruff voice bade him enter.

Dunford stood at a tall window gazing out at the gathering storm. He turned, his expression matching the weather when he realized who had entered. "You fool," he said bluntly.

"My lord?"

"I repeat—you *fool.*" Dunford slammed his hand on the window frame, the glass rattling from the blow. "It's bad enough that you killed that drab. But what on earth possessed you to kill the mother?"

He shrugged. "She was determined to marry her remaining daughter to your nephew, and was willing to use blackmail to do it. Did you really want to give in?"

"Of course not," Dunford snapped. "But neither did I want her to be removed in so public a manner. Good God, man, that was nothing short of barbaric. What is wrong with you?"

Another shrug. "She threatened to talk to the police and the papers. I did what I had to do."

"You did not need to mutilate her body," the marquis snarled. "There are ways around this sort of difficulty, civilized ways."

He made a dismissive sound. "Yes—marrying the girl off to someone made agreeable with a cash payment. I'm quite familiar with your methods, my lord. Except that the mother wouldn't accept your offer, no matter how you sweetened it. So I did what I had to do in order to protect your family."

Dunford glared at him. "You may well have damaged my family beyond repair with your ham-handedness. Too many people are aware of the links between Philip and that damned girl, and now I'll have to keep him with me up at Redhull for the entire term until things cool down."

"Is that wise, my lord? It does make him look somewhat weak."

"I would rather him be thought weak than be taken up by the constabulary for murder. A few months at Redhull, and the gossip will die down and he can safely return to the House. After that he'll be married and, please God, present me with a legitimate heir."

He went still for a moment. "A legitimate heir. That's all that really matters, doesn't it?"

Dunford snorted. "As well you know. So Philip will lie low for the term, and you will do everything in your power to implicate William Venables as the murderer before you leave Oxford. He's already been taken up by the constabulary on suspicion, thanks to a word in the right ears. I want to see him on a gibbet before Boxing Day."

He almost wanted to laugh. Almost. "You'd see an innocent man hanged in order to protect your nephew?"

"I would see *you* hanged, sir, in order to protect him," Dunford thundered. "Philip will be the next marquis after my death, God help him, and I must rely on him to continue the family line."

"That whoring, gambling excuse for a man is what you expect to carry on the family line?" He couldn't resist sneering, letting the contempt finally, finally come into his voice. "He can barely read English, much less Greek or Latin, and yet that wastrel's to gain everything while your own son—"

"I do not have a son!"

It felt as if he'd been struck. He had to fix his gaze on the Persian carpet beneath his feet while he regained control. "Of course," he murmured. "You have no son, and so Philip is your heir. And I am to make sure that William Venables pays for a crime he did not commit."

"Indeed you are, sir." Dunford glared out the window as if the foul weather was a personal insult to him. "Consider it your penance for your failure. And mark me—if Venables doesn't swing, I'll have words with the constabulary. I'm quite sure they'll listen to me if I tell them who really killed the Billings women."

It was as he expected. "May I say one last thing, my lord?" he said, already moving forward.

Dunford turned around. "What—"

He stopped in mid-sentence, trying to take in a breath and failing. Only then did he look down at the knife sticking out of his chest. A thick crimson stain began to spread, staining the white linen of his shirt. His mouth opened, but nothing came out.

And then something did come out of the marquis's mouth, yet more crimson to join the spreading stain on his shirtfront. He thumped to his knees, his hands fluttering around the reddened hilt jutting out of his chest, then fell over, eyes bulging as he stared at his attacker.

But not dead. At least, not yet.

The killer stood over him, a small smile on his face. "You do have a son, sir. And he will make sure that Philip inherits nothing."

Dropping into a squat, he wrenched his knife free, cleaning it on Dunford's coat sleeve, then took a moment to study his father's body. After all, he would only have one chance to select an appropriate souvenir. But what should it be?

Of course. He sliced open fabric, exposing the desired flesh, and began to cut.

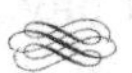

Eddy was unsurprised to find the Middleton carriage with its family crest on the doors to be a far more comfortable vehicle than the local hansom cabs. After a short journey through the city center, the carriage rolled to a stop in front of a stately townhouse. Built in the Palladium style, the lavish structure featured honey-colored stone and a graceful semicircular entranceway.

He waited until the footman opened the carriage door and helped out Lady Georgiana. Sir Richard exited after her, grumbling about the roughness of the carriage ride and the upcoming meal. "Here's hoping Dunford will settle on good English fare this time. Last time, he served some confounded Oriental slop, God help us."

Lady Georgiana smiled. "It wasn't that bad, Uncle," she said, "and eating with those sticks was rather interesting."

"Humbug," Sir Richard replied. "Nothing wrong with a good fork and knife, thank you very much."

Masking a smile at the family banter, Eddy got out and

followed the pair to the door, where they were greeted by a butler who waved for a waiting maid to take their coats and hats. "Sir Richard, Lady Georgiana, Mr. Poe," the butler said unctuously, ushering them into the foyer, "his lordship is unavoidably detained, but should be with you shortly. May I offer you a refreshment while you are waiting?"

A shrill scream echoed through the house, startling them all. "What the devil was that?" Sir Richard demanded.

The butler frowned. "I don't know, sir—"

Another maid came running into the foyer, eyes wide with fright. "Mr. Waverly, it's blood!" she gasped. "Coming from under the door!"

With an embarrassed glance at the newcomers, the butler grabbed the maid by an arm. "Get ahold of yourself, girl!" he ordered. "What blood and what door?"

"From his lordship's study!"

Eddy's heart went cold. *No, not yet, damn it all.* "Was his lordship in his study?" he demanded.

Waverly was taken aback by the question. "I believe he was, sir, but—"

"Then take us there, for God's sake!" Sir Richard barked.

Flustered, the butler nodded and led the nobleman from the room. Moving to follow, Eddy glanced at Lady Georgiana, who had gone pale at the mention of blood. "I think you should stay here, my lady. This may be unpleasant."

Grimacing, she nodded. "Perhaps that's best. But please send for me if Uncle Richard needs anything."

"I will." He hurried after the two men, following them through a paneled hallway. Two footmen joined the party as they arrived at a doorway. Just as the maid had described, a stream of blood was seeping underneath the door.

Sir Richard tried the handle. "Locked, blast it. Do you have a key?"

The butler shook his head. "But the housekeeper—"

"No time. We need to break down that door now."

Waverly gestured to the taller of the footmen. "Break it down, Danvers."

"Yes, Mr. Waverly." The husky young man stepped over the blood and rammed his shoulder against the door, then again. On the third try, the lock splintered away from the frame and the door swung open to reveal a lavishly appointed private office.

Sir Richard swore sulphurously. Sprawled in front of a large oak desk was Dunford, dead eyes staring at the ceiling. A spreading splotch of blood stained his shirtfront and waistcoat. The bulk of the crimson pool, however, streamed from the man's trouser fly, which was encrusted with gore.

Behind Eddy, one of the footmen retched at the sight, and Waverly's face had gone white with shock. "Oh, my God," he whispered. "Is ... is he—"

"Dead," Eddy said. He was becoming inured to the sight of yet another dead body. "No one could survive that amount of blood loss. Someone must call for the police."

"Y-yes, of course." Waverly turned and ran down the hallway, both footmen in tow.

Moving carefully so as not to step in the spattered blood, Eddy entered the room. "What are you doing, sir?" Sir Richard hissed in horror.

"Examining the scene before Furnow and his colleagues arrive and trample everything into chaos," Eddy replied through clenched jaws. With care, he knelt next to the marquis, studying the narrow slit in the center of the damp red stain on Dunford's shirt. "It appears that he was stabbed in the heart. Seeing as the blood is still wet in the center, the murder took place very recently, within the last half hour." Reluctantly, he turned his attention to the open fly, and the gaping wound beneath. "God almighty," he blurted, turning away and pressing his fist to his mouth.

"What is it?" Sir Richard asked, in a small, hollow voice.

It took a moment before he could bring himself to speak. "The marquis has been gelded." *And from the spread of the blood, the nobleman's heart had still been beating when his testicles were removed.*

Eager to get away from the mutilated body, he stood up and paced a circuit of the room. There were no obvious signs of struggle; the drapes were in place, all vases and other breakable decorative elements were still intact, and there were no scuffed tracks in the carpet indicating that the marquis's body had been moved after his death and impromptu castration. Surely a healthy, robust man such as Dunford would fight his attacker?

A sudden memory of his in-laws flashed through his mind. The marquis would fight—unless it was a surprise strike, by someone who was able to get close enough to the nobleman without arousing his suspicions. "Who did Dunford trust enough to allow near his person?"

Sir Richard, still stunned by the marquis's condition, shook his head. "His valet, of course. And Philip, I suppose—" He broke off, his cheeks mottling with red. "Oh dear God, you can't suspect Philip did this?"

"At the moment, the only men I'm sure didn't commit this crime are ourselves." Eddy crossed to the nobleman's desk, where an elegant leather blotter held an ink pot, quill pen, and a letter opener constructed to look like an Oriental sword. Pulse quickening, he picked up the opener and studied its gilded blade.

Sir Richard joined him. "Is that what killed him?"

He gingerly sniffed the blade, then shook his head. "I doubt it.

There are no traces of blood, skin or fabric, and while the canted tip might be sharp enough to pierce human skin and bone, the edge is far too dull for the butchery that was performed upon the marquis."

Replacing the opener, he turned his attention to the desktop's other contents. A few papers that appeared to be personal correspondence were neatly stacked on one side. On the other, an envelope addressed to the dean of Christ Church lay empty, waiting for its letter.

He went through the letters quickly, but none of them were addressed to Dean Gaisford. Before he could check the desk drawer, he heard a now-familiar voice say, "Sir Richard, I—*you*!"

Eddy turned and gave Furnow a bleak smile. "We must stop meeting like this, Constable. People will talk."

Furnow grimaced at Dunford's body. "God's blood," he muttered, before collecting himself. "Step away from the desk, Mr. Poe. It may contain evidence."

Raising his hands, Eddy did as he was bid. "In answer to your inevitable question, I was with Lady Georgiana and her companion from ten o'clock this morning to eleven thirty, at which point we joined Sir Richard and rode here in his coach in order to have luncheon with the marquis. I suspect if you ask the household staff, they will confirm that his lordship was still alive at the time I met up with the ladies. Ergo, I could not have killed Lord Dunford."

That earned him a glare. "You can be sure that I'll check with the staff," Furnow promised. "Right now, however, I must insist that both of you gentlemen clear out of this office until it can be searched."

"Of course." Careful not to step in the pool of blood, he vacated the room with Sir Richard. "Would you like to know what I noticed about the scene, constable?"

"Not particularly, no," Furnow snapped. "What I *would* like is for you and Sir Richard to wait in the library until we can ques—" He paused, noticing Sir Richard's sudden glower. "Until we can confirm details of your arrival," he amended. "Mr. Waverly will show you the way."

The butler, who had arrived with Furnow, nodded. "I took the liberty of showing Lady Georgiana to the library. If you two gentlemen will follow me?" he said anxiously.

Eddy followed Waverly and Sir Richard, breathing out through his nose to clear the stink of blood and torn flesh. *How refreshing it is to have an ironclad alibi.*

CHAPTER TWENTY-SIX

Waverly led them to a beautifully appointed library, lined floor to ceiling with polished walnut bookcases. Eddy tried not to stare at what had to be a small fortune in books, squelching a flash of writerly envy. *To be able to spend even one day browsing the luxury of these shelves...*

Lady Georgiana was seated in a comfortable wing chair but jumped to her feet as they entered. "Uncle," she said, rushing to Sir Richard and taking his hands. "The maid said that his lordship is dead."

Sir Richard was unable to meet her eyes as he nodded. "Murdered," he said heavily. "And in a most barbaric fashion."

"I think it's best that your uncle sit down for a spell," Eddy said, guiding the older man to the wing chair's mate before turning back to Waverly. "Could you fetch a brandy for Sir Richard, and some tea for Lady Georgiana and myself?"

Shock at his employer's death had turned the butler obsequious. "Certainly, sir."

With Sir Richard settled and Lady Georgiana fussing over him, Eddy paced along the bookshelves, mentally reviewing the bloody scene they'd witnessed. Dunford's murder was undoubtedly committed by the same madman who had killed the Billings women. *But to what purpose? Had the marquis threatened the murderer in some fashion over the previous deaths?*

A threat to call the constabulary would certainly explain the need to kill Dunford. *But if so, why mutilate the man, and in such a hideous fashion?*

An idea came to him as he passed a carved table that held some loose sheets of paper and a chased silver pencil box. Selecting a sharpened pencil and paper, he sat down and began to work out the deaths as if plotting a story. There was Jane Billings, pregnant by a peer's heir, who had the babe in her belly cut out. Elizabeth Billings had her tongue cut out; a most permanent way of silencing a threat. And the marquis had been gelded, losing what he most valued as a man.

If I was writing this as one of Dupin's cases, the killer would be someone who knew about Jane's child, was threatened by Elizabeth's tattling tongue, and unmanned somehow by Dunford.

He tried to juggle the facts of the situation, looking for links. There was only one person he could think of who fit each role—Philip Stiles. But while the undergraduate was undoubtedly weak, selfish, and spoilt, he still didn't fit the role of amoral butcher who had left a trail of gore and mutilated bodies behind him.

Still musing, Eddy glanced at the other sheets of paper. The top sheet in the pile had been blank; underneath it was another sheet that bore a carefully written cryptogram. The marquis's last challenge, obviously meant to be presented after luncheon.

Pulling up the sheet, he studied the scrambled letters, searching for the underlying pattern. *N is the most commonly used letter, which means it replaces an E, yes, and the first word, three letters—was? The? Ah, no—who. Which means that the Ts are O's, and that two-letter word must be 'to'.*

He jotted each correctly identified letter on the side, along with its replacement. Within a few minutes he'd cracked the code, reading the resulting message.

"You look perplexed, Mr. Poe."

He glanced up at Lady Georgiana, who now stood next to the table. "I believe this was the cryptogram the marquis planned to try me with," he explained. "I thought I would decipher it while we were waiting."

"What is it?"

He laughed once, humorlessly. "Quite appropriately, he chose a poem, but I don't recognize it, nor is the style familiar enough for me to ferret out its author."

The young woman frowned in thought. "The marquis was fond of some rather obscure writers and poets. May I?"

He handed her the paper. "Who sacrificed quiet to hatred, with a warrior heart," she murmured.

who did not stop at quarrels, struggles and slaughters,
is lying here in the coffin for all people to rejoice,
thy supreme pontiff Alexander, oh, capital Rome.
Thou, prelates of Erebus and Heaven, close thy doors
and prohibit the Soul from entering thy sites.
He would disrupt the peace of Styx and disturb Avernus,
and vanquish the Saints, if he enters the sphere of stars.

She frowned. "It doesn't sound very favorable for this pope, does it?"

"More of a warning to heaven, I suspect," Eddy commented. "I wasn't aware the marquis was an aficionado of the Romish faith."

"He wasn't," Sir Richard said from behind them. "But he did rather like Alexander."

They turned to the nobleman. "He'd recited that one to me before, you see," Sir Richard explained. "It was written by some Bohemian humanist, God only knows how his name is pronounced. The pope he's referencing is Alexander VI, one of the craftiest men ever to grace the Throne of St. Peter. Also the father of Caesare and Lucretia Borgia."

"He was the Pope *and* a father?" Lady Georgiana asked, sounding scandalized. "But I thought that Catholic priests were forbidden to marry."

Sir Richard spread his hands. "Oh, they are, my dear, but that didn't bother Alexander all that much at the time. He still took good care of his children, illegitimate or not."

Something glimmered at the back of Eddy's mind, a memory of his childhood under the rigid hand of John Allen. Caesare Borgia; an illegitimate child, unable to publicly claim a father but cared for nonetheless. The empty envelope, addressed to the dean of Christ Church. A powerful man, unmanned by his murderer. The connection was somewhere in there, he could feel it.

He wanted to growl in frustration when Furnow and two other constables entered the library. Between the two was a pale and breathless Dodgson. "We found Mr. Dodgson on the doorstep, demanding entrance and asking after you, Mr. Poe," Furnow said, pushing the undergraduate forward. "Sir Richard, have you or your niece seen Philip Stiles today?"

The older man shook his head. "No,"

"And you, Mr. Poe?"

The thought that the constabulary could no longer ignore Stiles as a suspect didn't cheer him. "I haven't seen him since you escorted me from Sir Richard's home, constable. But if you're presuming him to be his uncle's murderer, I fear that you're barking up the wrong tree."

"Thank you for that advice, Mr. Poe," Furnow said acidly. "As it stands, we've sent to London for a police detective from Scotland Yard to come here and take over the investigation. I'm supposed to make sure that all persons of interest remain in Oxford until further notice."

"Does that still include myself?"

The look the constable gave him was positively jaundiced. "The first murder took place across from your hotel room. You visited the second victim hours before her death, and I find you arrived for luncheon at the third victim's home. All in all, I would say that makes you a person of interest, if only because you seem to keep crossing paths with the murderer," Furnow said. "If we're very lucky, the blackguard might try to take a souvenir from you next."

A shiver ran down his spine. "You call that lucky?"

"As it seems to be our best chance of catching him, yes."

A constable entered at a trot, crossing to Furnow and whispering in his ear. He smiled grimly and nodded. "It seems to be your lucky day, Mr. Poe. Philip Stiles has been sighted in Jericho. With any luck, we should have him in custody within the hour. As that is the case, I would request that you go back to your hotel and stay there until we have him. And if I see either of you," his glare was turned on Dodgson, "within shouting distance of this investigation one more time, I'll have the both of you down to gaol, d'ye hear?"

Dodgson went milky white, but Eddy bristled at the threat. "On what charge?"

"Aggravating a sworn officer of the law," Furnow snapped back. "Now, with your kind permission, we have a murderer to catch. Sir Richard, Lady Georgiana." After a short bow to them and a final glare at Eddy, he left, the other constable in tow.

"Well, he's quite charming," Lady Georgiana murmured.

Dodgson sagged into a nearby chair. "I-is it true?" he stuttered. "Is the m-m-marquis d-dead?"

"Murdered, more accurately." Eddy headed to a side table

where someone had laid out both a tea service and a brandy decanter with matching glasses. Giving the decanter a longing look, he poured himself a cup of tea instead. "And yonder shining lights of the Oxford constabulary appear to have their sights set on young Stiles for the crime."

"S-stiles?" Dodgson spluttered. "That's prep-posterous."

"Our thoughts as well," Eddy said, gesturing with the teacup to Sir Richard. "I can only hope your annoying classmate has rock-solid witnesses who can vouch for his whereabouts from this morning onward, otherwise I suspect it will go badly for him."

"While Philip is hardly my favorite person, I can hardly believe him capable of murder," Lady Georgiana said, bustling past Eddy to the side table. She poured a dram of brandy into a glass and brought it to Dodgson. "You look positively peaked. This will do you good," she announced.

Dodgson looked as if she'd presented him with a vial of poison. "Thank you, but it's n-not n-n-necessary—"

"Drink the thing, lad, before you fall over," Sir Richard ordered.

With a wince, the young man accepted the brandy and sipped it. "I r-rushed here because a note for you was delivered to the Mitre," he said to Eddy. "From your, um, recent correspondent?"

"Ah, yes," Eddy breathed, glancing at the nobles. Sir Richard was lost in contemplation, but Lady Georgiana seemed determined to shadow Dodgson. "My dear lady, might I ask for a moment of privacy with my young friend?"

Aquamarine eyes flashed in irritation, but she reluctantly nodded and joined her uncle on the other side of the library.

Eddy moved so that he stood next to Dodgson's chair, muffling their discussion. "How do you know the note was from the murderer?"

"The handwriting. It slanted to the left, indicating that the author was left-handed. At the park you pointed out that the murdered was also left-handed." Dodgson flushed. "And I, er, opened the note. Unfortunately, I was too late to deliver the message."

He wanted to curse. "Another cryptogram?"

"Yes, but this time the decoded message turned out to be Latin." Dodgson gave him a bleak look. "'Sic semper tyrannis.' Often mistranslated as 'death to tyrants,' it actually means—"

"'Thus always to tyrants,'" Eddy said. "The phrase is part of Virginia's Great Seal, so I'm familiar with it."

"Oh, good," Dodgson said. "But it does cast even more questions on the identity of the murderer. If the message referred to Lord Dunford, who would think him a tyrant?"

"Most people who met him, I would think."

"Blakeney certainly did," Dodgson said. "Apparently he's been pulled out of the term along with Stiles. Dunford's been paying for his tuition, as it turns out, and now he's being punished for not keeping Stiles on the straight and narrow. And he all but told me that Stiles had done the murders."

Eddy stiffened as the younger man's words caused a bright tintinnabulation of bells to ring out in his mind. Pieces began to fall into place:

The diligence due to a bastard child.

The killer would be someone who knew about Jane's child, was threatened by Elizabeth's tattling tongue, and unmanned somehow by Dunford.

"He's being punished for not keeping Stiles on the straight and narrow."

With a final burst of heavenly music, the diverse pieces of the puzzle turned into one cohesive, damning picture. *Lord, it's so clear now. Dunford had a useless drunkard for an heir, didn't he? And a jealous bastard who was forced to watch as his unworthy but legitimate relative gains all that should have been his.*

Dodgson peered at him. "Are you all right, Mr. Poe?"

Before he could explain, there was a commotion in the hallway and Walton burst into the library. "What happened to his lordship?" the valet demanded, eyes wild. "They won't let me near his office."

Mind still blazing, Eddy studied Walton. Breathless, hair whipped by the wind, as if he'd rushed back to Dunford's manor for some reason. *On a task, or with news?* "I'm afraid his lordship is dead."

A flash of genuine grief surged across the burly valet's face. "No—he was healthy as a horse. He can't be dead."

"I'm af-fraid your employer didn't die of natural causes," Dodgson added, rising from his seat. "He was murdered."

Walton's grief was replaced with shock. "What? How?"

Glancing at Lady Georgiana, Eddy grabbed the valet's arm and towed him to a corner of the library, with Dodgson following. "His lordship was stabbed through the heart, then gelded."

The valet went white. "Gelded," he breathed. "Sweet Jesus."

"The constables w-ere already here," Dodgson added. "They're currently searching for his lordship's nephew to question him about his whereabouts."

Walton barked out a harsh laugh. "Philip? That useless twat? He could barely cut his own meat, much less—" He stopped, mouth working with some sort of realization, then spun on his heel and surged out of the library.

"Wait, the constables—" Dodgson said, moving to go after him.

Eddy put a hand on the undergraduate's arm. "No," he said quietly. "Give him a few moments of a head start."

"But h-he's going after Stiles—"

"Yes, I know. Now we follow him."

CHAPTER TWENTY-SEVEN

Charles and Poe grabbed their coats and hats from the shaken maid at the front door, setting out after the valet. The streetlamps had already been lit against the threat of rain, and the heavy clouds in the late afternoon sky promised a deluge at any moment.

"Mr. Poe, w-what are we doing?" Charles asked, dodging the other people on the street as he struggled into his coat.

"Locating the missing piece of the puzzle," Poe said, grey eyes gleaming with the light of impending battle. "We've been assuming all along that Jane was murdered in order to stop young Stiles from marrying her, and Mrs. Billings was murdered in order to cover up Stiles's involvement in her daughter's disgrace." He hefted his walking stick, swinging it like a mace "But the murder of the marquis makes all of that pointless—he wanted Stiles as his heir, no matter what, and was willing to withdraw him from Oxford in order to let the gossip to die down. So, let us assume that Stiles had nothing to do with any of the murders. Instead, what if he was the *target* of these heinous crimes? What if these murders were undertaken in order to disgrace Philip Stiles and prevent him from assuming the title of Marquis of Wells upon Robert Dunford's death?"

Charles stumbled slightly at the astounding theory, jogging a bit to catch up with the shorter man's determined stride. "You s-seriously believe that three people were murdered to s-stop Stiles from acquiring a title?"

"Oh, no. Three people were murdered so that Stiles would be executed for their deaths." Poe bared his teeth in a rictus grin. "Use your logic, Dodgson. The murder of the two women could be posited as an attempt to protect Stiles, but Dunford's demise, while instantaneously raising your young friend to the nobility, also attracts the attention of your constabulary and casts the shadow of the gibbet across him."

Ahead of them, Walton slowed, flicking a glance over his shoulder. The writer ducked behind a tree, dragging Charles with him. "This would be easier if the crowds were thicker," he muttered.

"With the impending storm, I'm surprised this many people are on the streets as it is," Charles said as Poe pulled him back onto the pavement. "H-how did you work all this out?"

"Elementary, my dear Dodgson. The murderer overplayed his hand with his methods." Ahead of them, Walton turned down a narrow street, and they followed. The buildings began to change character, becoming more run-down and weathered. "Jane's death, one could possibly attribute to a maddened lover. But the deaths of her mother and the marquis, and in such a barbaric fashion? Those murders smack of an individual who has the sangfroid to present a calm, smiling face to the public while a demon rages in his breast." He held a hand, indicating that they should slow now. "The murderer knew both families, and their secrets, and the layout of the marquis's home. He had an agenda of his own and was ready to not only kill but mutilate in order to achieve it."

Charles was quiet as he paced at the smaller man's side, ready to leap into a doorway at any moment. "You think it was Walton?"

Poe shook his head. "I admit, Walton recently joined my list of suspects, but the look on his face when he learned of the marquis's death was genuine shock. Also, he's right-handed—the man who cut out Mrs. Billings' tongue is left-handed. No, the marquis himself left us a final clue of his murderer's identity."

"How?"

Poe quickly explained the encrypted poem he'd found in the library. "Dunford admired a pope who took care of his illegitimate children, and at Sir Richard's soirée he commented to me about the diligence due to a bastard child. Stiles was his heir because he had no legitimate sons, but that doesn't mean the man had no offspring whatsoever."

They stopped at the edge of a dingy old building. Cautiously, they peered around the corner, just in time to see Walton disappear into a nondescript pub building halfway down the street. Above the door, a weatherworn sign featured a badly painted man waving from a barge.

Poe let out a satisfied humph. "You're the native, Dodgson. What's that place?"

Charles frowned at the building. "That's the Waterman's Arms. Some of the House men like to frequent it when they're in a mood to kick over the traces."

"Men such as Stiles?"

"Yes. I've never been there myself, but I've heard some stories about what goes on in the rented rooms over the pub. With women of, erm, questionable character."

"You mean whores?"

Charles felt his face heat. "Must you use such language?"

"Language is a writer's environment, Dodgson. If you do intend to become one, you need to expand your horizons. More importantly, we need to go in that pub. Now, will you follow me or not?"

He swallowed hard but nodded. "In the interest of expanding my horizons," he muttered, following Poe inside.

They were immediately met by the hazed aroma of spilled beer, smoke and unwashed bodies. An array of faces, all of them unfriendly, turned to watch them.

Ignoring the manic jabbering of his imp, Eddy went to the bar, where a thin man with a badly pockmarked face lethargically wiped glasses with a stained rag. "The man who just came in here—decent coat, looks like a bulldog. Where did he go?"

The barman shrugged. "Didn't see no man like that, gents."

Scowling, Eddy dug a shilling out of his pocket and tossed it on the bar. "The man?"

The coin disappeared and the man nodded towards a flight of rickety stairs in the back. "S'upstairs. Second door on yer right."

Gesturing for Dodgson to follow, Eddy headed up to the next floor. It was dark and stuffy, and boasted a collection of battered doors. He noted that the smell here changed to dust, mold and the sharper scent of spent passions.

They approached the indicated door, which was slightly ajar. A rustling sound, interspersed with low cursing, came from inside.

Steeling himself, he pushed the door open. "Stiles has bolted, hasn't he?"

Walton stood up from the bed, wrinkled bedclothes in one hand. He threw them back onto the stained mattress. "What are you doing here?" he growled.

"We followed you. It seemed logical that you'd head for Stiles's bolthole the moment you found out about the murder."

Walton gave them a long, cold look, then nodded. "He was here," the valet said, nodding at the bedside table where a tray of picked-over food sat. "Meat's still warm. Idiot boy always came here to get away from things. I thought he'd still be here, dammit."

"Unless someone convinced him that it wasn't safe," Eddy said, studying the room. Apart from the bed, a set of rickety chairs and a badly battered chest of drawers, the place was empty. He sniffed the air experimentally. Under the expected scents of dust, unwashed linen and ancient alcohol was something faint but familiar, almost metallic.

He tried to find the source of the odor. "Does anyone else know about this bolthole?"

"His lordship," Walton said. "And young Blakeney, I suppose. He's Mr. Philip's shadow, after all."

"Ah." Eddy dropped to his hands and knees next to the bed. The scent was stronger here. He peered into the darkness underneath the thin mattress and spotted a carved wooden box pushed to the back.

He pulled out the box, running one fingertip across the top. Unlike everything else in the room, there was no dust on it. "Do you recognize this, Walton?"

The valet frowned. "That's Mr. Philip's humidor. Dunno why it's here."

"An excellent question. Why keep a humidor full of expensive cigars in a place like this? Unless it holds something other than cigars." Steeling himself, he lifted the lid. "Oh, God."

Walton and Dodgson leaned in for a closer look. The undergraduate went white and spun away to gag in the corner. "Lord save us," Walton breathed, crossing himself.

Inside the humidor was a thick layer of rock salt. The white crystals clung to three pieces of flesh arranged in a gory tableau;

a tiny, curled thing that looked like an uncooked prawn, a tongue sliced off at the root, and two blood-soaked fleshy orbs.

"As I suspected, he likes to keep souvenirs," Eddy said grimly.

The valet shook his head, holding up a shaking hand to block the sight of the gory scraps of flesh. "I can't believe it," he muttered. "Not Mr. Philip. He's too weak to tie his own boots. He couldn't do this."

"He didn't." Eddy shut the humidor lid and put it on the bed's shabby mattress. "This was left here to make us think that he did."

A shaken Dodgson rejoined them, wiping at his mouth with the back of his hand. "T-that w-w-was h-h-horrible."

"Yes, it was," Eddy agreed, keeping his attention on the valet. "Three most malicious murders, performed by someone who has a personal grudge against young Stiles. Someone who, I suspect, has had to stand by for years and watch a foolish, foppish bully be given everything that should have been his, except for an accident of birth."

As he'd hoped, Walton twitched at his words, flushing a dull red. "That little bastard," the valet breathed.

"A bastard, indeed," Eddy agreed. "A final question, Dodgson. Stiles's pathetic companion, Blakeney—he wouldn't be left-handed by any chance, would he?"

"Well, yes, but—" The undergraduate's face was a study in dawning horror as he worked his way down the chain of evidence, twitching at the final link. "That's why the handwriting looked familiar. Oh, dear Lord."

"I assure you, the Almighty had nothing to do with this." Eddy turned back to the valet. "Mr. Walton, what do you know of Mr. Blakeney's parentage?"

The valet had been pacing the length of the room like a caged animal. Now he turned back, his face drawn and tight. "What the bloody hell does that have to do with anything?"

"Everything, I suspect. His parentage, Mr. Walton. Now."

Stiles stumbled along the tow path, barely pausing long enough to take a swig from the brandy bottle in his hand. "All that blood," he mumbled, mouth working loosely around the brandy. "All that blood."

"A terrible thing," Blakeney agreed, one hand gripped around his companion's arm in order to keep him upright. As he'd hoped, Stiles had come to the townhouse, taken one look at his handwork, and fled for his bolthole. After that, it was simply a matter of joining him.

Overhead, the heavens were already coursing down rain, driving people to seek what shelter they could. Even with the rapidly emptying streets, he'd taken pains to keep them to the narrow road leading from the Waterman's Arms to the towpath by the Isis. "And you argued with your uncle in front of witnesses at last night's party, even threatening retribution. The police are mostly likely after you this moment."

Stiles almost fell as his head whipped around, goggling fearfully behind them. Blakeney, half-turned by the violent movement, saw a flash of brown. He stared through the rain at the surrounding buildings, deciding finally that it was a shadow.

He tightened his grip, now, half-dragging the drunken undergraduate to the tow path. Once there, a natural dip in the ground led to a small copse in the surrounding foliage. He urged Stiles there, lowering him onto a fallen log.

Once released, Stiles curled over his knees, crying drunkenly into the dirt. "I didn't do it," he blubbered. "I swear, I didn't do it."

Blakeney waited, disgusted at the wretch huddled into a ball before him. "Of course you didn't," he said. "The very thought is utterly ridiculous." He sank into a crouch, wanting to look into Stiles's eyes when he sank his coup de grace. "I did it."

Stiles's head came up, and he blinked blearily. "W-what?"

"I did it. I killed your uncle, my dear cousin."

Stiles scrubbed the back of one hand across his mouth, clearly trying to focus on the one fact he could grasp at the moment. "Cousin? We're not related."

"Oh, yes we are, Philip. We're cousins," Blakeney said. "His lordship was my dear father, although he would never admit to impregnating my mother and marrying her off to one of the men in his regiment. While John Blakeney was perfectly happy to take his lordship's money, not to mention his lordship's castoffs, it turns out that he wasn't very happy about raising his lordship's bastard as his own." What a relief it was to drop the servile, fawning mask, revealing the real Martin Blakeney for the first time in their association. "Would you like to hear about my childhood, Philip? Would you like to hear about the beatings, and the times I went without food for days on end? Or how my so-called father cured me of thumb-sucking with a hot poker? Or what he did when I came of age and discovered the joys of Onanism? I promise you, they make Poe's tales seem like pleasant lullabies."

Stiles stared at him, his drunkenness meshed now with a growing horror. "You killed Jane."

"Yes, I did. I'm a monster, you see." He stood, pulling a well-used knife from his frock coat and looking at it contemplatively. "But I'm a methodical monster. The plan was to have you caught by the constabulary, tried and hanged for all three murders. But you're just like our dear departed relative, aren't you? You never could stand and face a situation like a man."

The cold rain was starting to chill his hands, making him look forward to the hot gush of Stiles's blood. "Which makes this even more believable, come to think of it. You drink yourself into a stupor, stagger off to a deserted place along the river, and kill yourself out of guilt over your heinous crimes. His lordship once told me a gruesome tale about the Japanese and how they slit their bellies open to appease their superiors if they fail in a task. That would be quite appropriate for you, don't you agree?"

Staring at the knife, Stiles struggled to his knees, dropping the brandy bottle to the ground as he clasped his hands in prayer. "Oh, God, please no," he babbled. "Please, no, Martin, don't kill me, please God—"

"Oh, Philip. Don't you understand yet?" Blakeney said gently, lifting the knife. "There is no God. There's only me."

He heard a gasp. Glancing behind him, he saw Maggie Billings staring at him horrorstruck, before she spun and ran back along the path.

With the intermittent cunning of drunks, Stiles seized the opportunity and scrabbled into the foliage, bellowing for help as he stampeded back towards South Street. Snarling, Blakeney started after him, then paused. The constabulary was undoubtedly in search of Stiles by now, and even if he threw themselves into their arms and babbled what he'd been told, nobody in their right mind would believe him. All the evidence pointed at Philip Stiles and no other—he'd made sure of that.

Which meant he had to stop the girl. Shoving the knife back into his coat, Blakeney set off after his new quarry. *Oh, what should I cut from you, you little bitch....*

CHAPTER TWENTY-EIGHT

"His Lordship never told me details," Walton said reluctantly. "But I knew Blakeney was his get. I figured his lordship had a bit of fun and married the girl off when she'd caught. But then her ladyship died in childbirth, and Philip had to be made the heir." The valet shook his head heavily. "A right sot, that one, and his lordship knew it. Someone had to keep an eye on him, so his lordship brought Blakeney up from Essex to be Philip's keeper. They've been like that ever since."

"So Dunford forced his illegitimate son to act as companion to his heir," Eddy observed. "That must have rankled young Blakeney."

"It did, but he hid it well. I never liked him," Walton admitted. "There was something wrong in his eyes. Reminded me of a mad dog I had to put down once."

"And now he's out there, somewhere, and so is S-stiles," Dodgson said. "Poe, we must go to the constables now."

"I agree." He glanced in distaste at the humidor and its gory contents. "And then—"

The door burst open and a sodden, filthy Stiles lurched in. "Oh, God, he killed them," the drunken young man sobbed. "He killed all of them!"

Walton was up like a shot, grabbing Stiles and easing him into his own chair. The young man's head bobbled as he stared at the valet, then at Eddy and Dodgson. “Blakeney killed Jane,” he sobbed again, hiccuping at the end. “He killed them all. He was going to kill me.”

“What happened?” Eddy demanded. But Stiles kept babbling about blood and death until Walton pulled out a half-full bottle of wine from a wardrobe and allowed the nobleman a single drink.

In fits and starts, Stiles explained how Blakeney had come to the Watermen’s Arms to tell him about his uncle’s murder, and how the constabulary now believed he’d killed both Jane and Mrs. Billings as well as Lord Dunford. “He said he’d get me away, out of Oxford,” the young man said, compulsively wiping the back of his hand across his lips. Eddy recognized the gesture and waved for Walton to give Stiles another drink.

He gulped the dregs gratefully. “He gave me some brandy—for courage, he said—and we started walking down near the river. He said we’d make for the train station, and that I should head back to Redhull where I’d be safe. And then I fell, and he pulled out this knife, this horrible knife—” The undergraduate shook his head like a drenched cur. “I swear, I never hurt Jane or her mother. And my uncle, I didn’t, I couldn’t. I swear, Maggie can vouch for me—”

“Maggie?” Dodgson leaned forward. “How is she involved in this?”

Stiles shrank into his coat collar at the focused stare from his fellow student. “I saw her on St. Alban’s this morning,” he confessed. “I told her I was Jane’s friend. She started crying. I didn’t know what to do, so I took her to the tuck shop and bought her some sweets. We talked about … Jane.” He dropped his head into his hands, scrubbing at his face. “What else could I do? I couldn’t bring Jane back, and I couldn’t do anything about her mother. So I left. Then she saw Blakeney and me on the towpath."

Eddy boggled at the thought of a twelve-year-old's testimony being the only thing that could keep Philip Stiles off the gibbet. "Where is she now?"

"She ... oh, Lord." Stiles shuddered. "She ran, and then I did. I think Blakeney chased her."

"You f-filthy coward!" Dodgson spat. "You left a ch-child out there to be hunted by that madman?"

"Dodgson, not now," Eddy hissed. "Stiles, where did you see them last?"

Stiles shook his head, eyes muddled with exhaustion. Without a word, Walton came forward and slapped him across the face, the report sharp in the small room. "Answer the man," he ordered.

The undergraduate clutched his cheek, but some of the dreamy terror leached from his eyes. "Downstream of South Street," he said, giving Walton a childish glare.

Eddy wished he knew Oxford better. A child, all alone on a towpath, and hunted by a monster. "Do you know where that is?" he asked Dodgson.

"I do," the young man said grimly.

"All right, then. You," he pointed to Walton, "drum up the constabulary and tell them what happened, then tell them to start looking for Blakeney. And for the love of all that's holy, give them what's in that humidor. If you try and get rid of it, you may well sentence your new employer to death."

The valet nodded jerkily. "Where are you two going?"

Overhead, a peal of thunder rolled through the stormy Oxford skies. "To find Maggie," Eddy said. "Before Blakeney finds her first."

Gouts of rain slashed down from the rapidly darkening sky, drenching the towpath and turning it into a chain of muddy puddles. Maggie splashed through them, heart thrumming in her chest as she searched for a way off the towpath. There was nothing but foliage, not even a light or the back of one of the little terrace houses that populated the area. Heavy bolts of lightning cracked and flashed overhead, the rolling boom intermittently drowning out the pounding of her heart as well as the rush of the Isis, stirred by the drenching downpour.

What she couldn't hear was the man behind her. She glanced over her shoulder, terrified that he would be right there with that evil smile and the long knife.

He was gone. She skidded to a halt in the mud, gasping for breath as she stared around the dark trail. She knew the towpaths well, both from walking them and from rides on her Pa's barge, but with the rain coming down everything looked strange and frightening. The only thing she could spot was detritus from the storm littering the reeds along the riverbank: an old paddle, a small hogshead barrel. Her breathing began to calm as hope grew. Perhaps the bad man had gone after Mr. Philip, or she outran him, or—

"Got you," Blakeney hissed, lunging out from the foliage and grabbing her wrist. Maggie screamed shrilly, slipping in the mud. One leg came up as she fell, her sturdy boot catching his knee with a sharp crack.

He howled and let go of her wrist, clasping his agonized joint. "Bitch!"

Sobbing, she scrambled backwards in the clinging mud, gaining her feet. There was only one sanctuary now—the river.

Throwing herself into the reeds along the riverbank, she cried out at the chill water biting into her skin. She managed to wrap her arms around the small barrel and kick off frantically from the muddy bank. The river's flow caught her, tugging her along.

Now remember, Maggie, if you fall in, always try to float with the current, she heard her father say, a long-ago lesson when he'd taken her on his barge for the afternoon. *Kick off your boots if you can, otherwise they'll weigh you down like anchors.*

She frantically toed at her boot heels, but they were laced too tightly to slip off. She wrenched her neck around, the wood of the barrel scraping her cheek, to look back at the riverbank. A blaze of lightening flashed, and she saw Blakeney there.

Smiling and stalking her along the towpath.

Move away, Maggie, as far away as you can. This time, it sounded like Jane's voice.

She kicked harder, trying to keep her mouth and nose out of the cold water as she struggled with the weight of her sodden boots and the makeshift life preserver. The tug of the river's flow pulled her under a narrow stone bridge, towards a triangular spit of land in the middle of the water. Realizing where she was, she started kicking frantically for the spit. Ahead of her to the left, the Osney lock blocked off the river for barges headed to the Osney Mill, effectively trapping her with a madman on the shore. To the right was the lock's weir, a low head dam that emptied into what would now be a churning pool. In either direction, she was dead; reaching the spit was her only hope.

Whimpering with each breath, she thrashed through the water, rapidly growing exhausted from fighting the current and her own clothes while clinging to the barrel. The smell of cold water, fish and mud filled her nostrils, almost choking her.

Finally, she felt the tip of one toe brush the shallowing bottom of the river.

You're almost there, my sweet girl. Mamma sounded so proud of her. *Now reach for a branch—reach, Maggie, and pull, hard as you can!*

Letting go of the barrel, she struggled against the pull of the river until she could grab a willow bough flicking back and forth over the ruffled surface of the river. She pulled herself onto land, clawing up and away from the river.

Sinking onto the wet dirt, she rested her head on her arm and burst into tears. "Oh, I did it," she whispered, not even feeling the scalding tears trickling down her cheek. "Mama, Jane, I did it."

All she wanted to do was curl into a ball and wait for Pa to come find her. But the bad man was still out there.

Maggie. You have to run. Run as fast as you can, sweetheart.

"Yes, Mamma," she whispered. Forcing herself to her feet, she stumbled through the gorse and willows until she reached another path running along the spit's eastern shore. Ahead, linked by a bridge over the lock's weir, was the small island with the lock keeper's house. Once she reached that, she was safe.

As she stepped onto the weir bridge, something hard slammed against her neck, pressing into the tender flesh of her throat. Gagging, she was yanked backwards.

Into the grip of the bad man. "Caught you, pet," he hissed.

Eddy and Dodgson exited the Waterman's Arms into a monsoon. Crossing South Street, they ran down the bricked path that led to the river. The barges tied up to the wharf pulled at their cleats, pushed about by the storm-swollen water.

"Which way?" Eddy demanded over the rushing susurrus of the rain.

Dodgson's jaw muscles clenched, and he pointed to the right. "Downstream," he shouted back.

They hurried down the towpath, slipping and sliding in the ever-present mud. "Where does this lead?" Eddy shouted.

"Down to Osney Lock," Dodgson huffed back. "I think."

"You *think*?"

"This is my first term here, dash it all," Dodgson shouted back. "I c-cannot be expected to know the whole of the city yet!"

"Yes, well—" Eddy slid to a halt, grabbing for Dodgson's arm to stop him as well. Ahead of them was a wide bridge leading over the river. Both glanced around at the sodden foliage, looking for any sign of Blakeney or Maggie's passing. There was nothing.

"Where do we go?" Dodgson asked, wiping rain from his eyes.

Eddy glanced around, trying to think. If they were upstream from a lock, there was undoubtedly a lock keeper's house somewhere close by, something that the daughter of a bargeman would know. Surely she would try for that haven rather than hide among the bushes and trees?

"Forward," he said, stepping onto the bridge. The boards underfoot were slick from the rain, and he was grateful to make the other side.

They were now on a narrow wedge of land that split the river like an axe head. To their right were willow stands and reeds right down to the gushing river; on the left was the continuation of the towpath, beyond which he could make out another, narrower bridge and a house. In addition to the hiss of the rain, there was now also a low, rushing sound.

And at the end of the towpath, revealed by a bright flash of lighting—a shape. No, two shapes on the bridge, struggling in the rain.

"There!" Eddy said, breaking into a run. Dodgson followed him. Before they could reach Maggie and her assailant, the girl sagged in Blakeney's arms, supported only by the elegant walking stick jammed underneath her chin that was strangling her.

Spotting them, Blakeney yanked his stick away and grabbed her by the back of her dress, whirling her about and pushing her to side of the bridge, close to the source of the rushing noise. Eddy realized it must be the lock's weir. "No!" he shouted.

Baring his teeth in a snarl, Blakeney heaved Maggie over the bridge railing. With an inarticulate cry, Dodgson accelerated past both of them to the edge of the bridge, clambering over it and disappearing.

Now we're alone. "You may as well give up. We know everything," Eddy half-shouted, trying to catch his breath.

Blakeney grinned, smoothing back his drenched hair with one hand. "And what exactly do you know, Mr. Poe?" he called back.

"That you murdered Jane and Elizabeth Billings, as well as Lord Dunford, and tried to frame Philip Stiles for their deaths."

"Ah, yes." Blakeney shook his head in mock regret. "The deaths. They were necessary, you see. I would say unfortunately necessary, but then again I found nothing unfortunate about them. Quite the contrary, they were all absolutely enjoyable experiences."

"You're insane. You gelded your own father, man!"

"I did?" Blakeney asked mockingly. "He certainly never claimed paternity, I can assure you." He lifted his walking stick, grasping the silver head and drawing it up. A length of silvery steel followed. "And now, those who have insulted me are dead, and Dodo and the little brat are gone, which only leaves you in my way, Mr. Poe. If you don't struggle, I promise I'll make this quick and painless."

Eddy registered the insane glitter in the other man's eyes. *Surely Walton would have called out the constabulary by now.* All he had to do was stall this madman. "I can understand your rage with your father, but how did Jane Billings insult you?" he said, eyes locked on Blakeney's blade. "Or Elizabeth Billings, for that matter? What in God's sake could those women have said to you that made them deserve such deaths?"

"Isn't it obvious?" Blakeney called. "Jane, the little trollop, thought she could better herself and gain my inheritance by getting in pup by Stiles. Her slut of a mother thought that she could blackmail me into pressing a suit between Stiles and the youngest bitch of the family. I merely taught them both a lesson they richly deserved."

"And Maggie? What did she ever do to you? She's a child!"

The madman shook his drenched head again. "That's quite the rich statement, coming from a jumped-up colonial who married his thirteen-year-old cousin. Or are you upset because you had your own plans for little Maggie, hmm?"

Eddy clenched his teeth at the all-too-familiar slander. "I would never harm a child!"

"Oh, I beg to differ, sir," Blakeney goaded. "After all, you *are* a fan of green fruit, are you not? How your wife must have wept when you breached her on your wedding night. Did she beg you to leave her be? Cry for her mother?"

All thought of waiting for the constables fled, replaced by a surge of rage fueled by the tension and fear of the last few days. *I am Edgar Allan Poe, a gentleman of Virginia, and I will not be insulted with impunity.* "Mention my late wife once more, you bastard, and it will be the last thing you do with that foul tongue of yours."

The mad humor left Blakeney's expression, replaced by rage

at the hated word. "And pray tell," he demanded, waving his slender sword like a conductor's baton, "how do you intend to enforce this injunction?"

Gritting his teeth, Eddy took his Malacca walking stick in both hands and pulled on the handle. Two and a half feet of blued Toledo steel slid out of the wood, a wicked point at the tip. "Like this."

"I see. Well, then—*en garde!*" Blakeney leapt forward, blade thrusting for Eddy's throat.

CHAPTER TWENTY-NINE

Charles scrambled down the slick, muddy slope leading to the weir pond. With relief, he saw that Blakeney's aim had been off by a foot. Instead of plunging to her death in the churning waters, Maggie had landed on the muddy slope, rolling down to the reedy bank where she now lay sprawled on her back.

Grabbing at wet foliage for handholds, he landed with a thump at her side. Her eyes were closed, and her face was pale as new milk. Desperately, he started patting her cheeks. "Maggie," he begged. "Maggie, wake up, please!"

Her eyelashes fluttered almost imperceptibly.

As gently as possible, he brushed dark, wet hair back from her face. To his dismay, a large goose egg stood out on her temple, undoubtedly gained during her tumble down the hill. He tried to remember what the nurse did when one of his brothers or sisters had a similar injury. *Put a cold compress over the swelling, wrap her up warm, keep her—*

"Awake," he said out loud. "Maggie, you have to stay awake!"

A low, pained noise was her only response. He glanced around the weir stream. There was no easy access off the spit of land other than the way they came, and from the clash of metal it sounded as if Poe had his hands full with Blakeney up on the bridge. Across the stream was another small island and the misty outline of the lock keeper's house. He had to get Maggie there, where she would be safe.

Except that they couldn't use the bridge to reach it. For the first time in his life, Charles wished he knew how to curse effectively. Trying to cudgel his exhausted brain into rational thought, he stared under the bridge.

And saw it—the thick rope barrier strung across the weir. The river's level had risen enough to almost obscure it, but he could just make out the twisted line along the surface.

There was no other way across. They had to get to the lock keeper's house, and from the feel of her clothing Maggie was already soaked. "Sweetheart, we h-have to go in the water, just for a little bit."

"Nooo," she whimpered, trying to curl into a ball.

"Yes, s-sweetheart. Please, b-be a good girl and h-help me."

Reluctantly, she rolled up into a sitting position. Grimacing, he got both of them on their feet, wrapping his arm around her thin waist and guiding her to the base of the bridge. From here, he could see the massive eyebolt screwed into the stone base and the rope barrier threaded through it.

Now they just had to reach it. "All right, then. H-hold on to me, and we'll b-be on the other side before you know it," he said, wishing that he felt as confident as he sounded.

With a little jump, they half-slid, half-plunged into the churning water. The chill hit his already-soaked body like a blow, and he gasped in pain. Maggie moaned and tried to squirm out of his grasp, but he held her fast, lunging against the river's flow as he reached for the rope.

His fingers skittered along the twisted hemp, lost their grip, then regained it. With a grunt, he pulled the two of them fully into the river now, hauling himself up so that the rope barrier settled under his left arm.

Clutching Maggie in his right arm, he slowly inched along the rope, kicking with his legs as necessary to resist the drag of the river pulling them towards the weir. The coldness of the water sapped his strength as surely as the efforts of the unusual exercise; he blinked rainwater out of his eyes, discouraged to see the bank of the other island still a good fifteen feet away.

Dear Lord, hear your servant in his hour of need, he began to pray, pulling them along inch by torturous inch. *Give me the strength to save us, not for myself, but for Maggie's sake. Please help me save her, if it be your will. Our Father, who art in heaven, hallowed by thy name, thy kingdom come, thy will be done, in earth as it is in heaven…*

His toes touched riverbed. He redoubled his efforts, puffs of chilly breath scoring his throat as he slowly dragged them into the shallows on the other side of the bridge, where a strip of land waited for them like a welcoming hand.

To Eddy's consternation, Blakeney showed skill with a sword, reinforced by his youth, strength, and longer reach. Eddy found himself falling back on old drills from his days at West Point, desperately parrying the merciless thrusts and searching for an opening in the other man's defense. The battle was made more difficult by the rain, now pouring down in an unremitting deluge and making the wooden boards of the weir bridge slick and treacherous.

Panting, he barely managed to deflect a vicious slash, his arm muscles burning from the constant movement. That and the cramping sensation in his calf muscles made it clear he couldn't keep up a pitched battle for much longer.

A memory of Elmira presenting him with the sword cane came to him. *Then again, perhaps I don't have to.*

He slid to one side, angling until he was close to one of the bridge railing's newel posts. *Wait for it, wait for it—*

Grunting enthusiastically, Blakeney lunged, aiming for his chest. Eddy dropped his arm, turning out of the sword's path. The force of the lunge drove the point of Blakeney's sword deep into the wood of the newel post, the slender shaft vibrating from the thrust. Groaning, Eddy brought his boot up and kicked at the blade, cleanly snapping it in half.

Blakeney snarled in rage, whirling and stabbing the broken end of the sword cane into Eddy's left arm. The agony was bright and immediate, distracting him from the cold rain and the madman he faced. He screamed when Blakeney withdrew the jagged steel, ready for one final slash.

No. His sword arm went down, then up and out, and the Toledo steel of his sword cane speared through Blakeney's chest. Distantly, he noted the faint crunching sensations coming through his sword as it pierced skin, muscle and a beating heart.

Blakeney staggered back in shock and pain, dropping his broken sword and clutching the mortal wound as the blade slid out of his chest. A dark bloom appeared on his shirtfront, spreading rapidly in the rain. "You," he slurred. "You drunken whoremonger, you sot, you *dare*?"

Breathing hard, Eddy lowered his sword. "I do."

Blakeney's expression changed, becoming bestial. With a growling scream, he launched himself at Eddy.

There was no time to bring his sword up again. The thrust of the dying man's charge rammed them both against the side of the bridge, and Eddy gasped in pain as the weathered railing slammed into his back.

Something cracked, giving way, and suddenly he was falling backwards, the maddened Blakeney still scrabbling for this throat. There was only time for a single thought: *I'm sorry, my angel—*

And then the cold water closed around him.

Dodgson dragged Maggie and himself onto the stretch of reedy turf below the lock keeper's house. Stiffening muscles aching from the cold water, he gritted his teeth and stripped off his frock coat, draping it around the girl as a meager shield against the rain. Through the downpour, he could see flickering lights coming around the lock keeper's house, bobbing towards them. The constabulary had gotten Poe's message.

"It's all right, Maggie," he said through chattering teeth. "Help is on the way. It's going to be all right."

The girl's eyes opened at that, staring muzzily up at him. "Is the bad man gone?"

He wiped the water from his face, searching the weir bridge for the forms of Blakeney or Poe. Neither was there, and he could see the broken section of railing. With a hollow feeling, he realized he and Maggie hadn't been the only ones subjected to the cold waters of the Isis that night.

"Yes, dear," he said heavily. "The bad man is gone

"Eddy? Open your eyes, dearest."

He obeyed, feeling like ten-ton weights were attached to each lid. The stormy environs of the Isis were gone, and he was stretched out in a pleasant meadow that he remembered near Richmond. Over him, a young woman with huge violet eyes and perfect alabaster skin hovered, as if waiting for him to wake from a nap after a picnic lunch.

She took his hand and smiled, the warmth of it leaching into his very bones. "Oh, my dear Eddy," she murmured.

A burst of the purest joy raced through his heart, dissolving the cold and fear from his fall into the river. "Sissy," he whispered, wrapping his fingers around hers. "Oh, my angel. I've missed you so much."

"And I've missed you, Eddy."

Her other hand came to rest on his brow, and every concern seemed to melt away, replaced by the most perfect sense of contentment. "It's finally over," he murmured. "The unending toil and care of the world, swept away to the shores of Eternity."

A sad smile hovered over her mouth. "I'm afraid it's not yet time for you to join me, Eddy. There's still so much for you to do, my dear, such magnificent things on the horizon for you to achieve. And you *will* have time to achieve them, but first you have to go back." Her head tilted to the side, a mannerism so familiar that it made him ache. "If nothing else, Elmira would miss you terribly."

Guilt twinged at the name of his second wife on his first wife's lips. "I'm sorry, Sissy," he said, bringing her hand to his mouth and kissing it. "I know I promised you I would never remarry."

Sissy shook her head. "You need someone to take care of you, Eddy, and Elmira has done a wonderful job of that. I don't begrudge her at all, nor do I blame you for marrying her." She leaned forward, kissing him on the forehead. "I'll be here when it's truly time for you to return. In the meantime, always remember that I love you. And keep writing, Eddy. Promise me that you'll never stop writing."

He gazed into the eyes that he missed so terribly. Even in death, she still held the key to his very soul. "I won't, Sissy, I swear," he said. "I swear—"

He couldn't breathe. He tried, but there was no air, nothing but thick, choking liquid. *Was it like this for Sissy, when she coughed away her life in the tiny bedroom at the back of the cottage? My angel, My poor, sweet angel.*

On instinct, he kicked, his face upturned in the search for air. Suddenly, he broke the surface, up into more water—no, rain. *Of course.* He'd fallen into the weir pond with Blakeney. Worse, he'd lost hold of Elmira's present, the blade undoubtedly sinking to the bottom of the pond. The coldness of the river water seemed to make the stab wound on his left arm burn even more.

Whipping the wet hair out of his eyes, he spotted the little island with the lock keeper's house on it and wearily started swimming towards it, his good arm doing the bulk of the work. *After all, I swam the mighty James River at its widest point. A mere stream should be nothing.*

Using the reeds to pull himself onto land, he heard voices and steered himself towards them. A curious tableau appeared out of the rain; a gaggle of constables huddled in a group against the downpour, with one man who appeared to be the lock keeper gesticulating frantically towards his charge. One of the constables leaned over to speak to a little girl—Maggie, thank all that was holy—who clutched a bedraggled frock coat around herself. And next to her, a very wet and bedraggled Dodgson in his shirtsleeves.

Eddy coughed once to clear his throat. "Have I missed the party?" he croaked.

Dodgson looked up, relief lighting his young face. "P-poe!"

"Indeed." He tried to bow and staggered with the gesture. Two constables came to him then, guiding him to the group.

And like dandelions emerging from the center of a well-tended lawn, both Collin and Furnow were in their midst. "You *are* something of a trial, Mr. Poe," the constable said wearily, water dripping from the brim of his hat.

CHAPTER THIRTY

The lock keeper, a Mr. Ainsley, brought them all into the lock house, Mrs. Ainsley clucking over Maggie and taking her upstairs to change into something dry.

Eddy wished someone would do the same for him, but Furnow politely asked Dodgson and him to sit down and explain the events of the evening. Aided by more kindness from Mrs. Ainsley, who bandaged his wounded arm once she'd finished caring for Maggie, the men donned hastily borrowed clothes from the lock keeper; as Mr. Ainsley was a good six inches taller and quite robust, Eddy found himself kilting the trousers up around his waist, the flapping hems rolled multiple times. *I must look like a boy playing in his father's clothes.* Even the tall but slender Dodgson flapped around like a living scarecrow.

With two large mugs of hot tea to fortify them, they recounted their movements since leaving the Dunford townhouse that afternoon. The color rose in Furnow's face as Eddy explained their decision to go after Blakeney and Maggie.

"The both of you are damned fools," he exclaimed sourly. "Did it ever occur to either of you that this madman could have been lying in wait for you, and killed you both before you knew what was what?"

Eddy's hackles went up, but before he could speak Dodgson leaned forward. "Mr. Furnow, we did what we had to do," he said, speaking slowly and carefully. "What kind of gentlemen—what kind of *men*—would we be if we did n-nothing while a monster snuffed out an innocent child's life?"

"Hmph." Collin shook his head at that, but Eddy detected a glimmer of reluctant admiration in the watchman's attitude. "And are you sure he's dead, Mr. Poe? I don't particularly want to order my men out in this wet unless we're sure we'll find a body."

"Ahem. I believe that would be the responsibility of the Oxford University Police," Furnow observed.

"Suits me," Collin retorted. "I wasn't in the mood to go swimming in any case."

Eddy remembered the feel of Blakeney's heart shivering on his blade. He nodded tiredly. "Believe me, gentlemen, he's dead. You'll find his body in the river."

As it turned out, locating Blakeney's body wasn't difficult; a young and very wet constable reported that the river current had swept the corpse down to the far end of the pond, snagging it on an overhanging bush. Collin headed out with a combination of constables and watchmen to retrieve it and take the physical shell of Martin Blakeney to his final assignation with the coroner.

Furnow's expression at this news was opaque as ever; only Eddy noticed the gleam of relief in the man's eyes. "So it wasn't a crime of passion, after all," he mused. "Only a madman wanting something he couldn't have."

"Exactly," Eddy agreed. "I must admit, I never would have suspected him if Dodgson hadn't told me that he was being paid to act as Stiles's companion. That was the final clue to the puzzle."

"Indeed, Mr. Poe." That sharp gaze took him in. "Perhaps it's best that you wound up embroiled in his plan. Otherwise, it's most likely that he would have caused the death of the new Marquis of Wells one way or the other and left Oxford laughing up his sleeve."

"Speaking of leaving Oxford, constable, what happens now?"

Furnow shrugged. "Mr. Walton provided us with the evidence," he grimaced slightly," and Mr. Stiles—pardon, his lordship the marquis—explained Blakeney's plot against him. As far as the university constabulary is concerned, the case is closed and you're free to continue with your lecture tour."

Eddy hesitated. "And, er, the circumstances of that night?"

"Are not pertinent to anyone who was not there to witness them." An ironic sort of smile flickered over Furnow's face. "Such as Mrs. Poe, who I understand will be arriving in town tomorrow."

Every muscle in his body seemed to give way at the same time. "Elmira is coming here?" he said weakly.

"In the company of a Mrs. Ponsonby, or so your Mr. Tomlinson informed me. Speaking of the gentleman, he's also pledged to keep certain events to himself, upon my personal recommendation."

Something loosened in Eddy's chest, a band of tension that he'd almost forgotten was there until it dissolved. "I cannot thank you enough, Mr. Furnow."

The constable smirked at that. "Go tend to your wife, Mr. Poe," he said, not unkindly. "And stay away from pubs for the rest of your tour, please."

The rest of the night passed in a blur. Somehow, the lock keeper had convinced a hansom cab to cross the bridge to the island, loading an exhausted Eddy and Dodgson into it. Half-dozing, Eddy leaned his head back against the firm leather seat and watched the rain-swept buildings roll by as the cab headed back to the city's center. *I know I did the right thing.* In the heat of battle, it had come down to himself or Blakeney, and he did the only thing any reasonable man could do. Nonetheless, the taking of another person's life rested heavily on his mind, and he knew it would do so for some time.

There was a quick, staggering disembarkation at the Mitre, a blurry farewell to Dodgson who was already dozing in his seat, a relieved greeting by Venables who passed along his newly freed son's best wishes and gratitude, and finally, finally Eddy was in his room, pulling on his own nightshirt and settling gratefully into the clean bed linen. He drifted off to sleep, the first stanza of a poem flowing through his mind. *When needs demand a martial stance/And men must heed Fate's clarion call...*

"You left us," O'Donnell declared in an injured tone, looking for all the world like an actor as he gestured towards the still-raining skies. "You left us, and didn't let anyone know where you were going, and proceeded to have a momentous adventure. *Without* us, I might add."

"O'Donnell, p-please," Charles begged. The Horsemen had been waiting for him at the St. Aldate's gate, overseen by a watchful bulldog. Grateful as he was for their concern, all he wanted to do at the moment was stagger to his room, shuck off his borrowed clothes, and crawl into a blessedly dry and warm bed. "I would have c-come back for you if there'd been time."

"But there wasn't," Hebron concluded for him, "and that's the end of it." He pointed a warning finger at O'Donnell, and the Horseman shut his opening mouth with a sulky snap. "You can tell us all about it at breakfast."

O'Donnell's mouth opened again. "Breakfast," Hebron repeated with emphasis.

"Oh, very well," the smaller man grumbled. "Breakfast, then.

But I refuse to go to a single class until we get the entire tale, Dodgson."

"I don't think that's quite the threat you think it is," Reade said. "But that reminds me." He reached inside his robes and brought out an envelope. "This came for you from Lady Georgiana, Dodgson. Luckily I intercepted it before O'Donnell had a chance."

Charles took it, shoving it into the nearest pocket. Whatever was inside could wait for later. "Thank you, Reade."

"You're not even going to open it?" O'Donnell complained. "Good God, man, if a beautiful young noblewoman was sending me love notes I'd be turning cartwheels through Tom Quad."

"I s-strongly doubt it's a love note. I shall tell you all everything in the morning, I promise."

He left Hebron and Reade to deal with O'Donnell's good-natured grumbling and shambled off to his room. Once safely inside, he took out the envelope and opened it.

A single piece of paper was inside. It was no love note as O'Donnell had suggested. Instead, it contained a list of polysyllogisms, with an addendum at the bottom inviting him for luncheon next Saturday.

Wearily amused, he put the list on his bedside table, then blew out the candle. *Well, then. Let the battle commence.*

The first signs of morning were a golden glow on Eddy's eyelids, and a soft, warm hand brushing a lock of hair from his forehead. He opened his eyes and saw a woman seated on the edge of his bed, her bonnet in her lap as she smiled down at him. "Good morning, my dearest," she said softly.

He struggled to sit up, ignoring the pain from aching muscles and his sword wound in his haste to embrace Elmira. "My angel," he murmured, covering her face with soft, enthusiastic kisses, "oh, my dear love—" He pulled back suddenly, choked with guilt. "What's the time? My dear, I'm so sorry—I should have met you at the train station—"

"It's quite all right, Eddy," Elmira said with a smile, resting a hand on his cheek. "Mr. Tomlinson wired us this morning and told us about your adventure. He met us at the station and has been ever so helpful to the Ponsonbys and me. We thought it best to let you sleep, but I'm afraid I couldn't wait any longer."

"Oh. That's quite all right." Eddy thought of the tall, red-faced publisher with discomfort; undoubtedly Tomlinson had told him all about the incident at the pub and kept him notified about the murder investigation. *Did he mention anything to Elmira? Is he here to inform me that the tour has been cancelled? Surely it can't be over, we haven't even made it to Bath yet—*

Then his wife leaned forward and kissed him again, and he forgot everything else in the world.

Washed, brushed and dressed with Elmira's help, he escorted her down to the tearoom where Mr. and Mrs. Ponsonby waited for them with Tomlinson. "My dear chap!" the publisher boomed, leaping out of his chair to shake Eddy's hand energetically. "I'm relieved that you're in one piece, sir. Gods, what a time you must have had these last few days."

"Yes, quite a time," Eddy replied, wincing at the strength of the handshake.

Mrs. Ponsonby, a plump, cheerful woman in a navy blue silk bonnet and matching traveling dress, tapped her husband on the wrist. "Henry, dear, do let the Poes sit and have their tea," she remonstrated gently.

"Of course, my dear, of course," Ponsonby said, affable as always. His wife, in her position as the senior lady at the table, poured everyone tea, pausing to determine their tastes in sugar and cream before handing them delicately steaming china cups. "Now, sir, I must ask, are you quite all right?"

"Oh? Er, yes." Eddy grimaced in the middle of reaching for a sandwich. "Well, to be honest, I'm a bit sore, and I suspect I'll need a doctor to look at this gash on my arm. Apart from that, however, I seem to be fit for further tour duty." Hesitant, he turned to Ponsonby. "That is, if the tour is still on?"

The publisher's face, already ruddy, turned an even richer shade as he burst into laughter. "Still on? My dear Poe, you're the hero of the hour!" he exclaimed. "The story of your detective work and derring-do is making the rounds of the country as we speak. We've already received requests to add Leeds, Hull and Manchester to the tour, and the Palace has made inquiries about a royal command performance once you return to London. I assure you, sir, there's quite a bit of talking still ahead of you while you remain on our shores."

The last nagging sense of worry evaporated, replaced with relief. "I would be delighted to oblige, sir," Eddy said, already thinking of what to put in his lecture. *I'll recite "The Raven" and "Annabel Lee"—oh, and perhaps that new poem, and the subscriptions to the Stylus will pour in—*

Elmira squeezed his hand. "There is one additional recitation, my dear, that has been requested," she said soberly. "Jane Billings's funeral will take place this afternoon at Osney Cemetery. Mr. Billings has asked that you speak during the service."

A sudden image of Jane Billings as he'd last seen her, young and happy with her secret love, appeared in his mind's eye. His delighted glow faded, and he nodded somberly. "It would be my honor."

CHAPTER THIRTY-ONE

The rains of the previous night gone, the cemetery appeared clean-swept and carpeted in a dew-dropped green, broken in a regular pattern by the somber grey, black and white of headstones. The wind from the west was cool and crisp, carrying the scent of autumn leaves and the inevitable turn of the seasons.

Eddy stood back from the lectern and bier, quietly surveying the mourners gathered there to remember the life of a young woman cut down in her prime by a monster. In the front was Mr. Billings, carefully holding young Maggie's hand. Both of them looked drawn but resolute, the two of them surrounded by family and friends. Further back, he noted Lady Georgiana, for once wearing a muted color in tune with the occasion, with Miss Grey at her side. Elmira, flanked by the Ponsonbys and Tomlinson, stood on the outskirts of the gathered folk with a weary-looking William Venables. A notable absence was Philip Stiles, but he suspected the newly minted Marquis of Wells knew full well of this event and was grieving in private.

And standing alone, his head bowed in silent prayer, was Dodgson. He looked up as if sensing Eddy's attention, his shadowed eyes blinking as they took in Jane Billings's plain pine coffin. For a moment, Eddy felt a strong sense of kinship with the young man. Neither of them would ever live a simple life, not with their shared tendency of always searching for pattern and meaning in what was formless and irresolute. *Perhaps we are cursed to see more clearly, but we are also blessed with the ability to consign what we see to words, so that others may understand the beauty hidden in the world around them.*

The vicar finished his homily and moved back, nodding at Eddy. Taking a deep breath, he stepped forward and began.

At midnight, in the month of June,
I stand beneath the mystic moon.
An opiate vapor, dewy, dim,
Exhales from out her golden rim,
And, softly dripping, drop by drop,
Upon the quiet mountain top,
Steals drowsily and musically
Into the universal valley.
The rosemary nods upon the grave;
The lily lolls upon the wave;
Wrapping the fog about its breast,
The ruin molders into rest;
Looking like Lethe, see! the lake
A conscious slumber seems to take,
And would not, for the world, awake.
All Beauty sleeps!- and lo! where lies
Irene, with her Destinies!

O, lady bright! can it be right-
This window open to the night?
The wanton airs, from the tree-top,
Laughingly through the lattice drop-
The bodiless airs, a wizard rout,
Flit through thy chamber in and out,

And wave the curtain canopy
So fitfully- so fearfully-
Above the closed and fringed lid
'Neath which thy slumb'ring soul lies hid,
That, o'er the floor and down the wall,
Like ghosts the shadows rise and fall!
Oh, lady dear, hast thou no fear?
Why and what art thou dreaming here?
Sure thou art come O'er far-off seas,
A wonder to these garden trees!
Strange is thy pallor! strange thy dress,
Strange, above all, thy length of tress,
And this all solemn silentness!

The lady sleeps! Oh, may her sleep,
Which is enduring, so be deep!
Heaven have her in its sacred keep!
This chamber changed for one more holy,
This bed for one more melancholy,
I pray to God that she may lie
For ever with unopened eye,
While the pale sheeted ghosts go by!

"That was a lovely poem, Edgar," Elmira said later that night as they prepared for bed. Already in her nightgown, she was propped up with fat goose down pillows and wrapped warmly at his insistence, despite her pointing out that he was the one with the injury. "I know our religious beliefs are not the same, but I feel you offered comfort to the family. It was a good and Godly thing to do."

He stepped out from behind the screen where he'd changed

into his nightshirt, wincing a bit as he moved his left arm. An unpleasant fifteen minutes with a local physician had left him with a neat row of stitches and a fresh bandage. "Thank you, my dear," he said, drawing back the coverlet and climbing into bed beside her. "God knows it was the least I could do for them, poor souls."

Elmira shook her head. "That poor child, having to grow up without her sister or mother. My heart went out to her, truly."

"I suspect the Billings clan will close ranks around her in support. She seemed to have an entire regiment of aunts and cousins fussing around her. And Lady Georgiana had said that she would take a hand in the child's education, so there should be no lack of feminine influence in her life."

His wife smiled hesitantly. "Lady Georgiana is certainly ... unique."

That was quite possibly the understatement of the century. "I believe she enjoys being noticed, my dear," he said diplomatically. "Of more interest is the fact that I suspect Lady Georgiana has set her cap for Dodgson. The poor man has no idea what's in store for him."

"I'm sure he'll be able to work it out for himself, eventually." Elmira turned onto her side, the candlelight from the bedroom table casting her dark blue eyes into shadow. "Which brings me to another subject, Edgar. I saw a physician while I was in Bath, one recommended by Mrs. Ponsonby. There's something we must discuss."

His heart seemed to still for a long second, then raced ahead on a wave of despair. "I was afraid—" He bit his lip, forcing back the memories of Sissy's last day and the emotions that had flayed him when she was finally gone. He reached for Elmira's hands, cradling them in his own. "We shall get through this, whatever it is, I swear to you. I won't leave your side, not for anything."

Her mouth puckered to an O. "Oh, Edgar—no, it's nothing like that," she said quickly, squeezing his hands. "I'm quite fine, my dear. In fact, I'm rather embarrassed that I didn't recognize this particular condition earlier."

His despair subsided. "You've suffered from this malady before?"

"Oh, yes. Twice, as a matter of fact. Which is how I know that I should recover fully in, oh, six months or so." Elmira's right hand gently slid from his grasp and came to rest on her stomach. "I'd feared that this was no longer possible, but it seems that the good Lord decided otherwise."

Her meaning slowly dawned. Now that he knew what to look for, he could see the gentle swell under her nightgown. "You—you mean—"

"Yes, dearest. You're going to be a father." The glow in her eyes dimmed slightly, replaced by worry. "That won't be a problem, will it? I know that we never discussed this—"

Her words were cut off as he pulled her into his arms, kissing her thoroughly. "My angel," he murmured against her lips, "you've given me the greatest gift a wife can give to her husband. How could something this wonderful be a problem?"

She gave him one of her lovely sunburst smiles. "I was hoping you would feel that way, my dear."

"Oh, indeed." He paused as a thought occurred to him. "Should you travel in your condition, Mira? Perhaps you should return to London with the Ponsonbys. We could arrange for a hotel room where you could rest in comfort while I tour. We could certainly afford it now."

She patted his hand. "I'll be quite all right, Eddy—I *have* experienced this before, after all. Once the morning sickness passes, I shall be right as rain. And even with the attractions of

London, I suspect I would miss you terribly if I let you go gadding about the country on your own."

He stilled at her words. If he was to be a father, he wanted to be a better one than David Poe, who had deserted his wife and three children, or John Allan, who dispensed paternal affection with the grudging grip of a miser doling out coins. And to be a good father, he had to start with the truth. "Mira, there is something I must tell you," he said quietly.

Slowly, with no quarter given to himself, he recounted the story of the altercation at Christ Church, and the pub, and how he'd gotten drunk and wound up in a hotel room not his own. "I have no excuse, only evidence of my own weakness," he concluded, bowing his head. He was too afraid to look Elmira in the eye and see the disappointment there. "I broke my vow to you, and I am heartily sorry that I've disappointed you in this way. If you wish me to live apart from you, I understand and will offer no objection." He paused, swallowing against the lump in his throat. "Although it will surely tear my heart in two."

Silence fell in the room, and he waited for judgement. When she removed her hand from his, the earlier joy of her news turned to ashes in his soul.

And then he felt her cool hand on his cheek, urging his head up. Her expression was solemn and slightly hurt but glossed nonetheless with a hint of compassion. "Firstly, I thank you for being honest with me, Edgar," she said softly. "I'd suspected that something had happened, judging from the way Mr. Tomlinson was behaving, but I'd hoped that you would tell me yourself. It does occur to me that if you hadn't stumbled into that hotel room, this Blakeney villain would have completed his plan and caused young Stiles to hang for all three murders. So in a way, your breaking of your vow caught a murderer."

"I suppose," he said hesitantly. "But you said, 'firstly.' Is there more?"

"Yes. Secondly, I am disappointed that you broke your vow of temperance, I will not deny that. I made that a prerequisite of our marriage for a very good reason, Eddy."

He nodded, the old familiar guilt gnawing at him. "Of course. No lady wants to be married to an irresponsible drunkard."

Her hand tightened on his cheek. "No. I asked you to take a vow of temperance because I didn't want to be left a widow again," she said quietly, but with force. "I've seen what happens to men who let alcohol dominate their lives, my dear. It eats at their bodies and souls, and leaves them as pitiful shells who die far too early for their years."

She leaned forward, touching her forehead to his. "I love you, Edgar," she murmured. "I've loved you since I was a girl, and thanks to Father's interference I was denied the chance to spend my early years with you. I must reclaim those years as best I can now, and I tell you that I will not release one of them, not a month or week or minute, not even a second before I must." She reinforced each measurement of time with a gentle squeeze of his cheek. "I intend to keep you with me for years to come, Mr. Poe, to help raise our child. To do that, however, you *must* abstain from the poison that drives your imp to such acts of perversity and regret. Now that you know of your impending fatherhood, can you make that vow to me once again, and keep it this time? Will you stay away from alcohol—not for my sake, not even for your own sake, but for the sake of your child?"

A scalding tear trickled down his cheek, washing away the shame and leaving behind a sense of release, as if some dark weight was finally cut free. "I swear," he said huskily, bringing her hands to his mouth and kissing them. "For the sake of our child, I will never drink alcohol ever again."

"Then I accept your vow, and I forgive you," she said, her

own eyes luminous with tears as she allowed herself to be pulled into his embrace. "Oh, Eddy."

"My angel," he murmured, full of wonder and gratitude as he stroked her hair, silently thanking Dodgson's God that this woman had seen fit to hitch her destiny to his own. Through no credit of his own, he had his wife back, and soon he would have a child (a child!) to add to their family. Surely a cooing infant would win over even the most holdout Roysters.

He fell asleep with Elmira in his arms, baby names dancing in his head.

CHAPTER THIRTY-TWO

Thursday morning dawned bright and clear, and a hired carriage provided the Poes with a pleasant viewing of the latest Oxford follies and fashions. Across from them, Ponsonby sat and reviewed a sheaf of schedules, with his wife next to him chatting amiably with Elmira.

"The 10:25 is an express train and will take you directly to Coventry," Ponsonby said, "where Mr. Carruthers will meet you at the station and take you to your hotel. According to the latest telegram from him, the local guild hall is already sold out. I certainly hope you're prepared to speak on the events of the past few days."

"I've made a few notes," Eddy admitted, giving Elmira a smile. "Although I still maintain that I'm not the hero people seem to make me out to be. Frankly, I was terrified out of my wits on that bridge."

Ponsonby tapped the side of his nose. "My own pater, bless his memory, was a sergeant major in the last of the Napoleonic wars. He once told me that a hero is simply a terrified man who still manages to do what is necessary. My suggestion is to keep quiet and enjoy your laurels, sir. Heaven knows you earned them."

The cab turned off Park End, passing the London and North Western Rail station in favor of the Great Western Rail station, coming to a stop in front of the newer station. After the Poes disembarked and handed their luggage off to a porter, Ponsonby handed the schedule through the cab window, along with an envelope. "Best of luck, Mr. Poe. Hopefully the rest of the tour will be much calmer, eh?" he called.

"Indeed," Eddy said with a wave, standing back and watching as the cab headed back to the L&NWR train station where the Ponsonbys would catch their own train back to the capital city. He turned his attention to opening the envelope, blinking at the contents. "Oh, my!"

Elmira leaned closer. "What is it, Eddy?"

"A bank draft, angel. An absolutely enormous one." He spotted a note tucked in with the draft and fished it out. The crest at the top of the paper was familiar, as was the tone of the note itself:

Dear Mr. Poe:

After your recent contretemps amongst the dreaming spires, and your peerless efforts to bring justice to those most foully slain, I find myself possessed of the greatest admiration for your determination and intellect. Any magazine with a man such as you at the head must surely succeed. To that end, please use the enclosed funds as you see fit. Both my niece and I look forward to our first issue of The Stylus.

Sir Richard Middleton

Eddy turned a beaming face to his wife. "Sir Richard has just funded *The Stylus* in full for the next year!"

"How wonderful!" Elmira exclaimed, a girl again for a moment, before returning to the practicality he knew and loved. "In which case, you must double your efforts to promote the magazine during the tour. We wouldn't want to disappoint Sir Richard, after all."

He took her hand and kissed it. "I bow to your wisdom, my dear. After all, it would be wrong of me to accept Sir Richard's generosity and not strive to make *The Stylus* famous on both sides of the Atlantic."

She squeezed his fingers affectionately. "I knew you would see things that way."

After checking to see how long they had until it was time to board, they stopped in at the station's small tea shop. Eddy found himself idly scanning the people streaming in and out of the station; he'd sent off a message to Christ Church before they left that morning, but Dodgson never showed up at the hotel. He felt a certain sense of duty to the young undergraduate that required a face-to-face farewell to be properly discharged.

To his pleasure, he spotted the lanky figure when it strode onto the platform. "My dear, would you like to meet the young man who provided me with such able assistance all weekend?" he asked.

A smile wreathed Elmira's face. "I would be delighted."

Offering her his arm, he escorted her out to the platform. "Dodgson," he called. "Over here."

The undergraduate turned, relief plain on his face. "Oh, good. I w-was afraid I'd m-missed you," he said, smiling when he saw Elmira.

"My dear, this is Charles Dodgson of Christ Church, a most stalwart young man if ever there was one," Eddy said heartily. "Dodgson, this is my wife, Elmira."

"Mr. Dodgson," Elmira said warmly, extending her hand. Blushing, the younger man took it, bowing awkwardly. "Edgar has told me much about your exploits these past few days, and that a great deal of credit for catching the murderer must go to you."

"Oh, it was n-nothing," Dodgson murmured, still pink. "Mr.

P-poe was the leader of this p-particular expedition in all w-ways. I simply supplied translation s-services."

"And acted as guide, and badgered me into doing the right thing, not to mention your single-handed rescue of young Maggie from a watery death," Eddy pointed out. "If I'm to be lionized for this weekend's work, you'll bear your share of the kingly hide, young man."

Dodgson smiled and shrugged in acceptance. "In that case, I was w-wondering if you remembered my request, sir."

Eddy noticed the young man had a sheaf of papers bound with ribbon in his hand. "I do indeed," he said with a sense of wry amusement. "I take it that's a selection of your work?"

"It is, sir. I apologize for the imposition, but I would greatly appreciate a c-critique from a poet of your stature."

"Such as it is," Eddy said, pointedly glancing up at the taller man. He grinned when a new flush of pink spread across Dodgson's cheekbones. "All right, young scholar, I'll review your work. But I must be honest if my critique's to be of any use. Do you think your ego can withstand the bite of my tomahawk?"

"If I have any hope of progressing as a writer, I suppose it must," Dodgson said, his doleful tone belied by a faint glint in his eye.

A blast of the locomotive whistle broke into their conversation. "I believe that's our signal to board," Eddy said, hefting the sheaf of poems. "You've included your postal details in these, I assume?"

"Yes. If worse comes to worse, simply address it to me, care of Christ Church College in Oxford," Dodgson advised, walking with them to the first-class carriage where other passengers were already boarding.

"I believe I can remember that." Eddy guided his wife into the rail carriage, then turned back to his young friend. "It's been quite the adventure, Dodgson," he said, holding out his hand. "I find I cannot adequately thank you for all your assistance."

"On the c-contrary, sir. Th-thank you for allowing me to assist you," Dodgson said, taking his hand and shaking it firmly. "And good luck with *The Stylus*. I look f-forward to more poems and stories from your pen."

"I hope you enjoy them." He'd already mentally allotted a subscription that would be shipped across the Atlantic to Christ Church College every month. With a final wave, he climbed into the rail carriage and took his seat next to Elmira. There was little chance that he would ever see his young friend again, but then again, who knew what the turn of the world would bring? And if Dodgson did turn out to have some skill at writing, he might even buy some of it.

For a modest payment, of course. After all, there was no point in throwing perfectly good publication money at a mathematician when there were real writers out there waiting to be discovered.

An hour later, the Great Western Railway engine chugged at speed through the Oxfordshire countryside, plumes of white smoke streaming up into the pale blue sky. Having finished the broadsheet he'd brought with him from the hotel and not trusting his traveling ink pot to the uncertainty of the track, Eddy decided to bow to necessity and start reading through Dodgson's scribbles.

He was halfway through the first poem when he barked with laughter. Elmira looked up from her own reading. "What it is, dear?"

He waved the paper. "For someone so stalwartly pious, Dodgson has a surprisingly droll turn of phrase," he explained. "Listen to this piece he calls 'Misunderstandings.'"

If such a thing had been my thought,
I should have told you so before,
But as I didn't, then you ought
To ask for such a thing no more,
For to teach one who has been taught
Is always thought an awful bore.

"How delightful," Elmira said with an appreciative smile.

"Yes. A bit unpolished and clanking, mind you, but our young mathematician may have a flair for the written word, after all." He read through the rest of the poem, then let the paper fall back onto the sheaf in his lap. *Misunderstandings are curious things, indeed—from something as simple as a mistake in phrasing to a father who has no comprehension of the monster he's spawned.*

After a moment he leaned back against the upholstered seat, gazing absently at the passing countryside. *If I was writing this as one of Dupin's adventures, I would have Blakeney driven insane by a cruel stepfather and helpless stepmother, the madness further driven inward by his posting as guardian to the boy who would inherit what should have been his. He would have learned early on to don a civilized mask, all the while a raging demon capered in his soul. And when he saw his usurper ready to claim all that should have been his, something inside him would snap, oh yes. But how best to strike back at his tormentors...*

When Elmira looked up again from her book, Eddy was already far away, plotting.

AUTHOR'S NOTE

So, why did I write an alternate history mystery starring Edgar Allan Poe and Lewis Carroll? Because of Jeffrey Combs.

Allow me to explain. Back in 2009 I was working as a contract technical writer for a telecoms company. This job would have driven Mother Teresa to drunken vengeance, but it also provided fairly decent health insurance. Since 1) the job wasn't permanent and 2) being able to afford my meds and the occasional doctor's visit was a good thing, I decided to suck it up and persevere.

That same year, I also learned that Stuart Gordon and Dennis Paoli were mounting *Nevermore*, a one-man play about Edgar Allan Poe, at the Steve Allen Theater in Los Angeles. *Nevermore* had been inspired by their *Masters of Horror* episode, "The Black Cat," and was their take of what might have happened during one of Poe's lectures.

Like "The Black Cat," *Nevermore* would also star Jeffrey Combs as Poe. As he's been one of my favorite actors for decades and I needed some kind of carrot to dissuade myself from running amok at the day job, I decided that I was going to see *Nevermore* come hell or high water.

And I did. Unsurprisingly, Mr. Combs is just as gifted on stage as he is on screen and was sublime as Poe. I returned to LA a handful of times to see the play again with an assortment of people in tow, and even got to meet the man himself after one performance.

It was on my third trip to LA when lightning struck. I was sitting at my gate at Bob Hope Airport and leafing through a Poe biography when it occurred to me that probably the only other English language author to catch as much flak about his personal life was Lewis Carroll (who wasn't a pedophile, nor was he afraid of adult women. That whole mess stems from a combination of well-meaning family members, unfortunate misunderstandings, and 1950s armchair psychology, but that's a whole 'nother author's note).

But that's when it hit me—what if Poe had met Carroll? To be honest, I don't think it would have gone all that well. Genius that he was, Poe was also a broke alcoholic who'd been tainted by numerous scandals and had a habit of borrowing money from friends and admirers, while Carroll was a devout Christian, more than a bit priggish, and extremely class conscious. Putting those two together would be the Victorian version of the Odd Couple.

Ah, but that would make their meeting even more interesting, wouldn't it? Upon such musings are novels created, dear reader.

When I got home, I did some Googling and discovered a problem. Poe had died under mysterious circumstances in 1849, while Carroll was still at Rugby, so it would have been impossible for the two to meet as adults. Well, boo.

Or maybe not. You see, there's sub-genre of speculative fiction called alternate history that explores what might have happened if certain historical events/figures/etc. turned out differently (e.g., if America had lost the War of Independence). In our reality Edgar Allan Poe died under mysterious circumstances in 1849, but what if he'd managed to survive? For one thing, he would have been able to marry Sarah Elmira

Royston, his childhood sweetheart and the woman he'd become engaged to shortly before his death. It's not hard to believe that Elmira, a firm-willed widow with money of her own, would have become the Susan Downey to Poe's RJD. Secure in a marriage to a wealthy wife, he might have settled down to the point where he could write more detective stories starring C. Auguste Dupin and even start his longed-for magazine, *The Stylus*.

At that point, the book outline pretty much wrote itself. Carroll (whose real name was Charles Dodgson) matriculated at Oxford in 1851. I decided Poe could travel to England that same year on a lecture tour and become embroiled in a murder while lecturing at Christ Church College in Oxford. Desperate to clear his name, he'd recruit Dodgson to help him translate a note in Ancient Greek on the victim's body, and hijinks would ensue.

All this, mind you, was in 2009. I picked at the story over the next nine years, slowly working on it while also launching my romance career as Nicola M. Cameron. By the time I finished *A Most Malicious Murder* in 2018, I had ten novels and eight novellas under my belt and was hard at work on new books for my assorted series. *Malicious* was reluctantly put to the side, with a promise to myself that I'd get it edited and published at some point.

And then COVID hit and pretty much set everyone's plans for 2020 on fire. By the time 2021 rolled around I'd cleaned out my pending backlog of Nicola books, thanks to being stuck in the house for fifteen months, and was desperate to do something different. Et voila—my alternate history mystery was a go.

I'm not going to lie; editing this book was a challenge. I'd written it over such a long period of time that my writing skills had changed dramatically, which meant I had to do a lot of improvements on the earlier sections. I'd also left a lot of gaps, intending to do research later on and fill them, which now had to be done. Luckily I have one hell of a good research library on Poe and Carroll (people kept giving me books on Poe and I didn't have the heart to tell them I wasn't a Poe fan so much as a Jeffrey Combs fan), and was able to fill out what I didn't know with judicious internet research.

The result is currently in your hands. I'm very proud of this book, and I hope that somewhere Poe and Carroll are entertained by the thought of their fictional adventure together.

A NOTE ABOUT REVIEWS

If you liked this book, then please leave a review on Amazon, Barnes & Noble, or wherever you purchased it. Reviews are love, and they help me sell more books, which means I can write more books. It's a win-win situation!

ABOUT THE AUTHOR

Melanie Fletcher is an expatriate Chicagoan who currently lives in North Dallas with her husband the Bodacious Brit™ and their five fabulous furbags JJ, Jessica, Jeremy, Jemma, and Jasmine, known collectively as the J Crew.

When not herding five cats and an engineer, she turns into SF Writer Girl and has the SFWA membership card to prove it. She has been writing professionally since 1995 and her short fiction can be found in a variety of anthologies and online zines. *A Most Malicious Murder* is her first novel.

ABOUT THE AUTHOR

[illegible]

[illegible]

CONNECT WITH MELANIE FLETCHER

Follow me on Twitter:
http://twitter.com/melaniemf

Connect with me on Facebook:
http://www.facebook.com/MelanieFletcherAuthor

Subscribe to my blog:
http://www.melaniefletcher.com/blog

Made in the USA
Monee, IL
19 October 2023